CASUALTIES
OF TRUTH

Also by Lauren Francis-Sharma

Book of the Little Axe
'Til the Well Runs Dry

CASUALTIES OF TRUTH

a novel

LAUREN FRANCIS-SHARMA

Atlantic Monthly Press
New York

FIRST EDITION

Published simultaneously in Canada
Printed in the United States of America

This text was set in 12-pt. Garamond Premier by Alpha Design & Composition
of Pittsfield, NH.

First Grove Atlantic hardcover edition: February 2025

Library of Congress Cataloging-in-Publication data is available for this title.

ISBN 978-0-8021-6378-3
eISBN 978-0-8021-6379-0

Atlantic Monthly Press
an imprint of Grove Atlantic
154 West 14th Street
New York, NY 10011

Distributed by Publishers Group West

groveatlantic.com

25 26 27 28   10 9 8 7 6 5 4 3 2 1

To Jen and Dad

The way to right wrongs is to turn the light of truth upon them.

—Ida B. Wells

CASUALTIES OF TRUTH

Johannesburg, 1996

The American girl had done some real damage. The policeman stood at the door of the breakroom, his kneecap pulsing and swollen. He tried to conceal his limp from his fellow officers but they had delayed the start of the game waiting for him, and now he felt the thick cloud of their irritation.

"Jissis, you look like shit." His ex-partner pointed at a chair on the perimeter of the poker table urging him to sit since the rookie had taken his usual seat. "Somebody steal your itty-bitty takkies? Is that why you made us wait so bloody long?"

The policeman grinned, trying to make light of the ribbing, trying not to draw attention to the searing pain in his leg. He told them he had been delayed by a kaffir bitch trying to steal petrol. This was not entirely true, but he needn't say more since the men had already begun turning from him, their focus directed at the television mounted on the cinder block wall.

The reporter, a thin-lipped blonde who hadn't yet been pushed out by the new Republic of South Africa's efforts to replace all the whites, offered a quick summary of the day's events at the amnesty hearings, then the screen flashed to Desmond Tutu in his red robe, his smug face nearly swallowed by thick glasses, his eyes narrowing as he stared at a former security officer who sat at the witness table offering half-truths about what took place during the Apartheid era.

"Era," they were calling it now. The work he had done to keep the Blacks from killing themselves and everyone else in the country was now considered criminal. His comrades at the poker table and those leaning against the breakroom walls mumbled, their quiet murmurs examples of the kind of silencing whites were suffering since de Klerk gave the fokken country away.

"Jissis, this is all they're covering now?" his ex-partner said in Afrikaans. "Testimony after fokken testimony." He sucked his teeth. "Complete rubbish. A commission for truth and reconciliation? What truth? They'll tell them what they want to hear, and then you watch and see how they'll throw the whole bloody lot of us under the jail. Fokken fools!"

As the other men nodded, the policeman wondered how much pressure he could have withstood if he was forced to testify about the things he had done.

"They should put it on that Black one. Zwane. Isn't that that double agent's name from the eighties? If they all blame him for every dead Black, then we can be done tomorrow."

His ex-partner slapped his hand on the table and the other men laughed, while the policeman silently questioned whether any of them had been paying close enough attention to what was happening in their country. They didn't seem to understand that the amnesty hearings and their new constitution and Mandela as president meant the end of life as they knew it. Nothing would be "done tomorrow."

"You didn't mention that she'd sucked you off, is it? Was she a vampire?" His ex-partner pointed to his neck. He slapped at the blood, surprised he didn't remember the American girl scratching him there. His heart quickened and he announced to the room that he wouldn't be joining the next game, that he'd forgotten he and Anne had plans.

He drove from the police station that November evening, thinking of the lie he would have to tell his wife when he arrived home. Almost as soon as he sat for supper, Anne asked after the knee and the scratch on his neck, but his shrug seemed enough to quiet her.

The next morning, the air was crisp and brazen. Spring was nearing its end, but still a chilled wind swept in from the south in a pitchy whistle over his carport. He turned off the outside porch light, setting the house dark again. Quietly, he closed the door behind him and zipped his jacket. Anne had had an eventful night with the colicky baby and he imagined she might sleep until a bit after the sun rose when she'd wake to pack lunches and get the older girls off to school.

Recently, she had told him that managing four small children was beginning to be too much for her. She had asked him to see about a schedule change but even with another child on the way, he wasn't inclined to do so. He enjoyed the early weekday shifts, and especially enjoyed weekend night shifts when Johannesburg enlivened. He had entered the force hoping to be a part of the chaotic frenzy: crowded bars brimming with drunken patrons; nightclub jam sessions bookended by brawls; sports arenas vomiting raucous fans; and of course, all the drunken girls. Last night, he had rolled down his windows on the way home and still Anne had sniffed his uniform shirt as if she could detect the American girl's perspiration. With the children at his knees, he'd hugged Anne tighter as if to dissuade her from inquiring more, her small bones feeling almost delicate enough to crush into powder. She had given him a weak, nervous smile and placed his supper on the table as the children ran about with plastic wands they'd won at a school raffle. "Look, Daddy, look!"

Now, he opened the rusty Land Cruiser door. In the glow of a new moon, he could see the bloody tissue he had left on the dash. He tossed it, along with his hat, onto the passenger seat. But as he sat down, he felt something odd, felt something wrong.

He climbed out and realized that the sooty roof of the Cruiser now sat four inches beneath its usual height, as if balanced only on its rims. Moving toward the rear of the car he found that the right tire had been slashed. Bloody hell, who would've done this? He should have hired someone to install a gate around the house. Every other white family had done it after the Blacks took over. Anne would tell him this again, for sure. He bent to feel the cuts in the rubber. They were deep and rough and snaking. If he had been investigating the scene, he would have quickly concluded that the husband had a scorned lover. Anne would certainly think so too.

The wind picked up again, dropping fat buds from the buffalo thorn tree that grew over the carport. They crunched beneath his boots as he moved toward the other back wheel. As he looked down to see that that tire too had been slashed, a hand clutched his hair from behind. His head wrenched back with such violence he could feel the tendons in his neck clicking to adjust. He punched at the assailant's leg but the knife had already pierced his throat, the initial penetration so acute, so agonizing, he could do nothing but part his mouth for a scream that would never be heard. The assailant dragged the blade up toward his right ear and created a most remarkable bloody necklace.

If the policeman had lived, he would have told the investigating unit—the one his ex-partner now ran—that as he lay there on the driveway's stone pavers, he could smell the strong perfume of petrol, could feel the brush of a hand reaching for the fallen knife, that he could hear someone softly weeping.

1

My humanity is bound up in yours, for we can
only be human together.

—Desmond Tutu

Washington, D.C., 2018

Swollen nuggets of ice fell from the August sky as if to announce
summer's refusal to be predictable. A streetlamp flickered through
the hail-battered windshield of their car as Prudence's husband,
Davis, slowed and turned with the road, hugging the edge of the
curb.

They were late for dinner. Their sitter, Alice, had arrived thirty
minutes after the agreed-upon time, and before leaving, Prudence
had needed to make sure Alice recalled all the steps for putting
Roland to bed: the music to be played, the position of his pillow,
the way his curtains were to be drawn and pinned. After, Prudence
and Davis had argued about which of the cars to take into the
District. Given the forecast, Prudence thought it best to drive
the minivan, but Davis insisted on the Porsche.

It was a 1959 Porsche Carrera Speedster. Cherry red. An exact
replica of the car in the poster Prudence had taped beside her
childhood bed, beneath the *Off the Wall* cover shot of Michael
Jackson. She had long dreamt of this car, and when they first
began discussing it, Davis admitted he had never considered
such a luxury. He had been easily persuaded, however, when he
spied the creamy leather seats with barely a crease. They paid the

previous owner with a personal check and the seller threw in an elegant pair of women's driving gloves, one of which Prudence now flipped inside out, using the fleece to gently wipe condensation from the windshield, as Davis reduced his speed.

"Damn, I can't believe how big this hail is," Davis whispered. "It's going to cost thousands to get these dents fixed."

"We should let the restaurant know we're going to be late," she said.

They were meeting the new "IT genius" Davis's firm had recently hired. Davis had been tasked with helping him onboard, with making him feel welcome, since he had recently moved from Sweden for the position. Davis seemed now to have forgotten all about the man, as the tail of the car began tarrying, the back left tire spinning like a pinball. He veered hard to the right, stopping forcefully alongside the curb. The car settled into itself, the engine at a low purr.

"Shit. Did you see that?"

Prudence rolled down her window, wiped the side mirror with the glove. In it, she saw the shadowy figure of something lumbering onto the sidewalk.

"Is it a child? Or a dog? I think maybe it's a fox." Davis turned off the engine. They were parked beneath a cherry tree with a thick canopy that deepened the darkness of that already-dark night. He switched on his cell phone light.

"What are you doing?" she said.

"I'm going to check on it."

"Then what? Perform CPR on a fox?"

"Pru, you don't leave a thing to bleed out."

Davis wrenched the door handle and rushed to the rear of the car. The streetlight flickered, illuminating broken tree limbs that dangled precariously over the hood. Prudence's annoyance was evolving, changing rapidly into anger as she considered Davis's impetuousness, his lack of forethought, as if he couldn't imagine what harm could come to a Black couple on a dark road.

Now, she heard the animal howling, the sound muffled yet urgent. She imagined its sallow eyes and hanging head, imagined the staggering profundity of its fear. A sickening feeling swept over her and she slapped her hands against her ears trying not to hear its cry, trying not to be reminded of all her own dead.

Davis returned. "A dog. So much blood." He was breathing heavily, attempting to switch off the phone's flashlight but his hands trembled.

"Do you have blood on your shoes?"

"What?" Davis said this as though suddenly waking. He wiped droplets of rain from his face.

"Blood." Prudence reached for his phone, turned off the light. "Do you want me to drive?"

As the streetlight flickered again, Davis started the car and Prudence made the call to report the injured dog.

"Does it look like someone's pet?" The woman's voice boomed through Prudence's phone.

"No," Prudence answered.

"Yes, yes, it does," Davis said.

Annoyed, Prudence began to push the phone toward Davis, when they heard a new, unusual sound.

"Hello?" the woman on the phone said.

There was a low, thick growl beneath the rumble of the Porsche's engine. Prudence peeped through the side mirror, thinking the dog had staggered to its feet, but she saw nothing before the streetlight went out again. The growl, however, blanketed them.

"Hello? Is everything okay?" the woman said.

The streetlamp flickered back on and flooded the road with a soft, creamy light, only to reveal a man at the front of the car. His reddened eyes seemed to rattle in his head until his sight settled on Prudence. Her breath suspended in her chest, the sound of it like a shovel scraping a large rock. Davis reached for her hand and together they watched the man. The wool of his coat lay flat and matted; the mud stains on his left cheek and across the backs of his large hands were caked and crusty.

"If you're still there, we'll send someone out as soon as possible," the woman said.

Prudence tried not to move, hoping this would deter the man from moving too. But he inched forward. She thought to tell Davis to pull off, but before she could get the words out, the man placed his hands on the hood of the car, leaning over at the waist, while the growling—his growling—grew all the more menacing.

Davis nodded, faintly, as if giving himself a pep talk before shifting the car into drive. Prudence felt the clunk-clunk of the transmission as the man's growl deepened into a roar. She could see into the dark and empty tunnel of his mouth as he climbed atop the hood, gathering himself on all fours, crawling toward them until he pressed his wet and liquored face into the windshield. Prudence thought she could hear his breaths through the glass, ragged and phlegmy. She wanted to leave, but if they drove off now, the man could be hurt. Davis made a sound, a sound she had never heard him utter—a small, sad grunt. He pressed the lock button for the doors.

"I really hope it isn't someone's pet," the woman on the phone said, as if an afterthought.

The wind blew hard, and the collar of the man's coat perked up beneath his menacing face, which now appeared exaggerated as he launched himself up into the damp air and back down onto the hood. He was stronger than his reediness suggested, and the car sank into the roadway over and over again as if refusing to resist him.

"Not everything is worth saving." The woman ended the call.

Terrified, Prudence reached for the steering wheel that Davis now gripped. She slammed her palm into the horn. It was a long and dull and desperate sound. A vehicle in the oncoming lane slowed. The man on the hood ceased his jumping to stare at the driver, as though to warn him that he could be next. The other car began to roll away, even as Prudence continued plunging her hand into the horn, even as Davis tightened his grip on the wheel.

A single piece of glass separated them from the man as he threw the first fist into the windshield. He pounded that wet glass with such fury that his hands brightened into a blood orange and water pooled at the corner of the man's eyes. Prudence's heart pumped and she threw herself back against the leather seat, as the man seemed to be punching only at the portion of glass in a direct line with her face, as though angry with her alone.

"I'm sorry!" she screamed. "I'm fucking sorry!"

When the man stopped pounding and his terrible face disappeared from view, Davis turned to her, confused. Then the streetlight failed once more and darkness overwhelmed Prudence and Davis until they felt the car rise as the man climbed off the hood.

2

After climbing a great hill, one only finds that
there are many more hills to climb.

—Nelson Mandela

Washington, D.C., 2018

The restaurant, a frequent haunt of theirs, sat a few blocks from
Davis's office. Days earlier, Prudence and Davis had agreed they
would cut dinner short so they could escape afterward to their
favorite bar. There, they planned to drink and gossip about the
IT guy and the girlfriend he told Davis he'd met on Tinder.

"Don't you think it's strange that he told you he met her on a
dating app?" Prudence had asked Davis.

"No, we were getting to know each other. Plus, he's new in
town and a man has needs."

"A man has needs?"

"Yeah." Davis had smiled.

"So . . . Mr. 'A Man Has Needs,' what does your Tinder profile
look like?"

"It looks like my wife's fist."

They had laughed, but now, inside the glass vestibule of the
restaurant, they were both feeling shaken. Neither had said a word
to the other after the man climbed off the hood. Prudence didn't
know what to make of any of it, so she brushed off rainwater
from her clothes and instead, searched for the familiar. Their
usual hostess was not working that night and her replacement, a

thick-lipped brunette, barely registered their presence. So, Davis made eye contact with the manager, who set down a leather-skinned bucket of ice where he stood behind the bar and hurried over to greet them.

"I was getting worried." The manager's luminous skin and bright teeth gave the impression of a man in his late twenties, but his body, soft and loose, signaled much older. He took Prudence's hand in his as if he might put her fingers to his lips. Prudence politely withdrew. Davis apologized, blaming their tardiness on the hail.

"Beat up my car pretty bad," Davis added.

"Don't tell me . . . the Carrera GT Speedster?"

Davis nodded and the manager put his fist to his chest, throwing his head back as if to mock being punched. He stood on his toes, stretching to peek at the condition of the car by the valet curb. Prudence reached for Davis's wrist and squeezed it. She didn't want him to mention the homeless man, no matter how much the manager queried him about the damage.

"I know a guy . . ." the manager began.

Prudence stepped away. Searching the dining room, she expected she might find the face of an acquaintance or two, but the crowd that night was mostly older and white, lacking the buzzy energy of D.C. lunches that she missed now that she no longer worked in the city. She turned back toward Davis, who was asking about his guests. The manager perused the electronic device perched on the gleaming mahogany podium where a small gold antique clock also rested. Reading the clock, Prudence realized they were twenty-two minutes late for their reservation. Their guests were even later, which became clear when the brunette passed a slip of paper to the manager who read the note aloud: "He is nearing." Discreetly, Davis offered the manager a tip. Prudence thought she would inquire later what reading three words had cost them.

Raindrops speckled the glass windowpanes as the manager led them to their usual table, which sat on one side of a Normandy stone half-wall. The wood volets leaned a bit toward the gothic, but all could be forgiven, as the food rarely disappointed. Even now, the smell of fresh brioche began to relax Prudence, as she breathed her first normal breaths since leaving home. This was to be short-lived, however, as she began to feel the weight of the other diners' gazes. With Davis one step behind her, she suspected they were now being mistaken for a well-connected Black Washington power couple. Which they were not. Or at least not in the way Black Washingtonians knew Black Washington power couples to be. They were not a part of the former Obama ball circuit, or the old Gold Coast family circuit, or the Duke Ellington School of the Arts circuit. Rather, they were on the fringe of Black Washington life, two transplants living in Bethesda, Maryland, in a neighborhood where little sold for less than $2.5 mil—a neighborhood that barely registered color, let alone Blackness.

And yet, Davis and Prudence definitely looked like Washington somebodies. Davis, with his refined heft, and Prudence, with her elegant, athletic litheness, gave off a general impression of courtliness, and this air, catching in the room, drew the other diners' interest as they watched Prudence sink into the Victorian button-back chair and place her Chanel bag on the hook beneath the tabletop.

"We're getting the hip-hop stares now," she whispered.

Years before, Davis had been approached by a stranger at a bar, a white guy with a drab ponytail and one gold hoop earring. He'd asked if Davis was a "music producer or something."

"Dude, you just have that look," the man had said.

After it happened several more times, it became the couple's private joke, a way to mask their irritation at the intensity of the questioning glances they encountered far too often in upscale places.

"Hova and Bey, baby," Davis said, but his smile faded as he tucked his phone into his jacket pocket and sat down.

"The car can be fixed," she said.

"It's not just the car."

"The dog?"

Davis frowned. "The man. Not the dog."

"The man is fine. He was having a bad reaction."

Prudence had been flustered, sure, but now she was choosing not to be. Davis tended to dwell too long on things.

"Really, Pru?" He searched her face. "I probably killed his dog. The man is probably not fine."

"He has more concerns than just that dog."

The sudden quiet between them landed like a heavy thud. There were some topics even Davis didn't want to broach, and the fact that Prudence had been without a permanent home for a long stretch of her childhood was one of them. He wouldn't argue with her any more about the homeless man's plight.

"This IT guy is ridiculously late," Davis said, as if he were forcing himself to redirect his annoyance with her.

"Could you imagine, back in the day, being invited by a firm partner and showing up this late?"

"The IT department is its own beast now," he said. "We hired this guy, Mat, hoping he could make our back office a powerhouse. He has to be on site for one year and if he meets performance metrics for the next three, he can earn close to a junior partner salary."

"Who made that deal? He doesn't even have to be in D.C. and he gets paid? That's insane."

Prudence knew by the sidelong gaze and the way he bit his lip that Davis had been in on the negotiations. He was no longer able to hide his displeasure with her. Perhaps he was upset because she'd been right about not driving the Porsche in the bad weather, or maybe it was because of how quickly she had dismissed his feelings about the man and the dog. Whatever it was, she couldn't win with him tonight.

"You always do that." He stared at the middle of her forehead, his expression wavering between contemplation and a barely concealed acrimony. "Mat's already been hired and your criticism isn't helpful at this point since we can't undo what's been done."

She didn't appreciate his tone, his finger-wagging, or the fact that he had driven her dream car into that hailstorm, but she needed to let it go, to salvage the night.

"You're right. I was wrong for saying it."

Her back teeth were clamped shut when the manager arrived with the menus. Two decorative sheets and a leather-bound book filled with selections of mid- to top-shelf Tuscan wines. She would order a simple glass of Sangiovese when Davis ordered a bottle for the table, and she would ask about the dinner specials to give the waitstaff something to recite for their guests, but from their summer menu, at least for her, there was only the beets and salmon roe with chervil yogurt, and the crispy soft-shell crabs with sugar snap remoulade. The Peruvian-born chef, a James Beard Award winner, had made it on the cover of *Bon Appetit* at twenty-three years old with his signature arrowroot pan-fried crabs. Often, she asked Davis to pick up an order on his way from work, she loved them so much.

Davis checked his watch. The manager had switched the restaurant's playlist so that Al Green crooned faintly in the background. As their wedding song played, she turned toward him to bring his attention to the music, but his left cheek was already dimpled into a near-smile. She looked around, noticing for the first time a couple with a newborn baby and a preschooler in a booth across from their table. Davis loved looking at babies. She grinned warmly at the mother, who didn't seem to notice her and who didn't seem to appreciate how lucky she was to have two children she could easily bring to restaurants. Their son, Roland, was sometimes . . . challenging, and though his autism diagnosis had been unsettling, it had also been a relief to have a name for the language and development milestones that regressed in his second year. And yet, if she were being completely honest (which almost no one ever was about parenting), nothing had fully erased the emotional discomfort of raising a neurodivergent child, particularly since she hadn't yet been able to stop wishing for what could have been.

"Are you looking at the baby?" she asked Davis. "It's a girl, right?"

Davis looked surprised, as if noticing the family for the first time. He offered Prudence a wan smile before dropping his head back down to study a menu he could have recited by memory. She swiveled in her seat and caught a redhead with freckly arms staring.

"Aah . . . I see . . . you have an admirer."

Davis pretended not to have noticed, and Prudence fiddled with the votive at the center of the table, almost regretting that she had ever agreed to join him for this business dinner.

Prudence and Davis had met at a business lunch in Manhattan the year after she'd left Cambridge. Still reveling in her academic successes at both Harvard Law and HBS, as well as a resume-building semester abroad in South Africa, she had landed a consulting job in McKinsey's New York City office. They were the only two Black people at Gramercy Tavern the afternoon they noticed each other. Davis, dining with two partners from his midsized law firm, leaned across his table as if to consider what one of them had said, and glanced in her direction. Within minutes they had both excused themselves to meet near the entrance of the restrooms. There, Davis told Prudence for the first time, though not the last, that she was the most beautiful woman he'd ever seen. It was so cliché, straight out of a bad eighties movie, and yet with the softening of his eyes and the quiver in his cheek, she found herself quite smitten.

Now, Davis looked over at her and set down his menu. "Ready?"

The baby across from them wailed and the little boy hopped down from the booth as if the shriek of his sibling had frightened him.

"To leave?"

"The sitter has to go in, what? Two and a half hours? With this rain, traffic is going to be a nightmare, so if we want to save this date night, we should drop the credit card number with the manager and tell Mat and his woman that dinner's on us." Davis stood up. "Plus, that little kid is about to blow."

Prudence happily reached for her bag. As Davis led them to the door, she noticed that the vent of his sport coat had creased, and as she reached down to fix the fold, he stopped mid-stride and held up his hand as if to acknowledge someone Prudence could not yet see around his frame. He turned on his heels and gently prodded Prudence back toward their table.

"Damnit, we were almost out of here," he whispered.

The little boy across from them hopped back up on the plush velour booth as Prudence slid again into her chair, her back to the door. As their guests were being escorted to the table, Davis remained standing and Prudence drank from her glass of water, wetting her lips enough to smudge her lipstick back into place.

Davis greeted the IT guy. "Hey, man!"

As Prudence went to re-hook her purse under the tabletop, it slipped from her hand and burst open, spilling its contents onto the floor. Davis called her name. "Pru. Pru, come meet Mat and . . . I'm sorry . . . what's your name again?"

She asked Davis to hold a minute and as she reached under the table for her belongings, she couldn't help but notice the muddle of mess on the floor. Restaurants, once, were expected to tidy up after each party, replace tablecloths, dust chairs, vacuum, but Prudence was now staring at discolored and threadbare carpet, covered in a thick layer of crumbs. She was embarrassed by her own disappointment. She expected a certain level of decorum, a certain predictable refinement in places where she'd chosen to spend the little free time she and Davis managed to squeeze out of a month. Where there was inelegance or even uncertainty, Prudence wanted to beat it back, replace it with order and augustness.

She reclaimed the last of the items—her driving glove—and shoved it into her bag, then slid the purse across the table to claim a new seat, one facing the door. She felt slightly embarrassed that the night with these people had begun at such an awkward turn, and stood to greet the IT guy and his Tinder girlfriend.

"Prudence, this is Tara. And you've heard me refer to him as the 'IT guy,' but this is Mat."

"Actually, it's Matshediso." The IT guy turned toward her, and the restaurant clatter seemed to grow quiet. Prudence could feel her jaw clench as if it intended to shut permanently.

The man, Matshediso, clucked his tongue and squinted as if to focus on her better. "Have we met before?"

"She's definitely got that familiar kind of look," Tara cut in, touching Prudence's forearm as if they were old pals. "Thanks so much for inviting us. It's really nice in here."

Prudence turned to face Tara, intending to say something polite, intending to say something at all, but she could only manage to press her fist into her stomach while the woman, Tara, said something about traffic and maybe some words about Prudence's green Ferragamo sandals. Prudence might have half grinned at the woman but she couldn't be certain, for she couldn't process anything over her own leaden breaths, over her own clamorous mind.

"Let's sit," Davis said.

Prudence put away her purse and Tara took the seat across from her, swinging one leg over the other, in slow, orchestrated movements that seemed designed for applause. An oval-faced, light-skinned woman with big, sensitive blue-grey eyes, Tara could certainly pass for white. Her highlighted hair fell limp at her shoulders and as she tucked strands of it behind her ears, she smiled at Prudence, and instead of reciprocating with a smile of her own, Prudence took another sip of water and fidgeted with the tablecloth, watching Matshediso as he peered at the little boy who was skipping across the carpeted floor behind him.

"So sorry we were late," Tara said. "Weather was so bad."

"No worries. We were late too." Davis reached to claim his water glass, grazing the platinum candleholder, jarring its base enough to make it shudder. Prudence had the urge to steady it, to steady something, but when she felt her brow lambent with sweat, beads of perspiration forming, she took two gulps from her water glass instead. Her throat felt like oxidized coals.

"Crazy drive in," Davis continued. "Got caught in a hailstorm. And had a little run-in with a dog."

Why couldn't he forget about the dog, forget about the man?

"A run-in with a dog?" Tara leaned forward, her cleavage a bit much for the occasion, while Matshediso smoothed the fabric of his cashmere summer sweater. He had a taut runner's jaw, and his skin, an acorn brown, seemed flushed beneath the tamed shadow of his beard.

"I think I hit it," Davis added.

"You think?" Matshediso said.

"My God." Tara covered her mouth in the dramatic fashion of an actress in a home-produced porn. "I would've been so upset. How were you able to keep driving?"

"It was a dog, not a human being, ja?" Matshediso shrugged and Tara winced.

"Mat's from South Africa," Tara said. "They don't know how to treat animals in Africa."

"Oh, no?" Matshediso grinned and rubbed Tara's back.

"South Africa? I don't remember seeing that on your resume," Davis said. "I thought you were from Sweden?"

Matshediso's hand climbed up to Tara's bare shoulder, his brown skin stark against hers, the bracelet of his gold wristwatch drawing Prudence's eyes. "I moved to Sweden when I was thirteen."

The server with sticky hair and too-big glasses approached and offered Tara and Matshediso their menus. Another server with the word PERU tattooed on her wrist stood beside him, refilling Davis's and Prudence's water glasses, signaling that she'd return with two additional ones for Matshediso and Tara. When she turned to leave, she nearly tripped over the little boy, who now grazed behind Tara's chair, hopping across the carpet like a bunny. The waiter apologized for the disturbance and whispered that the family would soon be paying their bill.

Davis looked again at Matshediso then peered at Prudence. "South Africa, huh? Prudence lived in South Africa for a short while."

Prudence nodded, forced a smile, but still no words came. She reached for her refilled water glass, her thirst seemingly unquenchable. Then, the restaurant lights flickered, reminding Prudence of the streetlamp on the drive in. Nothing about this night felt right.

"South Africa must've been amazing, right?" Tara leaned forward again, predictably intrigued.

"I bet it's so different there," Tara continued. "Did you feel like a new person when you got back to America? I heard that happens when you go to Africa."

Prudence didn't want to talk about South Africa, not there, not then, but she nodded again, politely, hoping the woman would get the hint.

"Was it like that for you?" Tara pressed on.

"It was, wasn't it?" Davis was silently pleading with her to engage, to help him get through this dinner. He was usually the big talker, the gregarious one at outings like this, so she knew that the dog, the man, the dented car, had affected him more than he'd let on. Prudence slowed her breaths and steeled herself.

"Yes, it actually was. It changed my life more than I can say." She spoke with her corporate voice now, bold, assertive, even deeper in tone. It was a cloak she needed more than ever, as Matshediso, for the first time since they'd taken their seats, looked at her directly, holding the stare, cocking his head and twisting his mouth into a near-imperceptible smirk, a smirk Prudence remembered all too well.

3

Where you stand depends on where you sit.
—Nelson Mandela

Johannesburg, 1996

Prudence felt like a proper adult, living in another country at twenty-four years old with her own car (albeit a scrappy one) and her own apartment (albeit with a roommate). She had traveled to South Africa with nine law school classmates, six of whom—including Prudence's flatmate, Nadia—had internships in or near Johannesburg. She had been in the country for almost a month when she arrived at her internship's downtown office, greeted both the receptionist and Bandile, the security guard, to find that Sheryl, her boss, had made special arrangements for her day.

"Sit, sit," Sheryl said.

Prudence moved aside a box from a chair and another from the conference table to get a clearer view of Sheryl, who in addition to being a brilliant advocate, was also a bowtie connoisseur. That day, her color was green. Olive green. She wore them always with crisp button-down shirts and matching cat-eye glasses, her blonde bangs curling just over the top of her frames, frames that she now set down on a thirty-six-inch stack of paper, as the desk surface likely couldn't be found even with radar. It was a sinking barge in a sea of paper. Its swollen drawers creaked under the weight of legal pads and books that had all grown heavy with dust. The unseemliness of Sheryl's office and the magnitude of its disarray was a shock even to Prudence, who'd once lived in a car. No doubt, Sheryl had noticed Prudence's fastidiousness from the first day of her internship, and had designated Prudence as the office's organizer-in-chief, so when Sheryl told Prudence that she should walk to City Hall that morning rather than to the office file room, Prudence felt confused.

"What's happening at City Hall?" Prudence asked.

"You must read the dailies while you're here, darling. The Truth and Reconciliation hearings are being held only a few blocks away, beginning today." Sheryl pointed to the front page of the paper.

"So, we're not going to the jail this afternoon?"

Sheryl laughed at Prudence's visible disappointment.

Most afternoons, Prudence accompanied one of the firm's two lawyers, Sheryl or Barbara, to a prison the locals wryly called "Sun City." There, she helped prepare amnesty applications for members of the African National Congress party, inmates who had been incarcerated, often for petty crimes, who hoped to tie those crimes to the resistance movement. Prudence knew that for most of those men, the relationship between their transgressions and the ANC resistance efforts—a requirement for amnesty—were tenuous at best, but Sheryl told her that it was not her job to judge people who'd had no opportunities in an Apartheid state, it was her job to give the young men the best chance at freedom. So, on behalf of many of the men who had never been taught to write and read in any language, much less English, Prudence drafted well-written fictions and, on occasion, true stories that nearly broke her heart. And as she wrote application drafts and sent them back through the prison system with queries and requests for clarifications, she knew the chances of those men ever seeing their papers or ever being granted amnesty were mighty slim.

"So, you've been working on amnesty applications but you're not excited about attending the amnesty hearings. Do you know anything about the hearings?" Sheryl studied her, seemingly hopeful that Prudence would impress her.

"I did a little reading before coming here," Prudence lied.

What did Prudence know about amnesty? She knew that after Mandela was released from prison, when South Africa finally had free elections, the country's new leaders had to contend with the human rights violations committed during the Apartheid era. A newly elected parliament set up a system where citizens could lodge complaints and perpetrators could request pardons for the horrible things they had done. Some of the testimony would be made public and some of that testimony would be televised. The country's new leaders wanted the world to see that in only its second year of existence, the new government of South Africa was doing something never done before—forging the most progressive democracy ever envisioned while also making amends for past horrors for which they were largely not responsible. That's what she knew. Which, in fact, was not very much.

"Ach, read this, then go. You'll need to be early to get a good seat." Sheryl handed Prudence a stack of papers and waved her off. At the top of the stack was a coffee-stained document titled *The Promotion of National Unity and Reconciliation Act 34 of 1995*. Prudence looked at the stack but was certain she wouldn't be reading pages of legal jargon unless it was for a grade.

"You can't be here and simply pretend to understand us," Sheryl said.

Prudence's face crumpled at the word "us." Who was the "us" Sheryl believed herself to be a part of? Prudence had rarely thought of herself in the context of an "us," and since she'd been in South Africa, she hardly understood how to think of herself at all. Despite believing she might feel some sense of belonging in Africa, she, in fact, had felt more alone than ever. And the work with Sheryl in the prisons didn't help. The visits had been affecting her deeply. Seeing the young boys there reminded her of the air of dread that hovered over Baltimore after crack poured into the city. Some afternoons inside those prison walls, she felt terribly sad and oddly guilty for how far removed she was from the prisoners' plights. And it unsettled her, maybe even angered her, when the South African boys and men in those prison meeting rooms questioned her with eyes that expressed a preemptive disappointment, as if they knew that she, like others, had come there not to help, but to say only that they had tried to help. Sure, her Black Americanness afforded her privileges in South Africa, maybe setting her apart from Sheryl's "us," but it also complicated things for her, inviting particular understandings and misunderstandings that Sheryl, a white South African woman, might never comprehend. Prudence would go to the hearings, she would listen attentively, but how different was South Africa from Jim Crow America? From a barely decolonized Caribbean? Was Sheryl really trying to tell her about an "us"?

"You must understand what's happened here to understand who we are." Sheryl slammed the top of a stapler, as if annoyed with her.

"But South Africa is more than just Apartheid, right?"

Sheryl's face tightened. "Yes?"

Perhaps Prudence meant her words to be a challenge, but she wasn't eager for an extension of Sheryl's lecture, so she quickly thanked Sheryl for the opportunity and left her office, heading to the conference room, only to run into Bandile, who'd overheard the entire exchange.

"Lucky, lucky," he said. "You get the day to sit in an air-con building and watch people talk."

"Isn't that what you do all day?" she shot back.

Bandile smirked, stuffed his hands into his guard uniform pockets, and watched her as she hurried into the conference room. There, Prudence filled her briefcase with her camera, legal pads, pens, and of course, the papers Sheryl had given her. When she arrived at Duncan Hall, she found herself impressed by the grandeur of the place. Though it was only a fifteen-minute walk from her office, she had never before taken note of the City Hall building. It was a sprawling stone structure in a bright golden hue marked by a dozen or so Corinthian columns. A turret and a clock tower helmeted by a jade-green copper dome seemed to be the crown jewels of the building, until she walked inside, where Prudence was met with mottled marble staircases not to be out-done by cast-iron balustrades and deep-green walls sparkling with gold fretwork. The bright-red carpet, along with its heavy paneled walls and desks of stone inlay, made the room feel like an impe-rial court, and from the seat that she found in the balcony, she admired the scrolled and carved wood fixtures and the recessed ceiling beams of blues and golds, all of which broadcasted the kind of enduringness the country seemed then to need.

The new democratic government had restored the building only two years earlier. Forty-three years of state-sanctioned Apart-heid and nearly four hundred years of oppression, demanded that old places be made new again. The high-backed wood benches and the sunlight that made its way through stained glass added to the pomp of that Edwardian building, which was only heightened by the attendees, all of whom were dressed for the significance of the occasion—blue and grey suits, starched and colorful shweshwe dresses, ties and fancy scarves and formal hats and polished shoes. From what she could see, South Africans seemed always prepared to re-create, to survive.

Come to order, come to order.

It was warm inside the hall that morning, and the air seemed a mixture of breath mints and burnt hair. The place hummed with

a nervous energy, as it was the first time the Amnesty Committee was seated in Gauteng Province. A few of the Committee
members, running behind, hurriedly made their way to the wide
dais at the front of the hall. The Chief Judge, a grey-haired Indian
man, seated in the center and tallest chair, ordered everyone to
attention again.

Order, order. Order, order. The Chief Judge wore reading
glasses that hung on a silver chain about his neck. As he spoke,
the glasses swung beneath his greying beard, tinkling softly
against the mic.

*We have before us six applications for amnesty. Before we begin
we would like to make sure each of the applicants understand that
the Committee will only consider acts committed between 1960 and
December sixth, 1993.*

Prudence hadn't known the amnesty window would be so
broad. Thirty years of crimes could be wiped away if someone
only told the truth about what they did?

*Do the applicants understand that if amnesty is not granted, the
testimony provided here may be used to incriminate them? Omis-
sions and inconsistencies will be frowned upon in our final determi-
nations. The Committee is most concerned with truth.*

There was movement down below. The kind of movement
that gave off an air of performative confusion. Prudence raised
herself from her seat to get a better look. She removed her camera from her bag, as the lawyers conferred with their clients.
She snapped a photo while the media cameramen click-clicked
too. She realized only then that some people wore translation
headphones and that live translators sat in grey boxes off to the
far left of the dais.

*If the applicants are prepared to testify, please have them stand
and raise their right hands.*

Prudence counted only five standing men. They varied in size, though none of them were small. Each wore handlebar mustaches and gave off the distinct impression that they were surprised to find themselves there.

The first to testify stepped toward the witness table to the right of the dais. The man, pink-faced with a hooked nose and a jutting lower lip, told the Committee in Afrikaans that his name was Johannes van der Mool. His lawyer, a slim man with spectacles, faced the Committee as he spoke on his client's behalf.

Former general Van der Mool will be testifying to the context in which the South African Police functioned and operated, providing evidence needed to establish political motive, as required by the Truth Commission Act.

The English translation was immediate, ringing out from hidden speakers. Prudence jotted down each word she could, making note of everyone who surrounded her, including the two white women who, before the proceedings had begun, had pointed to her notepads and said how lovely it was to meet a Black journalist. Prudence had not corrected their assumption.

Van der Mool slipped on his headphones, adjusting them for fit, and began what seemed to be a practiced recitation about police procedures. Chain of command. Recruiting of informants. Verification of information. Then he said, *The training of the South African Police met with the jobs required. We were trained to target activists. We used counterinsurgency tactics, war tactics.*

War tactics? Prudence thought it strange that a police officer would use this language.

Van der Mool continued by telling the Committee about their attempts to cool the resistance. *MK had limited capability but it enjoyed Black support.* Van der Mool's lawyer raised his right index finger, as if to remind him of what they'd practiced. *Yes, uh, MK stands for uMkhonto we Sizwe, which was the armed wing of the ANC, the African National Congress. As I was saying . . . we in the SAP worked hard against them. Most Blacks didn't like police.*

There was a shift in the mood of the crowd, as if the audience gleaned the irony of his words. Van der Mool didn't seem to notice. He spoke over the murmurs. *In 1983, the ANC reconciled that some civilians would have to be hurt. They began placing bombs in public areas. The long-term objective was the destruction of the South African state.*

Prudence was trying to make sense of what she was hearing about the ANC resistance efforts with what she knew about America's Civil Rights Movement. The resistance in South Africa felt different. Maybe more mobilized, maybe more violent, and she felt a certain pride listening to Van der Mool describe the ANC's shift away from nonviolent protests to AK-47s.

They wished to make South Africa ungovernable. The People's War, they called it. Van der Mool adjusted his tie, and for the remainder of the next hour, he fiddled with it as he spoke on the structure of the Security Branch of the SAP. *One hundred and ten branches. One division for the Black population, another for the other population groups, another to deal with MK, and so on. Various desks were assigned to specific people.* He spoke proudly. It had been a well-oiled machine. Organized. Exacting. Precise.

General Van der Mool, in your statement you mentioned that meetings were held once a month in Pretoria? The Committee's counsel, with a mass of thick dark hair and heavy glasses, leaned toward the witness table as if trying to make Van der Mool look him in the eye.

The meetings were known as TREWITS, Van der Mool said.

To Prudence's ear the name sounded like "Trevitz." She wrote it down, spelling it as best she could.

Can you tell us more details of TREWITS and how it worked? You said it was a national structure to get information on targets?

The newspaper that Sheryl had shown Prudence indicated that at least one of the six men testifying that week was expected to implicate the country's Defence Force in their testimony.

Van der Mool sat more erect now. *TREWITS included the Security Branch, which was state police. It also included MI, Military Intelligence; NI, National Intelligence; and the Defence Force. Teenrewolusionere Inligting Taakspan. Counter-revolutionary Intelligence Target Centre. It was founded in 1985 to identify and place activists on the priority list.*

Priority list?

Our goal was always to persuade the Blacks to work with us. When this didn't work we added people to the priority list of targets.

Targets? You said this word previously. Targets for what?

Van der Mool's lawyer nodded as if to urge him to proceed.

Targets that we intended to eliminate.

Prudence's body stiffened as she repeated Van der Mool's words to herself. A national elimination meeting? Is that what he was saying TREWITS was? They met monthly to determine who they would murder? She felt foolish for the shock until the Committee's counsel also took a deep breath, as if he, too, were trying to absorb the information.

Do you mean kill?

Van der Mool looked over at the other applicants seated near his lawyer. *Yes, to kill.*

The international journalists stirred but none of the South Africans in the audience, at least not the ones near Prudence, visibly reacted to this.

Do you still have lists of such targets?

Van der Mool shrugged. *Once the country turned, we were instructed to destroy all documents.*

For many more hours, Van der Mool testified about the sort of documents they created and relied upon for fifty years, the same files they summarily destroyed in 1994. Prudence wrote and wrote, and took more photographs, and by the third morning, she was one of the balcony regulars. Folks smiled when she walked in, offered her creamers for her coffee, adjusted themselves to make space for her, the "American journalist." Whenever she returned late to her seat, women gathered up their skirts and men's pocket keys jingled to give her the place at the corner of the second row.

But on the third afternoon, when she returned from a formal break in the proceedings, she found a man seated in her spot. The only thing immediately notable about him, outside of the fact that he was sitting in her seat, was a gold watch he wore on his right wrist, a fine watch that seemed a serious departure from the rest of his apparel, apparel that lent him little to no distinction.

She glanced at the other balcony regulars questioningly. They shrugged, as if they had been powerless against the skinny young Black man. Prudence was almost certain they had not told him the seat was taken. She intended to make that clear now.

"Excuse me." She pointed at the space he occupied. "This was my seat."

The man, like her, looked to be in his early to mid-twenties. He had a strong jaw and closely shaved hair with thin lips that seemed stuck in a sneer. And though she perhaps couldn't explain it to anyone who hadn't spent time looking at Black faces, by his phenotype, she knew he was South African, probably Sotho or Ndebele.

The man didn't acknowledge her.

"Hello?" she said, waving her hand before him.

Without looking at her, he nodded, ever so slightly, but did not budge. Prudence moved to the empty seat in the row ahead of him, seething. But there was little time to waste thinking about this miserable man, as Van der Mool returned to continue his testimony.

Are you willing, in light of the Commission's requirements of full disclosure, to give the names of those who attended TREWITS meetings and those who ordered the destruction of documents?

Van der Mool shrugged but Prudence could see by the way he looked far off that he was trying to determine how to best answer the question. *Anyone who had delegated powers from the Commanders could have attended.*

He said this as if the meetings were no big deal but it was too late for TREWITS not to be a big deal. Van der Mool nodded at his lawyer and the lawyer stood and handed the Chief Judge's assistant a stack of papers. Presumably, it listed names, but Prudence couldn't be sure.

You have to understand that with the elimination of ANC activists, many of us were given medals. This strengthened the perceptions of perhaps illegitimate actions. Our officers became confused.

The man behind Prudence sucked his teeth and the public gallery audibly fretted. No one seemed to believe that those in the Security Branch or the Defence Force had been confused about the illegality of their actions.

The ordinary officer's perception must be remembered. Security Council never stated that this was to be a military war but no doubt we all believed it to be a war. He licked his lips, then the Chief Judge spoke to him directly.

Did the government ever say that it wasn't a war?

Van der Mool shook his head. *No, I can't remember a time when the government tried to counter this perception. It wanted us to believe it was a full-scale war. Because they knew that in war, people must die.*

4

There is only one way to eat an elephant: a bite at a time.
—Desmond Tutu

Washington, D.C., 2018

At the table across from theirs, the little boy's father had accepted a phone call. Seeming to grow bored with his parents, the boy found his way beneath the table and sat with his arms crossed and the balls of his feet touching. Prudence had a clear view of him, and as she watched the boy, she tried not to think of Matshediso's smirk, tried not to think of how it had unnerved her. To distract herself, she studied that little boy with his hair trimmed tightly above his ears, sweeping to the right in a heavy combover that only a toddler and an octogenarian could pull off, and soon she found herself thinking of Roland.

Sometimes, contemplating her own child felt like heavy falling tree limbs landing in the pit of her stomach. She'd held off a pregnancy for ten years after their wedding, and her delay had nearly ended the marriage. Predictably enough perhaps, her son became the rope in a professional tug-of-war between her and Davis, a war Prudence couldn't win when the child developed something they couldn't at first name. Finally, reluctantly, Prudence requested a sabbatical from the McKinsey partnership she had fought so hard to get. It had been a hasty decision to take up the full-time mommy job, one she'd come to resent, as the grueling, needful days bloomed into months and years of whining and unpredictability, with only mere glimpses of the quiet, pleasant child she hoped Roland might become.

Now, the little boy across from her knocked at the underside of his family's tabletop and giggled. Trying to get his mother's attention, he instead drew the scrutiny of Tara and Davis, who grinned cordially, and Matshediso, who observed the child with a too-long glance that the boy's mother noticed, a glance that seemed to prompt her to peer beneath the table to ask her son if he'd be returning to his seat.

"No!" the boy shouted. "Leave me alone!"

The mother laughed nervously, and in watching the woman with her uncooperative son, Prudence thought that perhaps she and Davis had expected too much of Roland. She thought that if this dinner could miraculously be over, she might mention this to Davis, but he had already returned to the topic of South Africa.

"So, how did Sweden happen?"

"I was adopted. By Swedes." Matshediso scanned his phone as though hoping a call might come through.

"But you *are* originally from South Africa? Raised there?"

Matshediso grimaced at the word "originally," but Davis didn't notice.

"Ja. Born and mostly raised."

"See?" Davis elbowed Prudence. "A South African with an accent as watered down as yours!" Davis laughed his professional laugh and Prudence tried to smile but the smile felt too wide, stretching the corners of her drying lips.

"Prudence, when exactly were you in South Africa?" Tara asked.

Prudence shrugged, pretending not to remember precisely.

"It was '95, '96, right?" Davis said.

Prudence cradled her chin, her palm upraised, her eyes cast downward. "Yes, it was '96."

"Any time something crazy happens in the world, Pru finds a way to connect it to what the South African government did during Apartheid. Her face gets all red and she starts foaming at the mouth, talking about government conspiracies." Davis laughed. Prudence and Matshediso did not.

Of course, South Africa had been a turning point in her life, for more reasons than Prudence could say. But what she could say, though she wouldn't, was that she felt a sort of kinship with the damaged golden child of Africa. It was a place trapped within a tortured history that was not of its own choosing. She felt she understood its plight, felt that she knew what it was like to appear whole but, in fact, have so many disparate, incongruent parts.

"I'm passionate," Prudence said.

"Passionate about *some* things . . ." Davis added.

Tara's eyes flitted from Prudence back to Davis, leaving little doubt that she sensed the tension between them.

Thunder rumbled again and their server reappeared with two more water glasses. Tara, seeing that her napkin was the last on the table, set it quickly across her lap with a slight blush of embarrassment. Aretha Franklin fanned from the restaurant speakers as the four of them returned to their menus, reviewing them in silence. Prudence, feeling the relief of such quiet, considered offering entrée suggestions as a way to speed up a dinner that hadn't yet started but already felt well past its sell-by date.

"Would you like to hear the specials?" The waiter held his hands aloft, as if any moment he might set them on his hairy belly, which beamed from between the buttons of his ill-fitting shirt. He mentioned lamb and soup and said something about steak. Prudence was certain Tara would order the steak, well-done no doubt, and the waiter would pretend that the kitchen wouldn't scold him for bringing them such a shit request. Prudence had stopped eating red meat after returning from South Africa, so ignoring the waiter's recitation on beef gave her room to think on how she could get out of there more quickly. These thoughts were soon interrupted by the waiter's exclamation that the fish was "caught in Alaska just yesterday morning by the chef's best friend." Prudence thought Davis might question him, teasingly, about the mode of fish transportation—ask if the friend had rowed a small boat into D.C. to deliver it—but Davis was, instead, pressing forward, listening attentively, as if he might actually veer from his usual lamb order. He wasn't fooling Prudence, though. He had never been one for new adventures unless she prompted it.

The waiter left to "give them time to think," and while Tara moved her finger across the menu and while Davis examined a too-long wine list for what was certain to be an imperfect wine selection—for he rarely chose good wines—Matshediso set down his menu and peered at Prudence again. His glance was flat, expressionless, his eyes vacant, his mouth a vapid line, until he leaned toward her with a deep exhalation.

"Tell me, Pru, what did you do with your time in South Africa? You don't mind if I call you Pru, do you?"

Lightning brightened the room and her heart dashed, hurtling as if in a race with itself.

"I didn't tell him to call you that." Davis threw up his hands and smiled, and while the beverage server topped off their water glasses, Davis turned his attention to the table with the children. With the baby asleep and the boy a bit calmer, they could hear the parents asking if they could see the dessert menus. Davis rolled his eyes.

"So, Pru . . ." Matshediso began again. The corners of his mouth collapsed ever so slightly as he peered at her. She wanted to correct him, to tell him that she'd like to be called *Prudence* but she worried about what he might say next.

"Did you go on safari? A hunt? You look like a hunter. South Africa in 1996 was quite the year."

You look like a hunter?

"Why was it 'quite the year'?" Tara asked.

Prudence felt that sinking feeling of revulsion in her belly.

"The Truth and Reconciliation Hearings were going on," Davis said, as though an expert, as though he hadn't learned of this from Prudence.

"Wow," Tara said. "Did you play some major part in it?"

Prudence tilted her head, failing to fully conceal the condescension. She told Tara she had only been in the gallery, only a spectator at the hearings.

"Did you live in Johannesburg?" Matshediso asked.

The conversation was littered with traps. The political kind. And the personal kind.

"She lived in Sand- . . . Sand- . . . some fancy suburb. She talks about the mall there all the time. She once watched a tennis match while eating at some highbrow restaurant." Davis said this, as if the stories of her life in Joburg had bored him. It surprised her—his tone—because he had always seemed proud of the experiences she'd had in the years before they met. "She's always trying to get me to go to Africa for vacation, but I can't be on a damn plane for that long."

"Sandton," Matshediso said. "The name of the suburb is Sandton. And it *is*, or *was* back then, quite fancy."

"Well . . . she makes it out like it's Beverly Hills or something," Davis said. "Anyway . . . Mat, what part of South Africa are you from?"

Matshediso took a deep breath, as if he considered not answering truthfully. "KwaNdebele. Bantustan. Quite rural."

"But really beautiful. I saw some photos," Tara said. "They have gorgeous grasslands and, like, two hundred and seventy lakes or something and his tribe is the one who makes those pretty beaded dolls and who do that colorful block painting on their houses, right?"

Matshediso nodded at her, as if proud of her quick and simplistic summary.

"Oh, we have some of those dolls," Davis said. "Kwanda—what's it called again?"

"Kwa, meaning 'land of,' and Ndebele is the name of my tribe."

Prudence waited for Davis to ask about the climate or the village culture or some such typical American question, but they were all distracted by the redhead from earlier, who, passing their table now, swiped her fingers along their tablecloth.

Prudence looked to Davis, who shrugged, and though no one commented on the woman, Davis cleared his throat as if to force the conversation in another direction.

"And did you lose your parents there in South Africa or did you move to Sweden before that?"

Matshediso stiffened.

"That's too personal, Davis." Prudence hoped she could signal to Matshediso that they had equally as much to lose by the conversation proceeding as it was. It didn't work.

"No, it's not too personal." Matshediso was avoiding her gaze, looking directly at Davis. "It's difficult to explain to Americans how desperate a woman has to be to give up her thirteen-year-old son to a white journalist who came to take some photos. Back then, compulsory education for Blacks was only provided for six years. We rarely had books, so I could hardly read in any language until I was living in Sweden."

If there was any good cheer remaining in their glib little gathering, it was depleted at that moment.

Prudence thought now about how she too had been thirteen when her world was upturned. She tried to catch Matshediso's eye, to offer him something words couldn't convey, but then Davis did something Prudence hadn't expected. He chuckled. An actual chuckle. And he pointed to Prudence in what she later would regard as a sacrificial offering.

"Prudence knows a lot about brutal childhoods too," he said.

Tara's eyes grew wide as Davis reached for his water glass, seemingly oblivious, shaking his head, as if privately recollecting Prudence's tragic story: her murdered father, her mother's mental decline, the loss of her brother to leukemia. Prudence's eyes welled up in a deluge of rage as the redhead, returning from the ladies' room, walked past their table again, this time sweeping the edge of it with her A-line dress, her smell blanketing them with what could only be described as a thick cloud of pussy sweat.

"Really fucked Pru's head up," Davis muttered.

5

I dare not linger, for my long walk is not ended.
—Nelson Mandela

Johannesburg, 1996

On the fourth morning of the Johannesburg hearings, the sixth applicant was mentioned by name. This began a long lull in the testimony, as the very utterance of this name seemed to create some sort of shock across the proceedings. Papers were shuffled, people whispered, and Prudence scribbled the name as it sounded to her ear, wondering what kind of name it was, as it didn't sound particularly Dutch or English; it sounded rather indigenous, rather African.

Has the sixth applicant submitted his written statements? The Chief Judge pointed to the lawyers seated at the applicants' table.

Yes, he has, but he has chosen not to attend the public hearing. He is requesting in-camera *testimony.*

The Committee's counsel, seated on the other side of the aisle from the applicant's lawyers, looked up at the dais to see the reaction of the Committee. Four of the five members were stone-faced. The Chief Judge scowled before speaking again:

The applicant's name appears all over the statements submitted. We are encouraging him to make himself available for public questioning. Have you advised him that this is what we are asking of all applicants?

One of the lawyers, one Prudence hadn't seen before, nodded, then remembered to say "yes" for the record. He, too, was slim but much shorter than the other men. He wore a well-tailored suit and adjusted his jacket, though he remained in his chair. *It would be very dangerous for Mr. Zwane to appear here. Colonel Volter's testimony will provide more context about Mr. Zwane's role in several matters, including the disappearance of the Mozambique Eight. It is all in his written statement.*

The crowd stirred and Prudence, perplexed, turned to ask one of the balcony regulars what was happening. The only eyes she caught were those of the man who'd taken her seat.

"Mozambique Eight? Who disappeared?" she whispered to him.

The man's legs were trembling as though they'd been live wired. It was the first time she had spoken to him since asking him to move the day before, and when he didn't answer this time, she wondered if perhaps he did not speak English. Soon, however, she realized his expression was one of incredulity.

"The Security Forces were all murderers. They regularly made people disappear." He shrugged with disdain. "Did you come here expecting to see a comedy show?"

She couldn't stand this man, and to worsen matters, he hadn't even answered her damn question. However, before she could respond, the family of some of the victims began walking into the hall. Prudence squinted, trying to sharpen her view of the women dressed in red and black with chiming brass bangles and the older men with sharply pressed trousers who sat down, somber-faced, their lined hands planted and crossed before them.

The man behind her scooted forward in his seat. His breath felt hot on Prudence's neck. She sat back in the bench, forcefully, trying to make her annoyance apparent, but the man did not readjust himself. Instead, he began to whisper something that

Prudence couldn't quite make out, something that began with an "mm" sound.

"I wonder if any of them will be able to look the families in their faces," a woman behind Prudence whispered.

Prudence, suddenly, felt a sharp pain in her lower abdomen followed by a thick squirt of discharge into her panties. She feared her period had arrived early. Leaving her seat she raced along the mosaic flooring of the corridor with her briefcase in tow. As she peeled the backing of her maxi pad, she overheard two white women who'd only just exited the stalls.

"Truly, I can't believe they're letting him get away with this. Volter won't tell *all*. None of them will bloody tell *all*. And if Volter won't testify against that Black bastard, Zwane, what use is he?"

Black bastard? Who was this Zwane man?

Prudence rushed back to her seat as Volter was making himself comfortable at the witness table. He had been an officer in the counterinsurgency unit of the Security Branch, known as Vlakplaas. The women in the bathroom mentioned that he was expected to admit to the murders of at least thirty people, including eight missing men. Prudence pulled out the stack of papers Sheryl had given her on the first day, rapidly reading what she could before Volter began.

Before we begin on the specifics of certain cases, can you, Colonel Volter, tell us your views on Apartheid? Volter's eyes brightened as if he had been waiting for this question his entire life. He pivoted toward the television camera closest to him, cleared his throat. He could have been close to sixty years old, and was meaty and florid. He wore a blue suit that looked to have been purchased for the muscular build he once had.

I grew up during the Apartheid era. I believed Apartheid was right. I was indoctrinated. Our task was to combat Communism always. We must maintain Apartheid. This was the view of sub-ordinates and communicated by superiors. The struggle was never racially based. Whites and Blacks were dealt with the same way. It was not considered necessary to eliminate right-wing activists, but I was never involved in racism.

Unlike Prudence, the Committee members managed to keep straight faces as Volter spoke.

You were never involved in racism? This apart from the fact that you supported Apartheid?

Volter didn't seem to detect the irony in this question. He answered yes. *It was an unconventional war but war nonetheless. Some of my Black colleagues were shot dead. It was not about race.*

And are you a member of any political organization?

I used to be a National Party member. I am no longer. I don't want anything to do with them.

Prudence remembered reading that back in the early 1940s the National Party had publicly sympathized with the Nazis. She'd read that no one in South Africa believed the National Party would win that first election in 1948, especially not when they used campaign slogans like *die kaffir op sy plek*, "the nigger in his place"; *die koelies uit die land*, "the coolies out of the country"; and *eie volk, eie taal, eie land*, "our own people, our own language, our own land." A few mornings after the election ended, however, when all the white people's votes had been counted, Black people woke to find that their country would be run by Afrikaners whose platform rested on a program that codified a racial separation called Apartheid.

So, you never occupied a position in any political party?

Volter sat back in his seat as if to think over the question. *We weren't allowed to actively participate in politics, but the Security Forces was the National Party's iron fist, if that's what you are asking. We enforced policies.*

Which policies did you think was your job to enforce?

Volter scoffed, then seemed to regret the utterance as he shifted uncomfortably in his seat. *Which policies? All policies.* He threw up his hands. *Eighty-seven percent of the country's land was given to whites. The best mining jobs, the best neighborhoods, were reserved for whites. The Blacks were made to carry passes everywhere. The National Party forbade non-whites from voting, then took away the power of tribal chiefs. The Blacks were not happy about any of this and they made trouble. Like I said, we were needed to enforce policies. We didn't make work for ourselves.*

There was a break in testimony, and as Prudence waited, she realized she had only just begun to understand the history of South Africa after the arrival of the Dutch East India Company in 1652. She knew nothing about South Africa before this.

She skimmed the documents from Sheryl.

One hundred thousand years of Black Africans farming and hunting, isolated from the rest of the world. Many tribes; many languages; small, localized wars. The Dutch arrive. The indigenous Black population is eviscerated by a ravaging bout of smallpox. Same thing happens all over the world. Disease, death, resistance, manipulations. After the Khoikhoi people are nearly wiped out, the Zulu nation leads a series of battles against the Dutch Boers. The Boers head north, separate themselves, but the English soon arrive looking for gold. And with the help of a hundred thousand Black collaborators, the whites fight each other over Black people's land.

The hearing was called back to order. Volter had loosened his tie during the break so now it hung slightly to the left of his neck like a sports towel.

Colonel Volter, can you tell us what you know of the 1986 incident known as the Mozambique Eight?

Volter shrugged, not once but twice, as though exhausted with chronicling the same story. *Eight men who'd been involved in school boycotts in KwaNdebele came in contact with our agent, Andrew Zwane. Zwane told the men he would take them to Mozambique for MK training; they wanted to be resistance fighters.*

So, was this intended as an elimination from the start?

Activists had to be eliminated. Merely arresting them was not enough. The legal system was insufficient and cumbersome.

Counsel for the Committee winced. The Chief Judge spoke next. *Couldn't you stop them before they acted? Everyone who has testified has told us that the Security Forces were efficient and well run, one of the best in the world. Couldn't you foresee the acts?*

Volter raised his hand, and it occurred to Prudence that his counsel must have told him not to speak out of turn. *We couldn't always know. We had to act by eliminating.*

The eight boys ranged in ages from twelve to eighteen, is that correct?

Volter cocked his head. *I do not know the men's ages.*

The gallery grew eerily quiet. There wasn't a throat clearing, not an audible breath. Maybe, like Prudence, none of them knew until that moment that the Mozambique Eight had all been children. Prudence felt herself growing feverish as she thought of those young boys.

The Committee's counsel passed a sheet of paper to Volter. Prudence imagined the paper was an official record of the boys' ages. He glanced down at it.

You said the boys were involved in school boycotts? How did you know this?

Volter held up the paper, fanning it, as if it had little bearing on his testimony. *Zwane turned in written reports to the B-Section. B-Section handled Black power. As soon as a person became actively involved in political action, including boycotts, we would open a file. We derived this information from informants. We were told the men wanted to be trained. That was enough evidence.* Volter looked down again at the paper.

Enough evidence for them to be eliminated?

Volter passed the paper back to the Committee's counsel. *Yes, most certainly.*

The man behind Prudence placed his head on the back of her bench.

All right, let's move on to Zwane, shall we? A Black man who pretends to be a senior MK soldier. Did Zwane entice the boys under false pretense?

Volter lifted his chin, narrowed his eyes. *If Zwane wanted to entice them, he could have. We trained him well. Zwane had specific orders not to entice.* Volter said the words as confidently as one would say "shake" to a dog who'd been taught to lift his paw. It was smug.

Only one of the boys, Thomas Mahlangu, had a record of previous detainment. For handing out flyers to students. He was the eldest brother of three of the other boys killed that day. They were all students. Is that right?

Volter blinked quizzically. *Their relationship to one another and their ages wouldn't have mattered. We were acting in a preventative fashion. They were typical comrades.*

A preventative fashion? Can you please tell us what that means?

They would eventually have gone for training, Volter said. *For two years I raised war in Rhodesia, and then in Liberia. I saw young people who were able soldiers. These boys would have been no different.*

An older Black man on the lower floor stomped his foot in a thunderous and rageful response. Was he one of the boy's fathers? An uncle? His suit draped over him as though his body were a mere wire hanger. He shook his head, kept shaking his head. Volter didn't acknowledge the man.

So, you did, in fact, know them to be boys?

Volter cocked his head again. *I didn't ask for their ages.*

The reporters click-clicked their cameras and the man behind Prudence breathed harder, heavier.

Are you saying if you knew them to be boys, the outcome would have been different?

I didn't ask for their ages, Volter said again.

The man behind Prudence rose from the bench as if overcome. Several people behind her sniffled. The detached way Volter spoke of those children made every word uttered about them all the more gutting. Prudence felt desperate to know the other boys' names. Thomas would have been almost thirty by now. None of those boys had had a chance against that double agent, Zwane, no chance against that system of entrapment.

Soon, the lunch break was announced and the crowd swelled upward, a rush of subdued voices filling the hall as people moved briskly toward the doors. Down below, Prudence saw Volter shaking hands with the other men who would testify that week. They seemed to be congratulating him and she wondered if they were relieved that he'd said more than they would have or less than they had expected him to. One of the men offered him a piece of chewing gum. Watching Volter chew made Prudence feel hungry. She veered right after stepping out of the building, intending to walk to her usual lunch place, but found herself following behind the man who had taken her seat. His head was bent, his shoulders caved. Was he crying?

She double-stepped to catch up to him and tapped him on the shoulder, but the man didn't look up. She thought to leave him alone, but there was some part of her that felt guilty about his crying, guilty that she was not crying. Why couldn't she cry? The man's shoulders stuttered and he clasped his hands atop his head as if to try and tamp down his emotions. Prudence continued walking behind him until she got close enough to offer him a tissue. The man pushed it aside, not bothering to turn around to acknowledge her. In her humiliation, which was encroaching upon anger, she found herself inexplicably following the man down to a row of shops many blocks from City Hall.

Johannesburg, like other big cities, demonstrated both its deprivations and its riches on any given day. That day, the late morning rain had come and gone but the walkways shone with curdled, wet debris. Though downtown was dense with hawkers and high rises, many of which had long since seen their heyday, the city was also the most heavily wooded she'd ever seen. There were no majestic mountains, no big, teeming rivers, and the landscape was riddled by dormant mines, but trees were everywhere in Joburg, rumored to outnumber people two to one. This was a shock given that forty percent of the world's gold had once been excavated from Johannesburg hills. A loss felt not only in damage to the ecological system of the city, but also in the challenges to urban planning that the uninhabitable terrain caused. And yet, as Prudence followed the man, it seemed to her that the luster of all that lost gold had permeated the street murals and sidewalk art and paintings in display windows, all of which made Johannesburg one of the most colorful city centers of the modern world.

But there were no city centers in the history of mankind without an underbelly.

Sheryl had told Prudence that there were places in Joburg she should not venture, and Prudence had resented this comment, for it had seemed tinged with racism and classism. But now walking down that narrow, shadowy road, watching the man enter a drab little restaurant with its signage in disrepair, she felt as if she should have heeded the warnings.

She slowed, wondering if she should enter behind him, and this hesitation was all the men outside the restaurant door needed to begin calling out to her, reaching for her, slowing their cars to speak to her. Even stray dogs seemed to detect her foreignness.

When she opened the door to the restaurant, it felt like a great relief, though she soon found that inside was not as inviting as she might have hoped.

Mossy-green walls were spackled as if they'd been replastered and repainted haphazardly time and again. There were wobbly old Formica tables, peeling plastic flooring, duct-taped chair cushions, and yet, despite all that was unappealing, a buffet of hot South African home-cooked dishes made the place smell divine. Ravenous, Prudence moved into the line. She watched the all-Black group of customers eating stewed meats and rice and mealie and roast corn, and though she wasn't exactly sure what to order, given how she stood out, she was also too embarrassed to leave. Finally, with her order meticulously planned and memorized, she waited in line, two people behind the man she'd followed. Thankfully, he had yet to notice her, but when it was her turn at the front of the line and the woman behind the counter called on a man who'd only just entered, that all changed.

"Hey," Prudence said.

The newly arrived customer stepped in front of her.

"Wait. I was here first."

Her American accent sliced through the restaurant clatter. Heads turned, forks paused at mouths, but the woman behind the counter only smiled at the man, ignoring Prudence's cry. When it was finally Prudence's turn at the front of the line again, she told the woman she'd have only a Coke, as if remaining hungry would teach the bitch not to ignore her. The woman shrugged, pushed a warm bottle of generic cola toward her, while the man from the balcony, having collected his food, was already seated at a table in a far corner.

She walked toward him, asked if she could join him.

"Sit, if you will," he said.

She turned her body sideways, feeling a bit whiny and embarrassed, then sensing a clot of blood, hot and thick, pushing its way out onto her menstrual pad. There seemed to be no restroom in the restaurant, so she clenched her pelvis, trying to calm the panic she had about overflowing, while also imagining the blood coursing its way onto the too-small cotton surface of the second-to-last sanitary pad she had. When the discomfort grew bearable again, she looked to the man, chewing vigorously, his arms wrapped about the plastic tray.

"Hi, I was the one who was—"

"I know who you are," he said.

She thought she'd ask him about the hearings but his body language seemed closed to any line of questioning. He took another bite of his sandwich; thick layers of meat smelling of Indian spices hung from between fat slices of white bread. The man took a gulp of his drink and peered at the two women working behind the counter with aprons tied at their waists. They seemed to be snickering at Prudence.

"I swear I don't understand the women in this country. Have they never heard of the feminist movement? She skipped right over me like—"

"Feminist movement?"

"Yes, you have heard of it?"

"Ach, what use is the feminist movement to that woman?" He looked up, his gaze fixed on Prudence. "The only power she has is this job. She sees a man she knows, she sees you with your fancy shoes and handbag, and she thinks you can wait. Is that really affecting your life? That man may give her an extra piece of meat at the butcher shop to take home to her family. What were you going to give her?" He belched into his fist.

"It's her job," Prudence said. "In America—"

"You're not in America."

"I know. My only point—"

"You are going to say something about racial solidarity, ja?"

"No. I understand that South Africans know the principles of ujima—"

"Ujima?" He guffawed.

"That's not the point," Prudence said. "Race isn't the point. Customer service is the point."

"Is it? Customer service in America is not about race?"

Prudence felt even more foolish. How could he make her feel so foolish? And why was he so angry? Because she'd seen him crying?

"Look, all I'm saying is that we're all oppressed . . ."

"Aha . . . Black Americans always want to compare plights. But this was always our land. We weren't brought here." He peeled off the round edges of his bread, stuffing all of it into his mouth. "It's waking up one morning and finding animals in your yard. You think they're quite nice but as you approach, they bare their teeth and begin to chase you back into your home. They call their friends and every inch of your yard is now covered with them. You didn't think you needed to keep the kind of weaponry that could kill off thousands of these vicious animals, so for years you're locked inside with only the bare necessities as they graze on all the vegetables you planted and drink your fresh water. And now you have to ask permission to leave your home and they may tell you yes, but then they follow you with their jagged teeth everywhere you go, telling you that you're not allowed to do this, telling you that you're shit because you weren't prepared for their arrival, shit because you couldn't have imagined beasts like them. No, no, this is definitely not America."

Prudence might have argued more with this man, she might have mentioned the terrible plight of Native Americans or the horrors of chattel slavery or debated a dozen of the other insti-tutional villainies of the Americas, but the man was right—she would be leaving South Africa before the end of the year and would likely never think of that woman behind the counter again.

"I assume you know that woman, right?"

"No, we Africans don't all know each other." He took another gulp of his drink. Even the way he swallowed felt like mockery.

"But you live here so—?"

"I live in Stockholm."

"Sweden?"

"Yes, you've heard of it, have you?"

Prudence felt shamed by her surprise. She had thought his accent clearly South African, and he'd come across as exceptionally provincial in his brown pants and faded, flowery, Madiba-inspired shirt.

He smirked as if to tell her she'd been awfully predictable.

"So, I guess you're here on vacation?"

"Sure. One could say that I'm here on holiday," he said. "I assume the *New York Times* isn't giving one of their prize reporters a holiday here?"

"I wouldn't know." She winked but he offered her nothing, no smile, no sign that he knew she'd fibbed to fend off the nosey white ladies.

"Will you be in town for long?" she said.

"No longer than I have to be."

"So, you're here on business, then?"

He opened the lid to his cup. It covered half his face as he tipped it toward him. He chewed his ice. He didn't answer.

"I was just trying to be friendly when I offered you the tissue before."

He peered at her again. Above the strong jaw sat high cheekbones and naturally kohl-lined eyes with long, curly lashes. "I wasn't anxious to be consoled. My apologies."

She was surprised by his half apology, surprised by how delighted she was by it. She turned toward him more fully now, setting her hands on the tabletop, thinking perhaps they had reached some new understanding.

"You're not much of a talker, huh?"

"Particularly not when I've chosen to sit alone."

"Oh, damn." She had laid her own trap. "Well, if I leave now maybe I can finally have my seat back." Prudence rose from the chair, leaving her cola bottle behind. She walked toward the door and heard him lightly jogging after her. Pleased, she turned as if to courteously accept his more sincere apology, but on his face was an unmistakable smirk. He leaned in, too close, too familiar, motioning in a way that could be mistaken for both intimacy and intimidation, his breath slightly flavored with garam masala. He pointed at her pants. "Seems you're bleeding."

She was horrified but steadied herself. "I guess I should say thanks?"

"Only if you are thankful."

"So, what does a smart-ass like you call yourself?"

He reached into his wallet and retrieved a plain white stock card. The kind one could have had made at any copy shop in America. She tilted it, letting it catch a little sunlight, as it had turned out to be quite a beautiful afternoon. On the face of the card was the name of a company Prudence had never heard of, an office number, an email address, a cellular phone number, and beneath it the words STOCKHOLM and MATSHEDISO SAMUELSSON.

She looked up at him. "Mat," she said.

He seemed slightly amused by this renaming.

"Don't you want to know my name?" she asked.

"I'll call you 'the one who thinks she can call me Mat.'"

They parted ways and Prudence quickly returned to City Hall. Before the next testimony was scheduled to resume, she cleaned her pants as best she could in the restroom, then climbed the stairs only to notice that the doors to the balcony were closed. She pulled one open and found that the balcony had been roped off. With no guards in sight, she slyly slid beneath the rope and sat down before anyone else returned from lunch. She thought she might have a few quiet moments to read but soon realized there was a meeting being held down below. A Black man, three Committee members, and two of the lawyers she had seen earlier that morning were speaking. Undetected, she took a few photographs. Some of the photos were of the men below, but mostly they were of the hall, its decorative scroll detailing, its polished brass notes. Then, the Black man seated at the witness table began to speak into the microphone. It was clear that a question had been posed before she entered. Prudence sat back, listening, stunned by what she heard. The man spoke some of the most horrifying words she had written down all week, but soon, the returning crowd began to push against the doors and a Committee member said something about continuing the testimony at a later agreed-upon time. A guard tried to hurry the man toward the hall's exit, but the man walked coolly, his pace steady and easy as he re-buttoned his glossy black suit jacket.

6

A steady accumulation of a thousand slights.
—Nelson Mandela

Washington, D.C., 2018

The server returned before Prudence had a chance to take on Davis's comment.

Brutal childhood?

The waiter held a wire-bound pad, slouching as he paused for Tara's order. Tara droned on about not understanding how this was prepared and the accompaniments for that, while Prudence thought again about Davis's words. *Really fucked Pru's head up.* How long had he felt that way? She knew that Davis, the product of an untold cast of Black upper-middle-class Ohioans, had quietly judged her lower-class Caribbean roots. She'd seen how he held his arms about himself when they visited her mother in that dingy West Baltimore apartment she lived in when Prudence and Davis were first married. But now Davis had spoken of her with such derision that it seemed as though he'd been repulsed by the many dramas of her life, as though he thought she had chosen for things to be as horrid as they had been after her father died.

The waiter turned toward Davis now, and to Prudence's surprise he ordered the fish not the lamb. Discomposed by this very simple dinner selection of her husband's, Prudence chastised the server for not requesting her order before taking a man's. She then told him she would have her "usual."

The server flushed, apologized, wrote something down on his pad, then furrowed his brow. "Ma'am, I'm sorry, but I'm new here. I don't know your usual."

Prudence looked to Davis before glancing back at the waiter. "Please ask my husband since he seems to know everything there is to know about me."

Davis's right cheek trembled beneath the skin. He recited her order, remembering to mention her nightshade allergy and the precise temperature she liked her soft-shell crabs, and while Matshediso gave the waiter his order next, Prudence reached into her purse for her phone. She wanted to seem unbothered, and in the midst of this performance, she decided to check on Roland. A few years back, she had hired a security consultant to provide them with a defense plan for their home. She convinced herself that as Roland grew older, he would want more autonomy, so it was important that they could always keep an eye on him. She had the house covered by cameras, save the bathrooms and the basement storage room, the one Wi-Fi dead spot in their home. Now, from her phone, she spied Roland and the sitter watching television in the family room. Satisfied that all was well, she put away her phone and removed a tube of hand lotion from her bag. It was a candied scent that often prompted Roland to lick his lips when he smelled it. "Willy Wonka," Prudence would say to him, trying to get him to repeat the words.

Davis took her hands in his now, massaging the lotion into them. "I'm sorry," he said. "About what I said earlier. I shouldn't have said that." He turned to Tara and Matshediso, as if to make public his sincerity. "I didn't want Mat to think he was the only one who'd been through tough times. But it wasn't my place. It was out of line."

Nobody apologized like Davis. He had often modeled for Prudence what it was to be in intimate relations with other humans, how one can stay accountable for the harms we inflict upon those we love. But still, Prudence didn't want to let him off the hook. She wasn't sure she wanted to question him there, but she had to know where that hostility had come from.

And yet that particular concern was soon gone when she felt someone nearing. She presumed it was the waiter returning for another clarification with his dingy fourth-grade notebook, but instead it was a woman.

"Excuse me?"

There stood the redhead in a cloud of cheap apple-scented spritz, wearing fresh mauve lipstick and hot-pink rouge.

"I'm so sorry to bother you." The redhead cleared her throat to address Davis, while the couple with the children across the aisle looked over. "I know you must—I know you probably hate this, but I couldn't leave without taking the chance. I mean—I'm a singer—a pretty good one, I've been told—and—" The woman dug her freckly arm into her slouchy, shiny handbag and pulled out a computer stick drive. Davis waved his hand but the woman, not understanding, stretched her arm across Prudence to offer it to him. "It's a demo and I would really appreciate it if you could take a listen. I love your work, and I'm so sorry to—"

"I'm not who you think I am." Davis nudged the stick back toward the woman, his delight barely concealed. "I'm flattered, but . . ."

"Oh my—" The woman gaped at Tara, as though Tara might confirm better than Davis that he was not the music producer she thought he was. But Tara had by then covered her mouth, her laughter barely contained.

"Oh my God. I'm so so sorry. I thought—you might have noticed me looking—"

"Yes, we all noticed," Prudence said.

"I'm so so embarrassed and so so sorry. Please—"

"It's fine," Davis said. "It happens all the time."

"Oh my God. I'm so happy I'm not the only one who's done this. I feel so stupid."

"It's fine," Davis said again. "And good luck with your career. I'm sure you'll get a break soon."

As the woman scurried away, Prudence felt like she was watching her favorite tree being knocked over in a windstorm, leaves aflutter, limbs splayed and bouncing, roots slowly uplifting. She couldn't control anything about that night. She peered at the redhead and her friends, who were now gathered in a ring of mortified laughter at the restaurant entrance. The manager smiled at them as if overcome by the ambience of their youth. Outside, the awning lights, effulgent and dramatic, seemed to be expanding the appearance of the raindrops and they looked to Prudence like jumbo, diaphanous tears.

"Does that happen a lot?" Tara asked.

Davis blushed and seemed on the verge of explaining something, but the server reappeared bearing four canapé shells. He recited the descriptions the chef had given him at the midday service huddle—from where in France the goat cheese hailed, how exactly they crushed the Wisconsin cranberries, and which D.C. free-garden herbs they'd decided *not* to include in the dinner selections.

Tara reached for her dinner fork and Matshediso discreetly modeled how she should instead use the canapé fork, a delicate little piece of silver with a metal flower at its end.

"Did we order this?" Tara said.

"It's an amuse-bouche," Davis explained. "Like a little freebie."

Tara, bemused, stuffed the honied ball of goat cheese panna cotta into her mouth, chewing audibly with such exhilaration that none of them dared snatch away her pleasure with an appeal for propriety. Her large eyes rolled up, seeming to disappear into their sockets, and she put her hand to her heart, as if to say she was sorry but couldn't help herself. Prudence chuckled quietly, and Tara, taking note, covered her mouth, chewing hurriedly as if suddenly she had a thought, a burning question.

"So, I know Davis and Mat work at the same law firm." Tara sipped from her water glass and leaned forward, her breasts nearly grazing the tabletop. "But Prudence, what do you do?"

Prudence grinned tightly, her ears warming, her neck brightening. "I'm a strategy consultant. I used to work for McKinsey but now it's more freelance."

"Oh." Tara cocked her head, licked a bit of goat cheese from her finger. "So, you don't work full-time?"

"We have a child," Davis interjected.

"One child, right?" Tara sat back in her chair. "So, do you mostly stay home with your son? Are you a—what do they call it?—a SAHM?"

Aah . . . classic. The insignificance attached itself to any answer that couldn't be quantified with a substantial, regular paycheck. Prudence had three Ivy League degrees. She worked for two decades at the top of her field and was still being actively recruited. She had earned more money during those years than Tara would probably see in her lifetime, and yet, the choice to stay home with her child rendered her useless, impotent, invisible. Prudence couldn't tell Tara to go fuck herself but she wanted to. She could have told her that she'd gotten Davis the interview at his current law firm, and that the Harvard classmate who'd done her the favor had expected her to visit his suite at the Mandarin in return. She could have told Tara about the late-night strategy sessions with Davis in their bedroom, her at the foot of the bed, him on the sofa trying to conceal his tears after he'd been passed over for partnership, not once but twice. She could have mentioned the ad hoc management training she'd given him and many

other friends, the tips and tricks she'd helped them employ to better their careers. She could have informed Tara and Matshediso
that she made it possible for Davis to achieve what they had. But
Prudence didn't say any of this because Tara knew exactly what
she was doing when she asked that question, and no matter how
hard Prudence pushed out her chest, claiming the right to be at
home with her child, the moment never ceased to humiliate her.

Davis reached for her hand beneath the table. She gently pulled
away, angering again as she recalled his "brutal childhood" comment. It was Roland who would have had a "brutal childhood" if
Prudence hadn't stepped out of the fast lane. If Davis had shown
even half the care for Roland as she had expected him to, particularly after years of him longing for a child, maybe she could
have kept working.

But she couldn't say any of this, could she?

"Yep, that's what I am, a stay-at-home mom." Prudence grinned
with clamped teeth. "And given that Black women spent centuries
taking care of other people's babies, it's actually quite a shift in the
paradigm for me to be able to care for my Black child in this way."

Davis tapped her thigh as if to congratulate her for not kicking
that woman's ass. And Matshediso sat smirking, as if he'd enjoyed
every bit of her squirming, every bit of her attempt to not feel
small at a dinner she and her husband would be paying for. Then,
Matshediso peered at his phone and with an expression of concern, excused himself and headed toward the restaurant door.

"And what do you do?" Davis asked Tara.

Prudence didn't care what the Tara woman did for a living. She
was watching Matshediso, who first took the call in the vestibule,
but who now, despite the thunder and lightning, walked outside.
Where was he going? As she quietly prayed that his call was an
emergency, the sort that would take him far away from her, the
restaurant went completely dark. Prudence's phone buzzed with

a local storm warning and when the lights returned after forty long seconds, patrons clapped and the baby woke crying.

"That's quite some storm," Davis said, stretching his neck for any sign of Matshediso's return. "And I see you enjoyed that amuse-bouche, huh Tara?" He pointed at her canapé shell that had been swiped clean with her index finger.

Tara may have felt the sting of his judgment but Davis didn't give her time to respond. "None of us grew up eating this way. I'm a preacher's kid. We ate the same pork chops or chicken-and-rice every night because we spent most of our evenings at church." Davis pushed aside his shell. "Not a great way to live, but I do know how to pray, don't I, Pru?"

"Prayers up." She offered a little hallelujah wave, not looking up from her shell.

Matshediso returned, rubbing raindrops into the cashmere of his sweater and clearing his throat. He inched his chair closer to Tara's. "Sorry."

Another waitstaff member arrived to clear away their dishes. This young man grinned, as if pleased, as he collected Tara's shell.

"Everything cool?" Davis asked Matshediso.

Matshediso nodded, then their main server arrived with the wine.

With a flourish of his chewed fingernails, the server displayed the label of the Barolo Davis had chosen for the table. Davis glimpsed at the bottle, reasonably expecting that the restaurant would deliver what he ordered. The waiter nodded and began the process of uncorking, sliding the slender neck of the 2009 vintage beneath his armpit. Prudence was certain this would have warranted immediate dismissal if the manager had been paying attention. She grunted just audibly enough for Davis to tap her leg, signaling that he too noticed the armpit pull. If only for a moment, the two of them seemed to approach that familiar feeling of being in a perfect dance, that swift splendor of consonance achieved when one has been in sync with another long enough. Davis smiled and Prudence half expected he would offer to open the bottle himself, but instead, the four of them watched this most inelegant offense, as the waiter realized only after he had popped the cork that he had forgotten to deliver them wine goblets.

"Sorry," he grumbled. "Right back." He set down the bottle in front of Tara, who began reading the label aloud. Prudence suddenly recalled that the 2009 wines from Piedmont were reported to be thin and metallic, and she thought how the bad wine selection would be a perfect addition to the shitty night. Tara moved the bottleneck toward her nose and Prudence found herself wondering what other body part might touch the lip of that wine bottle before the evening's end. She and Davis smiled at one another just as the mother across from them pushed herself out of the booth.

"Charles?" the woman cried out.

No one but Prudence seemed to notice the woman searching beneath her table. Davis was evaluating the wine, smacking his lips, and by the way he pursed them, Prudence knew it had, indeed, been a poor choice. The waiter took Davis's silence as permission to dole, nearly overfilling Matshediso's glass and spilling wine over the side of Tara's, which he promptly absorbed with a sad-looking grey cloth that hung over his forearm.

"Was that a call from work?" Davis asked Matshediso.

"Yep. Things are going well."

"My man Mat here is a genius." Davis nodded and forced himself to take another sip, as though hoping the wine would open to an acceptable bouquet. Meanwhile, the mother across from them was now searching beneath the empty tables on her side of the restaurant, calling out repeatedly for "Charlie."

"Mat's developed new software, like real spy shit," Davis said. "He's already helped six firms double their billings by showing how inaccurate human timekeeping can be. When associates don't keep their time right, we lose ten percent of our billings with bad guesses. Mat has these little timekeepers that ask you every eighteen minutes if you're doing work, and it bills it to the correct client. It has a little tracker too, like those activity watches, where it can distinguish between work and play." Davis pushed his glass toward the middle of the table and clapped his hands, unwittingly drawing the attention of a few diners. He quickly lowered his voice. "He also figured out a way to detect when partners and associates bill excessive travel charges. Like booking extra days on the back and front ends for business development. Half that shit isn't business development. And now with Mat's software, we'll be able to stop it."

The mother moved toward the front of the restaurant, taking off her wedge sandals to walk more swiftly. She rushed through the vestibule, ran outside, then hurried back in.

"But what about employee morale?" Prudence said this even though she was still watching the mother and glancing at the father, who remained on his call. The baby in the car seat kicked her little feet.

"Morale? Every firm's gonna be doing this. Then, where are the low-morale employees gonna work?"

"But how do you actually do it?" Tara said.

"It's surveillance. Cell towers, cameras, computer spyware. We keep them locked down. Three law firms are already using it and their profits are way up."

Something about what Davis said made Matshediso blanch.

"Charles!" The woman's voice swept over the din of the restaurant's clatter. There was unmistakable panic in her voice. The manager arrived to speak with her.

"What's happening over there?" Prudence nodded toward the woman, as several other patrons turned to watch too, concern lining their faces. "Did she lose the boy?"

"He's probably behind the bar pouring himself a drink. Badass little kid." Davis sipped more wine. "Pru, I asked Mat if he can come over and take a look at that security system you had installed at home. He thinks he can probably optimize it."

"We're good. I already hired the best," Prudence said.

The boy's mother stalked toward them and was now leaning over their table, her long, unpolished fingers bracing its edge.

"Where is he?" Her tousled hair had formed a nest atop her head, and her husband, only now realizing that something was amiss, told the person on the phone he'd call back. He crossed the aisle, pulling his wife's hand, begging her to explain to him what was happening.

But she brushed him aside.

"I saw you. Saw you looking at him." As the woman pointed at Matshediso, Prudence saw members of the waitstaff rushing past the short Normandy stone wall, searching between tables for the boy.

"Where is he?" The woman's finger twitched with the weight of her shaking hand.

Matshediso said nothing, and the manager stepped forward, trying to convince the woman that they'd soon find her little boy, that she shouldn't panic.

"This couple dines here nearly every week," the manager added.

Of course, every week was an exaggeration, but Prudence appreciated the gesture. The manager told the woman that Davis was a partner at a "very respectable law firm" housed in a building "only a few blocks away." But this did nothing to persuade the woman to leave their table. By now the ambient music had stopped and the other patrons had turned fully to bear witness.

Davis rose from his seat, as lightning continued to flash outside. He skirted around Prudence's chair to speak to the husband, who appeared less feverish.

"Children play hiding games," Davis said. "We've got a rambunctious little boy too."

"Not Charles. He's never done anything like this," the woman said.

"The boy was hiding under the table just a little earlier," Davis said.

"He was under me. He always stays close enough that he can see me." The woman was seemingly trying to convince her husband of this too. The husband put both hands on his hips as if to keep himself upright.

"My wife told me that your friend had been watching Charles. That it made her nervous," the husband said.

"So nervous that you stayed and ordered dessert?" Davis replied. The husband's shoulders tightened. "Please, don't talk—"

"Listen, we were sitting here the whole time," Davis added.

"He left the table before the lights went out." Spittle formed at the left corner of the woman's mouth. She turned to look back at her baby in the car seat and scanned the restaurant again, hoping someone had found her boy, but there seemed to be no sign of him.

"Where did you go?" She pointed again at Matshediso. But still, Matshediso didn't answer.

"Ma'am." The manager was perspiring now, the veins in his neck purpling. "I can assure you that Mr. Gooden can vouch for his guest."

"So, you've never seen *this* man before?" The boy's father pointed at Matshediso. "He's not a regular patron, right?"

The manager's eyes widened and his mouth parted. "As I told you, Mr. Gooden is a trusted patron and this is his guest." The

manager glanced at Davis, concerned, then the father of the boy turned to Davis too.

"How long have you known this man?" the husband asked Davis.

Prudence knew Davis would never answer that question. Matshediso, of course, had only been working at the firm for a month, if not less, and they'd certainly performed a background check, certainly called each of his references, but Davis couldn't vouch for him, not personally.

"Can you tell me that he didn't grab Charlie's hand and take him outside to some waiting van? Can you? I want to see the security cameras. Call the goddamn police!" the mother shouted. By this time all of the diners had stopped pretending to eat. They were ogling Prudence, Davis, Tara, and most especially Matshediso.

"Do any one of you know this man? Can anyone vouch for this man? Any one of you?"

7

You can't hate the roots of the tree and not hate the tree.
—Malcolm X

Johannesburg, 1996

Thirty minutes after the man finished testifying in the private meeting, the official proceedings began again. Prudence searched the unusually large crowd for Matshediso. She presumed he had found a seat downstairs and he left her mind almost as soon as Volter resumed his testimony.

On the day of the Mozambique Eight boys' deaths, can you tell us what happened?

Surprisingly, Volter seemed more eager to talk after the lunch break, but there was nothing about his posture that suggested he was ashamed of the things he would say next.

Zwane picked up the men in the agreed-upon meeting place in KwaNdebele, a Bantustan—a Black homeland. He allowed the leader of the group to drive and gave the others alcoholic drinks. I followed behind the kombi. Zwane was instructed to tell the driver that they were meeting someone at a safe house for further directions. The other men stayed inside the kombi while Zwane led their leader inside. Two of our officers awaited their arrival. I joined them inside soon after I arrived.

What did you and the two officers do to the leader, the eldest brother, Thomas Mahlangu?

Volter put his right index finger into the palm of his left hand. *We were trying to get him to answer questions about his father. His father was responsible for destabilizing actions. Arson, boycotts. He was in the leadership of Mbokotho, an organization set up to promote KwaNdebele's aims of becoming independent from South Africa.* The sound from the mic seemed lower somehow and the entire hall seemingly pitched forward to hear him.

And did you electrocute Thomas to get the answers?

Correct, Volter answered.

Electrocute? Was that in his written statement? Prudence felt blindsided by the question.

In the meantime, the boys in the kombi were drunk. And this is when Zwane attached the bomb, correct?

No, one of the officers and Zwane removed the boys from the kombi one by one. They were quite inebriated by that time, so it wasn't difficult to pin them down.

Pin them down?

To inject them.

To inject them with what?

Poison.

A white man beside Prudence rose from his seat. Did white South Africans not know what was happening all those years?

And then?

Then, Zwane asked me to hold his cigarettes and his little trophy case while he worked under the kombi. The explosives were built so they wouldn't need to be lighted. They were attached under the cage. Fitted with clamps and screwed. Once the pins were pulled, they would activate thirty minutes later.

Prudence leaned back in her seat wondering why she was only now learning of this story. Those children had been baited by adults. They sat alone on a bus, waiting to be poisoned and blown up. And only now, over ten years later, was it breaking news. She understood, intellectually, that the South African government had controlled the narrative, controlled the media, but she couldn't help but feel the terrible shame of her naivete. And being in that hall, and watching those proceedings with their clinical, prosaic mood, was in deep contradiction with the staggering feeling she had of being bloated with rage.

Now, the advocate for the Committee stepped forward. *Colonel Volter, did you watch the detonation?*

Yes. We pushed the kombi over an incline and the detonation was successful.

Nearly everyone in the hall was crying. A woman in the section next to Prudence put her head between her knees. Volter seemed unflappable.

You mentioned a "trophy case"? What is this trophy Zwane asked you to hold?

It was a little tin that he carried. Volter shaped his hands into a rectangle. *Many of the men kept trophies of their successes against the resistance.* The Chief Judge nodded as though this had been heard before.

By the time of the detonation, was Thomas Mahlangu already dead?

I believe so. We removed the body from the safe house and strapped him under the kombi before detonation.

Volter wasn't speaking about these children like they had been real people, not even for the sake of the families, who were looking at him from the front seats. Was the Mahlangu mother there in that large crowd of relatives? Was she the woman who had pulled up her legs into the bench, twisting herself like an infant, the woman whose body seemed so broken Prudence couldn't bear to look at her?

Many in the country believed MK was responsible for the boys going missing; is this correct?

Volter nodded, as if he appreciated the question. *Yes, we wanted to leave the impression that the ANC was responsible. It would have suited the purposes of the government. To make whites think the Blacks were poorly trained and that Security Forces could win war against them with ease. It contributed to a feeling of trust in the Security Forces.* It was a small smile, but the cameras caught it. Prudence would see it later that night on the news and she would regret that she hadn't snapped the photo herself.

Did you receive verification that someone in charge, that the people higher up knew what you had done?

Volter nodded. *Afterward, commanding officer, Van Buren, went with me to KwaNdebele. We drove past the incline where the bomb was detonated. Van Buren said, "This is your monument." He didn't say if anyone at TREWITS knew. Our work was probably too insignificant.*

Paul Mahlangu, the father of four of the boys, died in an explosion at his house the morning after the boys were taken. It was reported that this may have been an accidental detonation of explosives that were to be used in terroristic activities. Did you or Zwane have anything to do with this detonation?

Volter paused and motioned toward his lawyer. They conferred while he remained in the witness chair, covering the microphone. When his lawyer returned to the counselor's table, Volter rubbed his face and began again.

I didn't know I was here to testify about that incident, he said.

Do you know if there was an order to eliminate Paul Mahlangu?

Volter shook his head. *I cannot recall.*

Did Andrew Zwane kill Paul Mahlangu? Zwane was a double agent, trusted in the community, isn't that right? Did he place a bomb in Mahlangu's house where the rest of his family lived? Did he know if his wife was in the house?

Volter reared back. The Chief Judge warned counsel about the pace of his questioning.

Zwane was not a double agent. He worked for us, and because he was a Black, the Blacks more easily believed he was a member of the ANC. He never worked for the Black organizations.

The fact that Zwane was Black and had easily fooled Black activists seemed to be a point of pride for Volter.

He was an askari, then?

Askari is a Nigerian military term. But it has a broad meaning, so okay, yes.

When was the last time you saw Andrew Zwane?

Volter squinted and glared at the Committee's counsel as though he were wasting his time. *Today. In the corridor. Just outside.*

A rush of reporters streamed out of the hearing, while Prudence became all the more certain that the Black man who had testified during that private hearing after lunch had, in fact, been Andrew Zwane.

The Johannesburg portion of the hearings ended later that week. In the following days, Volter's testimony would stand out as particularly horrible, but it was Volter's *and* Zwane's words collectively that haunted Prudence every day as she drove out of the city center, every day as she boiled eggs in the mornings, and worst of all, every night when she lay in bed. She couldn't stop thinking of those boys' faces that had flashed on the news, with their short-cropped hair and their handsome, solemn faces, wearing takkies that couldn't make them run any faster from their murderers. And at some point she found herself wondering what Matshediso had made of it all. She hadn't seen him since they had parted ways at the restaurant. She thought perhaps he wasn't the best choice for a new friend, but she called him anyway, asked him out for lunch, and there, in the dim light of a crowded pub in Orange Grove, she sat across from him, struggling to find commonality between them.

"So, what did you think of the hearings?" she asked.

"Is this an interview for the *New York Times*?" He didn't smile, though it might have been a joke.

"I'm trying to make conversation."

"Maybe I only wish to eat."

Every word felt loaded with this man, and even in the kitschy environs of the Radium Beer Hall—with its cheeky posters, its red plastic Captain Morgan's tablecloths, and its gregarious owner, Manny—the lunch had a sterile, businesslike quality to it. It was tiring, and she'd only been there for twenty minutes. She decided she would drink her whiskey, eat her hake, and get the hell out of there. After that she dropped her head, focusing only on her plate, until Matshediso tapped the table in front of her.

"Hallo? Hi. Hallo?" he said.

She eyed him.

"Can I ask a question?" He pushed his giblets across his plate and she felt a small breakthrough forthcoming. "What were you expecting? Out of this lunch? You must have had some expectations."

She frowned, wondering how to take his question. "I didn't have expectations. I just asked you to lunch," she said. "But . . . you can go. Leave. I can eat by myself. I can pay for my own lunch."

"Oh, you were expecting me to pay? I was expecting *you* to pay!" He laughed, and she found herself smiling. He held up his hands. "I'm sorry. All right?" His voice pitched, giving him a slight bit of boyish exuberance. "Being back here makes me feel—makes me feel plenty of things I don't want to feel."

"Do you still have family here?"

There was a rugby match streaming through the restaurant's televisions, and the crowd, cheering, moved to the back room where Prudence and Matshediso were seated. She leaned over the table to hear him better.

"My mother is here. There are others, but mostly it's my mother. I am her only child. I don't see her as often as I should." He bit his lip with a contemplative expression.

"I am my mother's only living child," she said. "And I don't see her as often as I should either."

He looked at her as if he weren't sure they meant the same things.

"And your father?" he asked.

"Passed on."

"Mine as well."

Though the crowd continued cheering around them, the two of them sat, trying to understand perhaps, how these very basic yet extraordinary facts about them—dead fathers, only child to mothers with whom they had challenges—could be so eerily similar.

"Do you like it here?" he asked.

"In South Africa? I'm not sure. It's a complicated place," she said. "I don't understand all the categories you have for people. Sometimes 'Black' means Black African, but sometimes 'Black' means Indian and Asian and Coloured. And what is this 'Coloured' category anyway? In America, light-skinned Black folks are considered just Black."

He nodded. "You know how people are always telling Black people that race is a construct, and we're like, ja, okay, sure? Well, 'Coloured' is the most construct of the constructs. The whites clearly needed a new category for their bastard children." He scoffed. "But it's confusing, ja. A boy with a white father and a Black African mother is not necessarily Coloured. You have to be mixed for generations. Coloured is its own culture. They have their own way of seeing the world, and they see themselves as different from Black."

When she thought on it, nothing about race and racism and their many iterations was original, and yet, she still found herself unmoored by it all.

"And what do you feel about this Truth and Reconciliation thing?"

He looked around, then lowered his voice, though it was unlikely anyone could hear them. "I understand they have to find a way to progress. This feels clean. 'Let's get on with it.' We are like this. South Africans get on with things. But because we are so busy 'getting on,' we sometimes don't take stock of the beatings we're taking and the things we're giving up until it's bloody too late."

"Do you think it's already too late?"

"I don't know," he said. "It feels as if we've all been in hospital after being beaten close to death and the authorities walk in and say 'we found the people who did this to you and we're going to take care of it. You get well,' they say. It seems kind, yes, but when you're out of hospital, you realize they've taken something away from you because all you want is some part in deciding how to hold the people who did this to you accountable. You want to have a say, a choice. And no, we're not all going to make the same choice but that's because each person's hurt is different." He paused as if to punctuate this point. "There's no accounting in this reconciliation process for how differently we all suffered."

"Do you know the writer James Baldwin? He says something like 'What is it you want me to reconcile myself to?'"

Matshediso nodded, as though he might have heard the quote before. "Malcolm X once said that South Africa was bet-ter than America because at least here we are not hypocritical and deceitful. We preach segregation and practice it, and in America you preach integration but deceitfully practice segregation." He laughed a rueful laugh. "I don't know if that's true and I don't know where this country is going. I know only that when I am here, surrounded by people who have done these horrible things, I don't think I can live in peace simply because they confess. We already know everything they are telling us. They killed our heroes, our families, so they could try and break the spirit of a whole people. Losing this country, they say, is justice enough, but those men testifying at the hearings are boastful, and sometimes I want to . . ." He clenched his teeth, and his fingers flexed and unflexed like a trumpeter's. Prudence was always acutely aware of moods, but particularly of anger, aware of its slight changes, its modulations, the way it could be unleashed in the most unexpected ways. The rage Matshediso exuded felt familiar, but it also felt like the sort that could birth a whole new and mightily unpleasant version of this man.

"You asked me if I liked it here and I think I do, but I am also afraid in a way I don't feel in other places. Your white people are different. It's like they haven't been neutered." She laughed but her laughter was a mask for genuine apprehension. "Last week, I saw a white man driving a Mercedes who cut in front of another guy for a parking space. When the other guy complained, the Mercedes driver got out of his car, dragged the guy onto the parking lot, and punched the shit out of his face. In America, old white dudes driving Benzes are not heavyweight boxers. The white men here are like deranged pirates."

Matshediso threw his head back in laughter. He told her he'd never heard it described this way before. "It's true, ja. Fucking hell, you must be careful with everybody here. A white man's violence has never been shamed in South Africa. And the propensity for violence doesn't disappear overnight. My problem is they expect us, who have become accustomed to living with that same violence, to simply adopt nonviolence as a way of life. You can't unring that bell. The peals echo for a very long time."

"Do you feel at home here?" she asked. "I don't know if I feel at home anywhere."

"A permanent feeling of dislocation." She was surprised at his words, surprised he felt the same way. "It's terrible how one can feel dislocated even in their own homeland. It's never about geography, ja, it's about who is waiting to embrace you."

He had seemed so emotionally unavailable, and yet, they had found some way with each other.

"I needed this talk," she said. "Thank you."

"Well, I didn't need it, but I'm happy to be of service." He laughed again, but this time it was a warm laugh.

He looked down at his giblets. "I should ask them for a take-away container."

They were ugly little things, but they smelled delicious.

"I can finish them if you won't." She reached for one, plopping it into her mouth. She felt starved much of the time, like there wasn't enough food in the world to fill her. She wondered what that kind of hunger meant about her.

"Come, take a ride with me? I want to show you something. I'll bring you back to your car when we're done," Matshediso said.

"Cool. And you definitely have to drive, because my Rent-A-Wreck barely made it here."

"A Rent-A-Wreck?" He said the words slowly, as if he had never heard the term.

"It was all I could afford, but now I can never tell when it needs gas or when it just wants to rest for a while." Prudence chuckled, as she followed him to his much nicer rental car.

The place he wanted her to see wasn't far from the restaurant. That part of Munro Drive was hilly, and he snaked around two sharp bends before parking next to a walkway of stone where dark-green moss puffed from its cracks. A Black woman and a bevy of children stood to take photos, while two white men climbed off mountain bikes to catch their breath and look out at the view. She followed Matshediso toward an expansive iron gate anchored by stone pillars that looked out over a valley of what seemed to be a thousand purple trees.

"Jacaranda," he said.

She'd read books where jacarandas were mentioned, but never had she seen one in real life, much less hundreds in one place. They were nearly neon in their purple brightness, and the way the afternoon sun played with the green trees that lay between them made the green of those trees seem greener than any she'd ever set eyes on.

"Jacarandas are not native to South Africa." He pointed down-hill toward more jacarandas that grew between slivers of houses. She wondered what it'd be like to live pillowed between all that wondrous purple. "They were brought from South America, but people come from all over the world to see them here."

"I read once that if a jacaranda bloom falls on your head, it will bring you good fortune," she said.

"In Peru, they tell this story of something called El Tunche, which I think means 'fear' in one of their indigenous languages," he said. "They say that the beauty and the fragrance of the jaca-randa will lull you into the jungle, only for this El Tunche, this tormented being, to devour you. El Tunche whistles when it has you in its sight." She froze, as if she could hear the whistle, but Matshediso couldn't whistle long enough because he was soon doubled over with laughter. She laughed at herself too. Then, he caught her eye, staring a bit too long and too deeply, as if wanting to make her turn from him.

"You've got real gallows humor." She was both trying to shake off the stare and trying to understand what the stare had meant to her and to him.

She looked toward his car. "Thank you for bringing me here. I wouldn't have known to look for this. This country is so full of surprises."

She didn't know exactly what was happening between them and wondered if he was attracted to her, wondered if she could ever be attracted to him. And maybe because she was desperate for companionship, desperate for connection, she invited him back to Sandton.

As he drove behind her car, she hoped this would be the start of something lovely that she hadn't anticipated. She was giddy with expectation, but in the end it turned out that he was far more interested in an anthropological study of Maxine, Synclaire, and Khadijah.

"Ach, this is what American women do?" He scowled at the television.

In another place and another time, Prudence might have argued the merits of *Living Single*, but that night she wanted intimacy, not a debate. She slid closer to him, her hand finding the underside of his thick, muscular thigh. She longed for attention, longed for touch, but Matshediso refused her, stiffening as she put her lips to his neck.

"You're a bit needy, aren't you?"

His nudge, but also this word—"needy"—felt almost violent.

"I only mean to say that something must have made you like this," he added.

Her roommate, Nadia, unlocked the door just at that moment, entering noisily. Prudence and Matshediso watched her clumsily bear the weight of a bouquet of red roses and a box of chicken.

Nadia glared at Matshediso, then searched for her last bottle of Castle in the fridge, as the backlight from the refrigerator drew attention to her cheap weave-in and her recently bleached skin. She'd made a spectacle of herself in her efforts to be more attractive to what they called "plaasjapies," which was a not-so-nice way to describe white South African farm boys. Now, as Nadia walked toward her bedroom, dragging her shoes at the heels, she said only, "Turn on the alarm after you let the garbage out."

Matshediso stood, dusted his pants. His lips were pinched, and he adjusted and readjusted the gold wristwatch she had first noticed in the balcony of the hall.

"Thank you for the hospitality," he said.

"Did Nadia hurt your feelings?"

He raised his hand, as though to make her stop speaking, as though Prudence's words were irritants.

"You don't like to feel rejected but you seem to enjoy rejecting people. I guess something must have made you like this."

8

I could conceive death but I could not conceive betrayal.
—Malcolm X

Johannesburg, 1996

Weeks passed and Prudence had decided not to bother anymore with Matshediso. She was trying also not to bother with thoughts of the hearings, though being anywhere in South Africa made that much harder, as snippets from the testimony seemed to be everywhere. However, as the weather grew warmer, intentional oblivion grew easier. There were weekend concerts at places like Kyalami Amphitheater, a green, hilly park where Black American artists like Tracy Chapman and Tevin Campbell performed songs for which she felt a particular possessiveness. There were new musical discoveries too—the sounds of Hugh Masekela and Mashamplani—artists whose global acclaim made her feel as though her life in America had been far too insular. She shared many of these moments with her classmates who had begun to reach out more often. Soon, she was spending much of her free time with them, along with a horde of progressive white South African lawyers, all of whom she'd meet up with at local pubs, laughing loudly and drinking as much as would be expected of any freedom-seeking, bookish American girls who had traveled abroad.

Four of her Joburg-based classmates—The Girls, they called themselves—had rented a home together on a little bohemian street in Yeoville, which was closer to downtown than where Prudence and Nadia lived. The Girls (all of them white except one who had a Korean grandfather) were the kind of women who wore Birkenstocks, maxi dresses, and overalls, the kind who she generally ignored at Harvard, but who she now gratefully had for companionship.

Before leaving Cambridge, she and Nadia had decided not to live with The Girls, though The Girls had kindly extended an invitation. They had rolled their eyes when The Girls insisted on finding a place to rent that was closer to a township so they could have a more "authentic African experience." Prudence and Nadia had already decided to use the advantage of the dollar-to-rand exchange rate to live in a way they could never afford in the Boston area. Granite countertops, sun-licked bedrooms, plush carpets, California King pillows, had all been there for the taking. There was no doubt upon their arrival in South Africa that the suburbs of Johannesburg had been borne of the same insipid desire by whites almost everywhere to escape non-white spaces, and no doubt that the choice to live among all those white people should have aroused some smidge of shame in them. But Prudence didn't feel ashamed. She reasoned that her classmates knew nothing of her "authentic" life outside of law school. How she had maxed out credit cards and manufactured an unspoken story of relative privilege by choosing well-fitted, understated clothes and not-too-worn shoes at poorly lit thrift shops. How her designer bags were solid knockoffs for which she'd paid a little extra to a Nigerian hawker in Flatbush. None of them, not even Nadia, knew the pleasure that little luxury apartment in Sandton brought her.

And yet, some nights she was desperate not to return there, desperate not to be alone.

The night before she would see Matshediso again, Prudence parked her Rent-A-Wreck in front of The Girls' house and after they returned from a night of clubbing, she decided to sleep on their couch. When she woke, it was already early afternoon on a resplendently sunny Sunday, a beautiful South African Spring day. As Prudence sat up, she observed tree limbs swinging listlessly over a street lined with houses in soft pinks and baby blues. People were happily milling about on small patches of lawns and paved walkways, pushing baby trams and jogging with Walkmans. It was a mixed-race neighborhood of mostly white-collar professionals, and she didn't quite know if what she was seeing was a post-Apartheid performance of progressivism or simply what the people had wanted all along.

After folding the sofa blanket, Prudence made her way across the expansive living room. Over the fireplace hung a black metal–framed photo of Mandela and de Klerk clasping hands in the air. In it, Mandela is smiling, his teeth prominent like little rectangular pearls, while de Klerk wears a strained grin, the sort one might see on newborn babies working to push out their first poop. She giggled quietly at the photo as she walked across the distressed floors, bleached white, and entered the kitchen where The Girls were already gathered. There, she was met by a sweeping plot of white cabinets, white appliances, white marble backsplash, and the backsides of The Girls who were staring out of the window, gawking at a broad-chested blonde who was tending to a braai in his front yard, guzzling a foamy beer.

"You're gorgeous even when you wake up," one of The Girls said, as they all turned to greet her.

Bluegrass played softly from the boombox as The Girls caught her up on their exciting projects at their various internships and, of course, on the people they'd recently slept with. They teased Prudence about a particular advocate, rich and handsome and much older, who had been handsy with her each time they'd all been together. Prudence couldn't tell them that she would have found it humiliatingly ironic to fuck her first white man while in sub-Saharan Africa. So, instead she laughed and traded more barbs and ate scrambled eggs and sourdough baguette, and after a few rounds of bad poker, the early afternoon turned into late afternoon, with the sun now skulking behind the neighbor's second story.

"I better get going," she announced.

She was certain Nadia wouldn't be home, and though she didn't wish to return to her lonely flat in Sandton, The Girls didn't insist that she stay. Rather, they began to disperse, offering her the one koeksister remaining in the box and telling her they would see her maybe the following weekend.

As she drove out onto the main road, Prudence took a bite of the koeksister and wiped the sticky honey from her face. The light from the setting sun made stripes on the car seats, and Prudence thought about what time of day it was back home in Baltimore. She'd only spoken to her mother once since she arrived, and she puzzled over where her mother might be staying now, whether with a friend or in a shelter or in a subsidized apartment the city admins had put her on the waitlist for. The state of her mother's affairs unsettled her in ways that made it hard to think of anything else, so she tried to push them out of her mind, which was just as well, since her Rent-A-Wreck began to cough, an indication that her gas tank was nearing empty even though the indicator still read FULL.

Prudence made a few turns and headed up a hill where she found the corner gas station with the full-service garage that she remembered seeing on an earlier visit. As she pulled alongside a pump, she noticed that the filling station house door was being propped open by a weedy boy with long, loose arms. He stood chatting with the attendant, a round-faced girl chomping on a large wad of gum, who seemed to be doing her best flirting—stroking her braids, batting her eyelashes, leaning her weight onto one thick and shiny leg. Unlike in most parts of America, you had to pump gas before you paid at the filling stations in Joburg, and though there was usually an attendant available to deal with this, the flirty girl didn't budge. Annoyed, Prudence climbed out of the car, clutched the pump, and when the tank gurgled with relief, she removed her credit card from her wallet and grabbed the long green sweater that had once been her father's, aware that she was still wearing "club clothes"—a short black minidress she had picked up at a yard sale in Boston. The woman who had sold her that dress told Prudence she'd met her husband wearing it but that "there were sixty pounds between then and now and two mistresses," and she had laughed the kind of laugh that had made Prudence pity her.

Now, guessing that the minidress looked far better in the dim lights of a bar, Prudence wrapped herself inside the cardigan, then locked the car, as a rush of night air swept in like cold, mad waves. As she approached the door of the station house, the cashier moved back behind the window and asked the boy to wait. Prudence handed the girl her credit card with a mocking flourish, and the teenager's jaws clacked as she said something to the boy in Zulu. The bright-purple wad of gum between the girl's back teeth came into view as she scowled.

"Cash only," she said.

Prudence rooted around in the pockets of her father's sweater, discovering three single US dollars. She held them up, knowing well that it wasn't enough for the gas, but all too often, South African cashiers simply didn't want to bother with credit card transactions unless forced to. "I don't have rand but I have dollars," she said, with not a little bit of derision.

The cashier, confirmed in her suspicions that Prudence was indeed a foreigner, rolled her eyes again. "Rand only."

"But I pumped the gas already."

The girl looked alarmed. "You took the petrol?"

"There's no sign that says 'Pay First' or 'Cash Only.' Do you have a bank machine in here?"

"Does this look like a bank?"

"You don't have to get smart." Prudence was losing patience. "Do you know if there's one nearby?"

The girl glanced at the boy who seemed to know, instinctively, that it was time for him to leave. The air outside roared and the door slammed shut behind him, as the darkening sky signaled that dusk was upon them.

"So, you don't have a credit card machine?"

The girl picked up the phone and dialed. She began speaking to someone in Afrikaans.

Prudence interrupted her. "If you can just tell me where the closest bank is, I'll walk there."

The girl turned from her and whispered something into the receiver.

Prudence tapped on the smudged plexiglass that separated the two of them. "Excuse me? How can we resolve this?"

The girl set down the phone and said nothing more to Prudence before adding another square of the purple gum to her already-thick wad.

"I'll leave the car and walk down to find a machine, okay?"

The girl chewed harder, pulling down her shirt, stretching letters further across her bosom. The shirt read COME HITHER. The girl pointed at Prudence. "Stay. You stole the petrol."

Seconds later, a South African police officer arrived. He wore the standard blueberry-colored shirt and droopy military-style pants, the hems tucked inside his thick boots. On his waist rested a black belt and a hefty holster with a flap that looked unwilling to conceal his gun. He spoke to the cashier in Afrikaans. Their chat was short, and Prudence, not yet worried, believed herself charming enough to explain everything to the officer.

But the officer did not look her in the eye.

Instead, he asked Prudence for her identification and for the rental car papers and began trailing her to the vehicle to retrieve them. She had had more than her fair share of interactions with police officers, and none of them had ever avoided eye contact. In fact, all of them had in varying degrees looked her straight on, as if to let her know they were watching her carefully.

"If you tell me where I can find a bank, I'll come back here to pay for the gas. You can even follow me there," she said, as he flipped through her papers.

The officer didn't give a reason for why he deemed her suggestion unacceptable. He only repeated the cashier's words. "It was payment by cash. You took the petrol." His Afrikaans-accented English made him sound angry, the harsh "k" like a warning. Prudence asked the officer if she could call a friend. He lifted his cap and nodded with an expression that seemed to suggest that she should have called a friend long before then. Prudence quietly berated herself. Cell phones were ubiquitous in South Africa but not yet at home in America. She'd hardly used hers since she'd arrived, but The Girls were nearby and Prudence was certain one of them could bring enough rand for her gas.

Prudence dialed The Girls. One by one. As their mobiles rang, she imagined the Bluegrass still playing in the kitchen, imagined that maybe they had gone as a group to purchase more koeksisters or coffee, leaving their phones atop the messy table. They wouldn't be gone long. Prudence left messages for each of them, then called Nadia, then Sheryl. The officer, growing irritable, reminded Prudence that he was doing her a favor by not immediately arresting her.

"How many friends do you have here?" he said.

"You want an actual number?"

He nodded and she pretended to count, her mind racing.

"Your friends should tell you not to steal petrol."

"In America, there are 'Pay First' or 'Cash Only' signs every-where. I didn't know they wouldn't have a credit card machine. What kind of gas station doesn't take credit cards?"

"You're not in America, you're in South Afreeka."

"I only mention it because—"

"How long have you been here? In the country?"

"A few months."

"And what do you do here?"

"I have an internship. I'm in school, back home."

"Working where? Where do you work?"

"A law firm."

"Which?"

"It's downtown."

"Which?"

Prudence lied about the name, fearful he would know her firm, know that it supported the ANC. The officer gestured toward her phone. "It seems your friends don't answer when you call."

"They're not far from here. If you let me walk there—"

"It's taking too long!" His outburst was harsh and unexpected. She tensed, and out of the corner of her eye, she spied the cashier spitting out the purple gum and quickly retreating into the little filling station house.

Prudence thought back to her very first encounter with police. She'd been thirteen when the uniformed officers pounded on the front door of their rowhouse. Their worried neighbors had come out too, staring from their small lawns, green hoses in hand. When her mother let the officers inside, they refused her offer to sit before blurting out that Prudence's father had been found dead.

"In a bag, on the shoulder of Reisterstown Road," one of the officers added.

"Upstairs!" her mother yelled at Prudence and her little brother. "Upstairs! Upstairs!" They hurried up the steps and Prudence's mother scolded the officers for not caring enough about the well-being of her children. But it was all too late. Prudence's brother began screaming into his pillow, asking Prudence questions about the kind of bag the officer meant. Prudence tried to soothe him, holding him against her chest, straining to hear the rest of the conversation downstairs.

"He's a teacher." Her mother sounded calm, as if she had quickly determined that what the officers had told her was a lie. On occasion, her father spent weekends in Atlantic City, his room on comp, and sometimes he'd bring back a blanket or a sweatshirt or a cup with the names CAESAR'S or BALLY'S stamped on them. Even when he lost money, he returned home with funny stories about rich tourists or old ladies with shopping bags of coins. They assumed he'd been in Jersey when he didn't come home on Friday night. "He's a high school math instructor," her mother added.

Now, the South African police officer drew closer to Prudence. He stood a few inches taller than her, but she could feel his breath on her forehead, warm, moist, and uneven.

"I have one more friend I can call. Can I get the number from my wallet?"

The officer didn't answer but he stepped back as Prudence reached for the car door. The wind picked up again, the breeze howling as if shocked by its own strength, while Prudence stretched across to the passenger seat floor, where she'd tossed her purse. She was worried that none of The Girls nor Nadia nor Sheryl would show, and she felt nearly breathless as the skin at the back of her legs grew damp with sweat. She had almost left Sandton without her wallet but had thought cherry-picking through it a waste of time, so she'd brought the whole fake designer bill-fold and now rifled through the interior zipper until she found the card.

"Matshediso," she said into the phone. It was the first time she spoke his full name, and she questioned if she was pronouncing it correctly. The Baltimore police officers had called her father "Kelvin" rather than "Calvin," and her mother had corrected them, angrily.

"Matshediso," Prudence repeated. "I'm leaving this message because I'm in quite a predicament. If you're still in the country and can help, I'd be really appreciative." She told Matshediso the location of the filling station, off Rockey Street, but knew it was unlikely he would receive the message before things worsened.

When Prudence pressed the end button on her phone, the officer told her to get out of the car.

"It seems you don't have *any* friends," he said.

9

... I was afraid of being carried away.
—Harriet Tubman

Johannesburg, 1996

Prudence tried to reach back into the car for her phone, but the officer blocked the door.

"Leave it and toss your keys inside too."

"Why?" Her heart raced but she did what she was told and pulled her cardigan closed, clutching it at her sternum. "Are you arresting me?"

The officer scanned the inside of her car to double-check that she'd done as he directed. The sun had almost set, though how much light remained was a question of perception. For the officer, perhaps there was too little, but for Prudence, who wished she could put the brakes on the earth's spin, the hazy pink varnish of the sky felt a little like hope.

"My internship is with a law firm because I'm a lawyer in the States," she heard herself say. "I've actually lunched with George Bizos. I'm sure he can attest to my honesty."

She sounded like her name-dropping Harvard classmates, and yet it was true that Sheryl had invited her cohort to lunch with Bizos during their first week in the country. Bizos was a friend and lawyer to Nelson Mandela, and part of the negotiation team for his release. When Sheryl first mentioned him, Prudence didn't recognize his name, but that afternoon over crustless tea sandwiches, he spoke to them about Mandela's brilliance, about the new Constitution and the hours the committee had spent on each draft, hoping it would be the world's most equitable and aspirational democratic charter. Bizos, with his bright-white hair, had taken a photo with Prudence, his face large against hers. It was a photograph Prudence would eventually lose, and yet it was a day she believed she'd always remember, because it had made her feel important, consequential, a part of something greater than her grievous past.

"I don't give a fokken shit about Bizos." The officer pushed his fist into her back, nudging her forward, past the gas pumps, and in the opposite direction of his patrol car. He was moving her away from the bright lights of the filling station's partial roof.

Prudence stopped mid-stride, lengthening her spine. She turned to face him. "Where are you taking me?"

He attempted to turn her around, push her forward again, but she tightened her core, planted her feet the way she had been taught by her father's old poker buddy, Sensei Keith, who had given her three lessons at his dojo for free.

"Move your fokken feet!"

Prudence had seen an episode of *The Oprah Winfrey Show* back when she was in college, in which an expert on crime had warned the audience against allowing an abductor to move them from the initial scene. "No matter what, never allow them to take you somewhere else. Crime scene number one to crime scene number two. Crime scene number two will be a remote location," the expert had said.

But the expert never told the audience, never told Prudence, what to do if the assailant was a uniformed police officer.

"I'm not moving until you tell me where we're going." Prudence glanced back at the officer's patrol car. He had parked it far enough away from the filling station house that a passerby might believe he'd only just left it there to run to a convenience store downhill.

"I want to make another call. My friends are probably back home by now."

She pivoted again toward the Rent-A-Wreck. The red scratched paint of the vehicle appeared almost shimmery in the dusk light, and she thought herself a fool for having left her phone inside it, a fool to believe that something horrific couldn't happen to her over a small misunderstanding. Misunderstandings were at the start of every heartbreak, every tragedy. Misunderstood people ended up dead every day.

"Turn around."

Prudence felt powerless. Following his command, she moved forward at a pace slower than before. She suspected she could not outrun him but perhaps she could reason with him, negotiate with him, buy time until one of her classmates showed. But now the officer, fuming at her stalling, snatched the back of her dress collar. She heard the fabric stretch, heard it tear, and she felt the burn of the cotton at her neck pinching her trachea. She fell onto the pavement and her dress flew up. The sizzling burn at her elbows took her back home to the alleys of Baltimore where she'd first learned to ride a bike. A pink Huffy with purple plastic tassels. She wanted to be there, with her father still alive, back before they lost the house, racing through the streets with her plaits flying behind her.

"Get up."

Prudence stood, rebalanced herself, and wiped the droplets of blood from her elbows on to her dress. She looked around to see if anyone was watching but she saw no one. Yeoville was a busy place, so how could no one be there to help her, to witness what was happening? She stopped again. She had wanted to believe that she could strategize her way out of this, and as she began peeling away the skim of terror that had only just settled over her senses, the officer, with a slight bend in his knees, removed his pistol from its holster. It seemed like one motion—the outstretching of his arms, his sausage-thick fingers clutching the black iron. The horizontal line of the gun seemed so faultless, so exact. Prudence wanted to cry. She felt a searing in her throat and heat at the corners of her eyes, but no tears came. Nothing but that bloated feeling, that sensation where one's body anticipates a release and yet it cannot actually let go.

"I told you to fokken walk."

She thought now about all the ways this could end. With her in a ditch. Biting a bullet. Perhaps he'd dump her at the edge of a township where the investigators would mark her as a Jane Doe. She didn't even know if "Jane Doe" was a term used in South Africa. She took a deep breath and threw her hands in the air, as he pressed the muzzle against her head, the iron snagging her sweated-out hair. How did she get here? Because she didn't have cash? She remembered, then, the three single dollar bills she'd waved at the cashier. She slipped her hand slowly into the pocket of her father's sweater. As the officer pushed the back of her skull, directing her to the shadowy rear of the station house, she began dropping the bills off to her left side, one by one. Then, a few feet into the distance, he stopped her near the mechanic's platform. A mucky patch of pavement where light would be spurned even on a sunny day. A patch made even darker by the shade of two trees that precariously balanced on the side of a small berm. There, they were hidden from both of the intersecting roads.

This was Crime Scene Number Two. She'd allowed him to move her to Crime Scene Number Two. *God*.

The area reeked of oil, of piss, and she could see only faintly the graffiti on the concrete wall of the station house that he'd backed her into. She imagined the cashier girl sitting on the other side of that wall, chatting on the phone, chewing a fresh wad of purple gum, awaiting the end of her shift.

"Take off the sweater."

A small utterance escaped her lips, her dread and imagination conjuring stark visions of what would happen next. She wanted to see his face. It might tell her what she suspected was true, and yet she was also too afraid to look at him again because she could hear his guttural, weightier breaths like a horn bellowing out from the back of his throat. Prudence couldn't feel daylight's warmth any longer, and when she removed her sweater and slung it over her arm, she immediately began to shiver. He reached for the sweater, threw it to the ground. It was the only one of her father's sweaters she'd taken before her mother was forced to sell his clothes on a folding table in the front yard. Her father had been a large man, but he had worn that too-small hunter-green sweater because Prudence and her brother had put it on layaway at K-Mart, paying for it with the cash they'd earned selling frozen cups to the neighborhood kids from their kitchen door.

Prudence felt her hands and her throat drying. She wanted water. A sip. She'd get her heart to slow if she could quench her thirst.

"Now the dress."

Prudence wanted to tell him to arrest her. She'd happily serve time in a Joburg jailhouse, "Sun City" if she must, with the smell of another's canned shit and cries of despair waking her every hour. But she knew now that the officer had seen an opportunity. He had seen *her* as an opportunity—a Black woman, a foreigner with few connections in South Africa. If she lived, it would be her word against his and maybe even against the young Black cashier who didn't see Prudence as an "us," as one of her own.

Prudence slowly pulled the torn dress over her head, the smell of it faint with the previous night's sweat and perfume. She hadn't yet decided whether to die or not, so she didn't resist, but she did wonder what her father felt before they shot him. Did he feel hopeful or had he accepted his death in the moments before?

"This is a drug crime, Mrs. Wright," one of the officers had said to her mother.

"My husband is not a drug man." From upstairs, Prudence could hear her mother's Trini accent filling their living room. "He has nevah, would nevah, could nevah, smoke reefer."

"That's not the kind of drugs we mean, ma'am. We're talking crack cocaine."

Prudence's mother, a woman raised in the high, thick bush of Trinidad, a woman who said her novenas at night and waved crucifixes and beaded rosaries at noon mass on Sundays, knew nothing of what had been happening in their city. But even at thirteen, Prudence knew. She had noticed the changes in their Northeast Baltimore neighborhood, noticed that the boys who used to play basketball with her in the alleys, and who on occasion hot-wired cars for joyrides, were now purchasing luxury vehicles with black-tinted windows and destroying streetlamps to conceal their activities from the old ladies who once babysat them. Change had been slow coming, but it had arrived. Right at their door.

"Cocaine?" her mother said.

Prudence remembered overhearing her father speaking to her mother about one of his students, a ninth-grader whom her father believed to be a math prodigy. "The boy's fadda is no older than twenty-eight, twenty-nine, driving a Maserati, June! A Maserati! You imagine why de police not pullin' dis young man over? You wanna know why? Because dey does know and dey does let him sell dem nasty drugs to dem kids. Then he come up to de school—my school!—and he does park that big ole car in de parking lot and wait for de boy to come outside. And all dem chil'ren, who ah is trying to teach to do the right t'ing, come outside and see dis young man with dis big ole fancy car and t'ink 'what de hell I doin' in school?' And dat young man's son could be somet'ing one day, ah tellin' you, June. Ah tellin' you, he could invent some big somet'ing with that mind of his, but the chupid fadda wanta interfere with de boy's studies. You know . . . I does have a good mind to call dat fadda into my classroom and have a good, long cuss about leavin' de blessed boy alone!"

Prudence remembered her father taking up his cassava in his spoon, then washing it down with her mother's thickly-brewed sorrel, shaking his head until he noticed Prudence peering at him. He smiled a soothing smile. "Your fadda loves his students, Pru. Dat's de passion you seein' here."

Now, Prudence looked the officer in his eyes. She would memorize the features of his face before darkness fully settled. If by some chance she lived, she wanted to remember everything about him so she could describe him to the police chief, to the American ambassador, to George Bizos, to Nelson Mandela, to anyone who might listen. And she wanted him to remember her face too—the dark-brown eyes she'd inherited from her father, her mother's high cheekbones and bronze coloring, the braids recently cut out, leaving only cropped hair with narrow waves like the Caribbean Sea. Prudence believed herself beautiful because her father had told her she was. "Pru, you's a lovely chile." She had long, well-developed legs, and muscled arms; she had delicate-looking hands, and a perfectly shaped head with a strong, narrow chin and full lips. Yeah, this motherfucker will go home and think on how the only way he could have her was with a gun. She hoped he would choke on the thought of all his inadequacies.

As she stared at him icily, the officer grinned and lowered the pistol to her chest. He reached for the waistband of her panties and yanked down the left side partway before stepping back so he could wedge his boot between the gap in her thighs. She was stunned by the ease with which they'd entered this forbidden place. The breeze rustled the leaves overhead, the night air crisp on her legs, the faint hairs stretching like yogis. Every sense was alight. Crickets rattled their spindly legs and she could smell the roast chicken that vendors hawked downhill. With the odor of burnt poultry skin hovering in the air, the officer pushed down her underwear the rest of the way, the tip of his muddied brogue sullying her Vanity Fair undies. She stepped out from one leg hole and felt as if she'd waded into dark, swampy waters. Only her bra remained. A linty tan-colored bra, greying with sloughed skin. She'd worn it the three days prior, too lazy to finish her laundry, and she wondered now if she would ever have the chance to tell a future daughter not to wear bad underwear because "you never know, dear, what the rapist-slash-murderer might think." She hated that her mind worked that way, the dark, dreadful humor walling off panic. She hated that, in that moment, she didn't fear the man before her so much as despise herself for being his choice, for looking or smelling or behaving too much like his perfect victim.

The officer smacked his tongue against the roof of his mouth, the noise salacious and unnerving, and Prudence weighed how much of her he could see now that the sun had disappeared from the sky. Her stretch marks? Her cellulite? He pulled at her bra now. It barely fit the plumper body she'd earned since starting at Harvard, where she'd eaten better than at any other time since her father's death.

He placed the barrel of his pistol on the top of Prudence's right shoulder and pushed down on it, the pressure as firm as if he were rolling dough. The metal felt warm against her chilled skin, as if plying her with the promise of comfort. She knelt. The coarse pavement beneath her was akin to knitting needles stabbing her, a terrible torture that distracted her so much that she almost failed to realize what he wished for her to do next.

"Black girls don't do that shit" is what her middle school friends had always said when the subject was broached. It had been a point of pride, a way to distinguish themselves from some of their white classmates who'd claimed purity despite making fellatio the common exception to their virginal status.

Prudence tried to unhear his zipper's teeth, his clumsy fumble as he rooted around in his trunks. The distracting sounds of the whirring cars downhill and the beep-beep of a horn reminded her that nearby, others were settling into a cozy Sunday night, legs outstretched on footstools, pots of meat boiling over. She imagined the bars were packed, patrons promising just one last drink, as a scoreless soccer game drew to a close.

He'd have to force her jaws open with that gun before she took him into her mouth. He moved his penis about her face, wiggling it as if to torment her like a dog clawing a beetle. Prudence shut her eyes and clamped her lips shut, her own groans of despair deafening her, the slime of his pre-cum just above her jaw.

She fell over.

God, she needed a second, just a second. She placed her hands on her neck, wondering if she could strangle her own self, wondering if maybe it was best to resist and die now. He sucked his teeth and reached down and tapped the barrel of the gun on the top of her head, as though she were a horse, as though she needed to be reminded of the labor she'd yet to do. She needed more time. Could she make it to the car? Could she make it down to the main road? Would someone help her if she managed to get there? She braced herself on the pavement, making as if to rise again, as if to please him, as if to nicely finish him off. She lifted her head, straightened her shoulders, grazing his bony knee, which was protected only by his thin police-issued pants. She remembered

Sensei Keith's lecture on eyes and necks and knees and crotches. "Vulnerable places," he had called them.

Prudence moved toward his penis, hoping his eagerness would distract him enough not to notice her balled fist. She charged his left kneecap with what she hoped was her most vicious punch. She heard a small pop. He cried out and she clawed at his neck before his body fell slack against the building with a thud. Prudence didn't hear his weapon plunk to the ground. He must have held on to it. He would be on her within seconds, but still, she picked herself up and sprinted toward the front of the gas station, where a swerving car blocked her way.

The headlights cast a blinding glare. Prudence squinted and could hear the tires braking, then she felt the shooting pain of a thin layer of dust flying into her eyes. Later, she would wonder why she hadn't thrown herself over the hood of the car and dashed across the lot to her Rent-A-Wreck, but in that moment Prudence could only think of the officer gathering strength behind her, cocking his pistol in her direction. She crouched down behind the stranger's car and heard the car door open.

"Hallo?" The man's voice was strong, and she knew by the tap-tap-tap of his hard-soled shoes and the crunch of the gravel beneath them that he was walking away from her, toward the officer.

"What's happening here, sir? Is there any way I can assist?"

Had she heard the man right?

The officer muttered something about the bitch taking his money. "Jissis, never fokken mind." She heard the uneven pace of the officer's boots hitting the pavement as he limped toward his patrol vehicle.

A tear rolled down her face as he drove away. She hurried over to the little stretch of shadowy pavement to search for her clothes.

She needed to find her father's sweater. The man, as if he could read her mind, cast the beam of a small flashlight that illuminated her clothes, which were crumpled in a pile. He waited until she slipped the dress over her head before approaching.

"You're all right now," Matshediso said, as if he was certain of this. "I came as soon as I heard your message."

10

When a person places the proper value on freedom, there is nothing under the sun that he will not do to acquire that freedom.

—Malcolm X

Johannesburg, 1996

Prudence climbed into his car and Matshediso immediately switched on the radio. An extended remix of "Ready or Not" by the Fugees played on a loop, Lauryn Hill crooned as Matshediso turned out of the petrol station and back down toward the main road, where Yeoville quaked with life. A meeting place for artisans, the canopied shops of Yeoville showcased handmade jewelry, downy textiles, halal meats, and herbal teas, while cafés displayed throw pillows on windowsills and brimmed with the dreadlocked and the head-wrapped. At nights, particularly weekend nights, people scampered from bar to bar, music trickled out onto the streets, video shops and spaza shops swelled with patrons, while along too-narrow walkways, dense rows of hawkers sold sandals, recycled wristwatches, hot boerewors.

Looking out of the cloudy passenger-side window, Prudence tucked her father's sweater under and between her legs as she watched all the gaiety that had teemed while she fought for her very existence. What a strange thing life was—to be so alone in one's travels and yet so in need of others.

Her first summer after college, Prudence had returned home to Baltimore for an internship at Baltimore City Public Schools' headquarters. She'd been directed to file papers, but the ladies in the office, ladies who had known her father, told Prudence to read a book instead.

"We know you work hard up there at Harvard."

The Budget Office ladies, who still wore pantyhose and kitten heels and brooches on sweaters, who smelled of roses and Jean Naté, and who called her "baby" and "honey" and "darling," were proud of her. And Prudence loved being there more than she loved being with her own mother. Some days those ladies brought her the only meal she would eat all day. Eggs on Styrofoam plates for breakfast, and for lunch they offered her fried or baked chicken or open-faced sandwiches, alongside fat cuts of silky pound cake wrapped inside oversized napkins they'd stowed away from some or another of the Superintendent's catered meetings.

One day, one of the women, Miss Jen, asked Prudence if she would ride with her to Lexington Market for a crab cake with "almost no fillin' in it." She needed someone to dash inside for the sandwich while she double-parked.

Though Miss Jen was a moody woman, prone to blocking off the entrance to her cubicle, she also had great humor and a laugh that often burst through Prudence, making her feel exultant, filling her with possibility, but that day everything about Miss Jen seemed more measured.

"You know, I used to make your father rum punch every Christmas and he told me how you and your brother used to steal sips from it."

"He knew?"

Miss Jen smiled, and rolled down her window to throw out old orange seeds. "After your father got killed, people had all kinds of theories, but this city is real real small." Miss Jen paused as if to collect her thoughts. "I heard about a man who was telling a few folks over in West Baltimore details about your father on his last day alive, details nobody shoulda known. So, I called a police friend of mine. An old boyfriend, actually. He came to my house that night to tell me I was never to speak about your father's murder again." Miss Jen sighed, pushing her left arm out of the window to signal to the car to her rear that she intended to turn. "I'm only telling you this cause I don't want you to go to your grave thinking your father did something wrong. He wasn't into no drugs. It was something else."

She asked Miss Jen to give her the name of the man rumored to have killed her father, and when Miss Jen refused, Prudence told her that she wanted the man to fear something the way she feared everything after her father's murder. Miss Jen reached across to squeeze Prudence's arm. "He already fears like that, baby. That's the only way he could do the horrible thing he did. Fear turns people into that. And your father ain't raise you to be fearful of nothin.'"

So alone for so long, Prudence had needed Miss Jen that summer, and now, looking over at Matshediso, she wondered why he had been the one to respond when she needed someone this time. She knew she'd never have an answer for this, so she tried to think only of the fluffy bed in Sandton, of the steamy shower she would take before climbing into it, and yet, she could not stop thinking about how she had journeyed all the way to Africa to be assaulted by a white cop. The irony of it felt jarring. So much of South Africa had reminded her of America, with its segregated neighborhoods, its inequities, and its police force with unchecked power. Before she left Cambridge, she had been warned to brace herself for the abject poverty, the needs, the wants of South Africa. "It's different there," she was told. And though some things were indeed different, there were many things that were exactly the same; she was still a Black woman, and still vulnerable to all the degradations and horrors and expectations of resilience that both womanhood and Blackness could bring.

But now, oddly, sitting in that warm car, wiping her face of the seminal fluid that she sensed, thick and crusty on her jaw, mostly she felt relieved that things hadn't turned out worse. She watched Matshediso sloping over the steering wheel, wearily, and she thought of how only weeks earlier he'd pushed away her advances. She was so grateful that he'd driven across town to help her, so grateful that she didn't have to drive herself home. Seated beside him now, she could smell the fresh oaky scent of his body soap and imagined that he had bathed just before hearing her message. This made her conscious of her own souring odor, and she pulled her father's sweater even more tightly across her spoiled dress. Matshediso glanced over as she did this, and she hoped he might say something, say anything comforting or distracting, but he only slowed the car for a woman crossing the road, releasing a small grunt when she waved to thank him, then picking up speed only to slow again and abruptly switch off the music.

"That's the car he was driving, isn't it?" He pointed to a patrol car, parked at an angle in front of an internet café that Prudence sometimes visited to type long emails to friends back home. Inside, as she remembered it, hung long white countertops bearing no fewer than ten boxy computer screens against a wall of sea blue. She stared at the vehicle but couldn't be sure it was the same one. At the filling station, the officer's car had been too far in the distance and too obscured by her mind's panic. But Matshediso seemed certain it was the same. He told her he'd slowly driven past it before noticing the dollar bills she left as a trail.

Matshediso parked his vehicle. She imagined herself shifting the car into drive and pressing the accelerator beneath his right foot; this is how much she wanted to be on her way to the apartment in Sandton. Her palms were sweaty, her neck pulsed; she needed to get away from the noise and the lights of Yeoville, needed to rid herself of the putrid smell of petrol.

"Can we go, please?"

"He must've stopped for the loo."

"I need to go home."

Matshediso jerked forward in the driver's seat as if preparing to leave, but then the officer appeared. The same officer from before, hurrying to his squad car with a distinct limp, slamming the door hard. She held her stomach as if the gesture might ease the vomit churning inside her. Matshediso pulled out onto the road again, and she felt a rush of relief that they were leaving, until she realized that he was, in fact, tracking the officer's vehicle.

She remembered her first safari. Sheryl had hosted her cohort for the weekend, and their guide, sloshing through fields of mud, had decided to track a lioness. It was the end of the day when the animal came into view. They had pulled over for a cup of tea and biscuits, and the lioness surprised them, alone and stunning in her velvety fur, tilting her head as if to make sense of them there in the wild before dashing off after a gazelle. The guide, who'd been paid for that kind of thrill, ordered them back into the truck, and they sped off at an exhilarating and frightening pace, chasing the lioness as she raced across the arid grasses between a boodle of trees, before eventually they lost sight of her.

She and Matshediso had been following the man for some minutes when she decided she'd had enough. "Please take me back to the gas station to get my car. I'll drive myself home."

"Don't you want to know what a man like that does after?"

"After what?"

She wondered if he'd say it—the thing she couldn't say. But he didn't.

"This isn't a game," she added. "It's my life."

"Precisely. You're not angry now, but you will be. After the shock, I promise you will absolutely be."

He didn't know anything about her anger, didn't know how she'd had to swallow it—that hard metal ball of it—and live with it kindling in her bowels. Her father had been murdered; Prudence knew what it was like to both be angry and to have no justice, and still she wanted Matshediso to turn the car around. But Matshediso kept driving, following the officer to the Yeoville police station, a small building with a stone foundation and cages for windows, whose cheery red roof felt woefully deceitful. He parked the car, and she sat in a stunned and uncertain silence. Did he want her to make a report? She watched the building's many visitors moving about chaotically, searching for something or praying for something or pleading for something. Prudence had been in South Africa for months now but had never been to that end of Yeoville, had never seen those multiethnic foot travelers whose shapes and faces and accents openly signaled the particular cut of the earth they called home. And though some of this scene felt familiar, reminding her of other cities and towns she'd known, what was also clear to Prudence was that she didn't know this city, didn't know this country. She was, in fact, a stranger there.

"Take me home. Right now," she said. "I don't want to be here."

Matshediso reached into his backseat and offered Prudence a Coca-Cola. He popped the cap, and the sound of the brown fizz felt like a drug. She took the bottle and before she began to drink, she dipped her finger into the neck of it, rubbing the liquid across the outside of her cheek, hoping the acidity of it would burn away any remnants of the officer from her face. She wanted to ask Matshediso again to take her back to the petrol station, but she knew he wouldn't concede. She had been rendered invisible, like the first day she saw him, when he didn't acknowledge that he'd taken her seat, or when she waved the tissue in his face on the walk outside. He was somewhere else now, somewhere she couldn't reach, and he would've remained so if a car hadn't pulled up in front of them, blocking them in.

Matshediso rolled down his window to ask the driver if he could please leave them enough space to pass. His voice was soft, he was polite, and the question itself gave her hope that they would soon be leaving.

"I'm coming straight back," the other driver said before dashing across the road.

Matshediso put his foot on the gas and gently nudged his front bumper into the side of the man's car. Onlookers gasped and the man turned around, ran back toward Matshediso who stepped out of the car signaling his willingness to take it further. "Move the car now."

The man climbed back into his car and drove off. But Matshediso did not return to his seat. He remained outside like a sentinel until, abruptly, he jumped back in and started the engine.

"It's him," he muttered.

Along the narrow path of the road, between pedestrians and double-parkers, a Land Cruiser slowly passed. Prudence couldn't see the driver but Matshediso drove behind him as if certain it was the same officer.

"Where are we going? What are you doing?"

For forty minutes Matshediso ignored her reasoning. He followed the car east until finally it turned onto a quiet road lined with modest single-family houses. The neighborhood looked to Prudence like it could have been in Indiana or even Tennessee. The front of the officer's house, brightly lit, sat behind a yellow concrete half-wall with stone pillars at its ends. Low, unruly shrubs spilled onto the sidewalk, and vine leaves the size and snarl of weathered hands crept along the base of the wide front porch. The Land Cruiser pulled into a narrow driveway of stone pavers, beneath a covered carport. Through white window sheers and white iron bars, Prudence could see a woman seated at a table with three young children. Matshediso circled the neighborhood, and at the next pass, the porch lights were off and she saw the officer inside, bending down to kiss the woman who was plump with an expected child. The woman gestured at the man's knee, the same one Prudence had hammered with her fist.

"You see? The fucker comes home to this nice place and pretends he's not a fucking animal." Matshediso spoke through clenched teeth, his right leg bouncing like a runaway tennis ball. He parked them across from the house, under the shade of a bush willow tree. Prudence leaned forward in her seat. The soda burned her chest, a chest that now pumped like a coal-fired ignition.

"This is my last night here," he said. "I didn't visit my mother."

Prudence didn't know why he was telling her this but she watched him closely. His warm breath fogged the driver's-side glass. He wiped it with his sleeve, as he continued staring into the house.

"After Volter testified, I kept thinking of those boys, ja. The Mozambique Eight. I was a small child when they disappeared from my village, and it wasn't until that day at the hearings— eleven years after the boys left home—that I finally understood they were never coming back."

Prudence thought that maybe Matshediso hadn't finished speaking, thought that maybe he might explain what those boys had to do with this police officer or explain why they were sitting in front of this house, but instead, he reached over her legs and removed two buck knives from the glove compartment.

"You can stay in the car if you want."

He handed her one of the knives, then disappeared into the murk of that dark road.

11

The future depends on what we do in the present.
—Mahatma Gandhi

Washington, D.C., 2018

Charlie's mother pounded her fists on their table. The candle votive leapt and the light extinguished, while Davis continued to try and reason with Charlie's father.

"Please, let's just—" Davis was saying.

The woman asked again, this time her voice louder, her tone more insistent. "Can *anyone* at this table vouch for this man?" Prudence couldn't admit now that they'd once known each other. Even if she did, what would she say about the kind of man Matshediso was?

"Charlie!" the woman shouted. "Charles, Mommy is looking for you!"

The boy's father gripped the woman's shoulders, promising her that they would find him, reminding her that every person on staff was searching for their child, but the woman could not be assuaged. Their baby began wailing, and though the mother quickly turned to set eyes on her, she seemed unwilling or perhaps unable to offer the child comfort.

"Are you from here?" She wrenched herself from her husband, turning again toward Matshediso. Her eyes twitched, filling with tears. She looked down at Tara, desperate, but Tara avoided her stare, looking instead at Davis, as if trusting that he could manage the situation. But Prudence felt less hopeful about a coming calm. She knew how she'd feel if it were her boy missing. Maniacal. Untethered. And knowing Matshediso as she did, he would do nothing to soothe that woman. He would not defend himself, would not explain himself, would not try to please those people with an excuse for why he had walked outside just as the lights went out in the restaurant. By now, some of the other patrons had begun gathering their things, leaving warm dinner plates behind, settling their bills with haste. Davis caught the manager's eye, conveying his desire for someone to wrest control over this disturbance. The manager offered free drinks to everyone.

"You're African, aren't you?" The boy's mother said "African" as though the word were a weapon.

Davis shook his head at the woman, shook his head at her husband. "No, you're not gonna do that." They'd gone too far, crossed a line, but the husband bristled at Davis's rebuke, doubling down, squaring himself beside his wife.

"I want to see your identification." The man outstretched his arm, crossing over Tara's chest to get his fingers closer to Matshediso's face.

Matshediso rose to his feet. Davis asked him to sit back down. Matshediso smoothed his sweater and remained standing, his fingers tented on the tabletop. Prudence knew the rage that roiled beneath that expression of his; she knew what he could do, would do, what perhaps even he should do, if pushed too far.

"I want to know where you work and where you live. When the cops get here, you're going to have to answer all these questions."

Matshediso smirked and stepped toward the boy's father. Davis put his hand up to discourage Matshediso from moving any further. The boy's father turned to Davis. "You're a partner at a law firm? What firm?"

Davis took another deep breath. "Listen . . ."

The boy's father, nearly as tall as Davis but not as broad, swallowed hard, pulling back his shoulders as if primed to square off.
Prudence thought about how this would look on the cell phone
recordings that were likely to be posted online. She stood, not yet
sure what to do, and Tara stood too, placing herself between the
boy's mother and Matshediso. Charles's mother, perhaps now feeling trapped and surrounded, elbowed Tara in the chest as if to
clear herself some space, knocking Tara off-balance and into the
table, rattling dishes, spilling a glass of wine. Tara, shocked, stared
at Prudence as if to ask what she should do, but Prudence was more
focused on the manager, who suddenly turned and left. As Tara
sat down again, soothing her chest and her pride, six cops moved
toward the back of the restaurant with their fingers on holsters.

"Whoa, whoa!" Davis held up his hands, and Prudence, trying not to have a dead husband, trying not to have a fatherless
son, turned quickly to face the officers, hoping to shape the story
before the boy's mother got to them. It was then that little Charlie came bounding between the tables with the manager running
behind him. He was weeping as he climbed into the booth to
calm his baby sister's cries.

Fifteen minutes passed before things cooled. The policemen
left the scene, the manager brought another bottle of the same bad
wine, and Charlie's parents escaped, with not one word of regret
despite learning that Charlie had been napping under the dining table of the private room, his face pressed against the chilled
brass base.

They were all seated again when Prudence reached for her
purse. "I think it's time for us to go."

After everything, she was wondering about Matshediso. He
had gone to the restroom but was now back in his seat with his
watch off, rubbing his wrist as he looked about the room, his
expression defiant and vexed. He locked eyes with Prudence for

a moment, but quickly looked away, as though he remembered that she knew him in ways he wanted to keep hidden.

Davis breathed deeply. He didn't want to leave. He insisted that they not allow "those people" to ruin their night, even as the remaining patrons were continuing to glance over at them with guilty, quiet stares of apology. Tara agreed with Davis, though she was still rubbing her chest and nervously dabbing the spilled red wine with her napkin.

"Mat, you really kept your calm." Tara's voice was just above a whisper now. "And Davis, you kept everything under control too."

Davis unbuttoned the top of his dress shirt. "Mat, you alright, man? That's some fucked-up shit to go through."

Matshediso's nostrils flared and he scoffed as he placed his watch back onto his wrist. He nodded, then rubbed his face. "I'm fine. Fine. Fine."

"Davis?" Prudence said, softly.

She couldn't do it. She couldn't stay there any longer.

"What? What's wrong?" he said.

"Let's call it a night. We can do this another time."

Davis looked over at Tara and Matshediso, as if to ask for their support. "Pru, it's pouring outside." He nodded toward the window. The newest bout of driving rain pelted the restaurant glass like fastballs. Thunder clapped.

"And plus, it's not right," he added. "They don't get to just do that to us. Let's eat. Okay? Let's just eat."

Davis's forehead glistened with perspiration, and Prudence sat in that fancy upholstered chair and watched her husband try to resume some semblance of normalcy. This was what was required, expected, she knew, and yet she was existentially tired, tired of the Black-people-can-handle-anything bullshit.

"So anyways . . . you and Matshediso," Davis said to Tara. "How did this all happen?"

Had he forgotten it was Tinder?

Tara's face flushed but Prudence had to give her credit for being a good sport.

"I was telling Davis earlier that I used to teach seven-year-olds in second grade, but there isn't very much money in teaching, so I earned my paralegal certificate," Tara said.

"Our son is seven." Prudence had felt guilty all night that she'd hardly mentioned Roland to Tara and Matshediso. She made this omission more often than she cared to admit, fearing the typical queries that would lead to having to explain that he was on the spectrum. She didn't always want to watch the expression on people's faces that meant "Thank God that's not my kid," or "Poor, poor things."

But neither Tara nor Matshediso nor Davis seemed interested in talking about Roland.

"So where do you work now?" Davis took a sip of wine. "At a firm? Or are you in-house?"

"Well, actually . . ." Tara turned to Matshediso and touched his arm. "We met online because we both wrote that our favorite street in D.C. is Pennsylvania Avenue. So weird, right? And thanks to Mat, I just started working on Pennsylvania Avenue. At your firm."

"At Wilbur?" Davis peered over at Prudence, as if to ask if she knew of this. He blink-blinked, wearing a heavy half smile. Prudence assumed he was now replaying everything he had uttered about the firm, about morale, about surveillance and their business plans, worried that Tara might make his words fodder for the firm's administrative staff. Davis eyed Matshediso as though to ask why he would have withheld that information, but Matshediso still wore that blank expression, the one that made Prudence feel anxious not only then but twenty-two years earlier.

"So, you're like a nepotism kid?" Davis chuckled. It was a forced chuckle but Prudence felt him reaching for something other than anger.

"A what?"

"You know . . . like when people get jobs and favors because of who they know."

Tara giggled, the tension in her face easing. She turned to Matshediso, whose far-off expression suggested that he wasn't paying much attention, but it became clear he was listening when he eyed Prudence again.

"So, were you a nepotism kid in South Africa, Prudence? You never explained how you ended up there."

They were back to South Africa? Why?

Matshediso grinned tightly, and Davis grinned too, though Prudence could tell Davis was disappointed that his joke hadn't lifted the mood quite as much as he had hoped it would. She felt sorry for her husband. He had no idea of all the intrigues at that table, no idea how he would not be able to save that unsalvageable dinner even after bravely stepping into the fray with Charlie's parents, even after trying to help them laugh their way past that shitty night.

"You're South African," Prudence answered. "You should know better than me how nepotism works there, and how it's definitely not for Black Americans."

Matshediso's nose flared before he threw up his hands in a lighthearted mea culpa.

Davis jumped in again. "There's so much I don't understand about South Africa. Prudence was telling me that the Apartheid government had such sophisticated and organized processes for suppressing the resistance and how they kept so much of it secret."

He went on to tell Tara and Matshediso what she had told him long ago about the South African Defence Force meetings in Pretoria, about how the South African intelligence agencies would compile their long list of "agitators" before selecting those who would be harassed, threatened, or disappeared.

"Imagine every morning deciding who should live or die," Tara said.

Matshediso sat back in his chair, prayer hands perched at his chest. "Everyone has that power."

"Who has that power?" Tara said.

"Each of us can go out any day and decide who will live or die. Look at what those people did tonight. Look at how everyone began to believe I had taken that boy. They used their power."

He was incensed. It was palpable now.

"But in a place like South Africa, during Apartheid, it was the state doing it," Davis said.

"Every unjust and unpunished act of an individual is a government act. America condones murders by drones and cops. Those six who barged in here with their hands on their guns came because white people who level accusations are never punished."

"That's what you wrote about in your independent study paper, isn't it, Pru? About how the hearings were all bullshit because nobody got convicted?"

Prudence didn't want to talk about the merits of the Truth and Reconciliation hearings. South Africa wasn't her home country, and the subject was too close to what she'd been trying to avoid all night. She pretended to hear her phone buzz and began digging for it in her purse.

"I don't know if I think they were bullshit." She muttered this while still rooting around in her bag. "My reaction, as an outsider, was that truth may have been too little a price to pay for the kind of injustices the perpetrators meted out."

"You wrote a paper? Did you ever get it published?" Tara said.

"My wife's got a mind like a machine. She's a true intellectual, though she won't claim it." Davis reached for her hand and Prudence could feel him trying to keep her from typing on her phone. "The law review published her paper. You can probably find it somewhere on Al Gore's internet." He laughed and Prudence unlocked her phone with her other hand.

"Did you take notes? During the hearings?" Matshediso asked.

He knew very well she'd taken notes. She shot him a punishing glance that she hoped only he noticed.

"Our basement storage room is filled with boxes of her stuff. Notes and photos. She should've been the official stenographer for the hearings."

"You have photos? Of the hearings? And you kept them all?" Matshediso sounded almost earnest.

"She thought she was gonna write the great Ameri—no, the great South African novel," Davis said.

This time Prudence bristled at his joking tone. What she had wanted when she returned from South Africa was for someone, someday, to understand, through her notes, how the media could still be turned, how the world could offer a blind eye to suffering, how a government could still undermine truth, how quietly and secretly resistance fighters could be put away, blamed, even murdered. But now, more than twenty years later, even her own husband, an educated Black man, didn't seem to care anymore about the sophisticated and undercutting institutional machinations that had been inflicted upon non-white South Africans. The country was Black-run now, everything was fine, that was what everyone thought. But how could that be completely true? How could all that pain, all that trauma, all that social programming and systemic injustice just disappear? After she returned from South Africa, nobody wanted to hear the stories. Everyone told her to put it all behind her, to get on with the business of earning a living, so she did. She worked her way into the McKinsey partnership, which afforded her and Davis their annual Park City trips, their weekends in the Hamptons, their weeks on Sea Island. They had moved three times in the intervening years, each time to a bigger house until they landed at their ten-thousand-square-foot home on a half acre of overpriced suburban greenery, where they had their nanny, their three cars, their three full floors of living space, finished with a gym, a wine cellar, six bedrooms, a movie theater, and a spacious storage room where she had stowed away notes and photos, as well as the journal she'd stopped writing in the night they followed the SAP officer home.

She looked down at her phone again and pressed the message icon. There was one new message from an unknown number. The timestamp said it had been delivered before the craziness with Charlie's parents. She was almost certain it was another weather warning until she began to digest the capital letters, emblazoned across the screen:

WILL YOU TELL HIM HOW WE KNOW ONE ANOTHER?

12

History is a people's memory.
—Malcolm X

Johannesburg, 1996

Prudence stepped out onto the road behind Matshediso. The air, colder than it had been at the petrol station, swept under her dress, attacking the bare parts of her, reminding her that the thing she never wished to speak of again had happened only a little over an hour before. As she crossed the street, an owl hooted and she realized they were near a nature reserve she had visited one lonely Saturday afternoon. The safari guide had named the twelve owl species found in the Republic of South Africa. The Giant Eagle Owl was the largest of them, the guide had said. It hunted mammals, some the size of young warthogs. On the way back to her car, Prudence remembered marveling at all the unknown dangers any one night could hold.

Now, staring through the officer's front window, she could see his seated silhouette painted by the shimmery blue light of his television. She thought of her father, who, after grading papers, would often bathe in that light too. The officer hadn't moved from his armchair since his wife and children went to bed, and the thought of him resting with such ease, unconcerned with what he'd done to her, moved her toward his driveway. She didn't see Matshediso until she had nearly crashed into him at the front end of the Land Cruiser. She could almost feel the excitement rippling from his skin. He had already slashed the front left tire, and the hiss of the releasing air was growing louder. As he moved toward the front right of the vehicle, she hungered for a sliver of that sort of revenge and moved to the left rear of the car, where she stabbed the tire, and dragged the knife Matshediso had given her around it, pulling it out only to stab it again and again. The unrivaled elation she felt was almost matched by imagining the officer's reddened and furious expression the next morning. At the last tire, Matshediso stood with his hands folded, waiting to give her the honor. She pierced that one harder than the first, pulling her arm in a wide arc around its inner tube, the resistance of the rubber all the more exhilarating. Afterward, she kicked the tire and the two of them hurried back to Matshediso's car. She expected he would turn over the engine and they would promptly leave, but he sat in the quiet of that night, near motionless, watching the Landie sink slowly to meet the carport's broken stone pavers. The night air filled Matshediso's car with the sillage of a sickly sweet flora. What they had done felt as delicious as the air smelled, and while Prudence waited for Matshediso to ready himself, she leaned back into the passenger seat to savor all of it.

After some minutes, his eyes began scanning her and he seemed on the verge of asking her something but appeared to think better of it. If he had asked how she felt about what they had done, she would've said she was thankful, glad for the opportunity, even if it would only be a small inconvenience for the policeman. What they did to his tires didn't measure up to the horror he had put her through, but Prudence knew that this was the best she would get. She had learned long ago that justice rarely felt compensatory.

She took a deep breath, preparing to ask Matshediso to leave, when she noticed the officer rising from his chair.

"Fuck."

They slid lower into their seats and crossed their arms over their chests. Despite their efforts, their breaths seemed to grow breaths of their own, the car filling with the sound, the windows fogging. The officer parted the sheers and peeked out. A tree limb at the left side of his window bounced against the pane. The officer flinched and he cast his eyes about, before pulling the drapes closed and turning off the television.

"Fuck," she whispered again.

Matshediso slid upward like a Push Pop, his breaths finally easing.

"You can drop me back at the gas station. I can drive myself back to Sandton."

He stuck the key into the ignition, perused the darkened road, then removed the key. "I think we should wait a while longer. He's still awake. I don't want him to hear the car turn over."

He was right. They should stay fifteen minutes, maybe twenty, then he could start the car slowly and casually. As they sat, the air between them felt bloated with something that seemed ready to burst. Matshediso was the first to speak.

"Did you think you'd die?" he said.

She hadn't expected him to be so direct, and the burn of tears knotted her throat as she considered his question. She had been scared. Terribly so. But until that moment in the car with him, she hadn't remembered how close she'd felt to her end. She wasn't sure if she had thanked him for coming, so she did so and he was quiet in response, as if he didn't feel he deserved gratitude. And as they sat in another bubble of silence, she knew there was something new between them, something neither of them could articulate, and she began to tell him the story of her father's death.

"I don't know why I'm about to tell you all this." She hugged herself, and with each word she spoke, she could feel him focusing, listening, hurting for the little Prudence that she had once been.

"Daddy had been a teacher in Trinidad, but when you come to the US, they don't accept degrees from developing nations, so he went back to school and eventually got a job at a high school for math and science."

"He had a brilliant student. A really smart boy who was quick with numbers. Daddy said he'd never seen a kid with such a mind. He was so excited by this boy. And the boy's mother was excited too. She didn't have a college degree and she really wanted her son to have a chance to go. She used to bring him to our house on Saturdays so Daddy could tutor him. He was a nice boy, really shy, but the boy's father was very flamboyant. Everyone said he sold drugs. But in Baltimore, they used to say that about every Black man with a nice car. The boy's father would pick him up from school in his big, fancy car, pulling him from class sometimes. The boy finally told Daddy that he was 'pushing' for his father, so Daddy confronted the man, told him he needed to be a better father to the boy."

Matshediso made a hissing sound, as if he already knew the ending.

"I saw the man's car down the street from our house every day the week before Daddy died. Daddy told me not to worry about it. He told me not to tell my mother."

Under the bush willow tree, the moonbeams scattered between branches and the light found its way into the car. Matshediso looked different under this light. Soft, vulnerable, open. His face reflected the agony she felt inside as she said the thing she had never said to anyone. "It was my fault. I should've told my mother. I should've gone up to that car and told that man to leave us alone."

Matshediso didn't tell her that her self-recrimination was childish or that it was an output of grief or that it wouldn't have changed anything. She was relieved by his silence.

"We don't know exactly what happened, but they found Daddy's car in another state and found his body on a road about twenty minutes from my house. They shot him in the head, then they cut him into pieces, and left him in a bag." She hated saying it, hated speaking of her father's beautiful body, his beautiful face, his beautiful hands and legs, in that way. "He left home for school on a Friday morning and I never saw him again. He was so smart, so funny. He had these big, straight white teeth and this big smile and when he chuckled his whole body bounced with joy. I was thirteen. Most nights he still read to me. This was the kind of man he was to me, to my brother, and to his students."

She wanted to stop. The tears were in her throat marching their way up.

"I found out who did it. I heard that the police wanted him to testify against another drug dealer, so they didn't arrest him for Daddy's death."

Her voice broke. Matshediso climbed over the gearshift and slid himself into the seat with her. He held her to his chest.

"My mother couldn't keep up the house payments and she just wasn't herself anymore. It was like Daddy's death had scooped out all her insides. And my little brother . . . he kept saying he wished he could take Daddy's place, wished he could give up his life to make Daddy come back home. What seven-year-old says this? Four years after that, my brother died of leukemia. Things were so heavy and so dark for so many years. I mean . . . I was just starting to see myself again . . . and now . . . this man . . . this fucking policeman did this. He was going to kill me. I knew it. It was like how you know, when you wake up, that the sun will be out. I was that sure. And I was so scared. Under my breath, I kept asking Daddy to help me get away from him, but I didn't think even Daddy could do it. But then you came . . ."

As the officer's house sat like a lake in the distant darkness with all manner of things deep beneath its surface, Prudence and Matshediso wept together. She didn't know why he cried alongside her but she felt she would never again experience this sort of compassion.

After some time, Prudence told Matshediso that it was time to go, time to get off that road, lest sunlight meet them there.

"Hold on just a bit more, ja. I want to see his face when he comes out and finds his tires flat." Matshediso climbed back into the driver's seat, taking on that formal upright posture from earlier. She adjusted her seat, pushed herself forward.

"But if you can see his face, he can see yours," she said. "We can't be in this neighborhood when the sun rises."

"He could have an early shift."

"He won't. He worked late last night. And if it's dark, you won't even see his face. You're not making sense."

But she knew Matshediso didn't care about reason.

"Is it?" he said. "I'm not making sense? A man walks outside and finds all his tires slashed . . . his whole body will let us know how upset he is. It'll be a good show."

"I have to pee and I wanna bathe and I don't wanna stay here. I told you this was one of the worst nights of my life. Please let's go." She was near whining and Matshediso stiffened.

"Piss here." He held up the empty Coke bottle, flinging it in the air at her.

"Are you fucking serious? I wanna go home."

He gripped the steering wheel as though he would punch it. "What home?" he said. "That flat isn't your home. All I want is a chance to see what it looks like to get back at one of these fuckers, these fucking rock spiders."

It wasn't about her. It was about him and his country.

"Look, take me to the gas station and then you can come straight back here. He'll probably be sleeping for a few hours more."

She was trying to reason with him like one would with a tantrum-throwing child. He pushed his fist into the steering column, as if considering it. "You can't know that. What if I miss him when I take you back?"

He was scaring her now. He had this desperate, agitated look about him. He was not the calm man who had handed her the buck knife, not the sweet man who had just held her for an hour.

"Pee in the bottle and go to sleep. If he's not out in an hour, I'll take you back to the station."

"You're holding me here against my wishes. If we get arrested for vandalizing that car, that's what I'm gonna tell them."

He chortled, the sound like a growl. "Oh yes? Well, you maybe shouldn't tell them about the petrol station and what he did to you. They'll make you disappear." He glared at her now, his eyes watery holes that shimmered like glass in the moonlight. "To save one of their own, to make sure the international press doesn't humiliate them, you'll have to be killed." He nodded intensely as though he intuited that she didn't believe him. "You sat through a week of testimony and all of it was about murder and torture. All of it. You think a place like this changes overnight? Mandela, our Madiba, has been in charge for two years, and still the cops are ninety-nine percent white. What's changed for people like you and me when we have a run-in with the police?"

She couldn't change his mind. She climbed into the backseat and did her best to get all her urine into the bottle. She'd done this many times before, inside her mother's car, and she had promised herself she'd never have to do it again. But she knew in that moment that history had the shortest memory of all.

13

When the water starts boiling it is foolish
to turn off the heat.

—Nelson Mandela

Washington, D.C., 2018

When Prudence first returned from South Africa, she replaced
some of the horrible truths of her time there with exciting reports
of "winning amnesty applications!" and fantastic tales of "amazing safaris!" and "whitewater rafting trips to Zimbabwe!"

Often, however, when she replayed the events of that half year
in her mind, what she remembered most fondly was the way
Matshediso had tried to soothe her fears that night in the car,
which was why she couldn't understand what he was thinking
when he sent her that text in the middle of dinner.

Prudence tried to excuse herself from the table, but before she
could leave, the server and another waitstaff member arrived,
finally, to unload the first course. As their server began describ-
ing Tara's cucumber bavarois, Prudence managed to squeeze past
him, moving toward the front of the restaurant with the excuse
that she needed to call the sitter.

She stepped into the vestibule and released a few full breaths,
regretting that she did not tell Davis earlier that she knew Matshediso. As she began to dial Alice, she noticed in the building across
the street from the restaurant, a single dim desk light on an upper
floor. She wondered who was there, wondered if they, like her,

sat waiting for the rain to ease before heading home. She recalled her many late nights at work, soaked in the scent of stale coffee, and thought of how she had willed the life she had now, bending and twisting and molding herself, consistently, regularly, so that no one could ever question how she'd gotten there. That steely version of Prudence she knew well, but the version of Prudence who now stood in a glass cube of a restaurant foyer, quaking at the reemergence of some man she once knew, disturbed her, or maybe more like disappointed her.

She had to shake this off. She had to shake him off.

Alice answered on the first ring. "How are things?" Prudence asked.

"Everything's fine except Roland can't find his blanket. You know the one?"

Prudence knew the one. The green blanket her mother had knitted from pieces of her father's tattered sweater when Prudence was pregnant. The same sweater she had taken to South Africa. Prudence and Roland often liked to cuddle under that blanket. It was theirs. But the last time Alice babysat on a date night, Prudence came home to find the two of them snuggled beneath it, watching YouTube clips of *The Backyardigans*. The sight of them—her child and the sitter—beneath her father's sweater had done something to her that even she couldn't explain. The feeling had been so primitive, so raw, that it prompted her to hide the blanket in the linen closet. She had pushed it into a far corner at the very top.

"I can't imagine where it'd be," Prudence said to Alice now. "Did you check Roland's bedroom closet?"

Alice put Prudence on hold. This pleased Prudence, as she wanted nothing more than to have a good reason for a prolonged absence from the table. As she waited, the vestibule vent blew icy air overhead, and when she moved from it, she had a straight line of sight to their table. Davis was pushing his scallop tartare across his plate, his brow in pleats.

"Oh my God, I found it!" Alice screamed into the phone. "It was all the way at the back of the laundry room closet. The cleaning lady must have put it there. Roland will be so happy!"

Alice's cheery voice made Prudence feel ashamed. "Won-der-ful," she said.

Now, the manager opened the vestibule door, welcoming Prudence back into his hellscape.

"Not such a good night, huh?" He said this with his hand to his heart, which she now knew to be part of his schtick. She wished he'd shut the hell up but she half smiled anyway. The crowd in the restaurant had thinned to three tables of two and their table of four. Prudence's beets sat untouched on a plain-white plate beneath a handful of sad-looking fish roe. Davis wiped his mouth with his napkin and looked up at her, questioningly.

"Is everything okay with Roland?"

"He's fine. He misplaced something."

She could see Davis's relief followed by a faint flash of disappointment. He had wanted her to come up with an excuse for them to leave. She hadn't even thought of telling a lie, putting an end to this fetid affair. She'd been so distracted.

"Mat was showing us some of his photos. He went back home a few months ago," Tara said.

"Sweden?"

"No, South Africa," Davis answered.

Prudence squinted at Matshediso. "Oh."

A server arrived to take away the appetizer plates. The young woman frowned at Prudence's untouched beets.

"She didn't finish yet," Davis said to the woman. He was always concerned when Prudence didn't eat. He told the server to leave the beets, while Matshediso reached for his phone, swiping his finger across his screen to again find his photos.

"It's so beautiful there," Tara whispered, rubbing her chest, which she had made so red that it looked as if Charlie's mother had punched her rather than simply elbowed her.

Davis stuck a fork into one of Prudence's beets and nodded with approval. Matshediso seemed to arrive at a photo he wished to share with them. He tilted his mobile, the photo now in full-screen mode. Then, his phone rang.

"Sorry, I have to take this." He rose from his seat, but this time he walked toward the restrooms. Tara gazed at her own phone and Prudence reached for Davis's forearm.

"I'm tired," she mouthed. "Let's go."

Matshediso returned quickly, and as he passed her chair on the way back to his seat, she smelled the deep oaky scent of him. She remembered that scent. Could it be the same?

"I think we're going to call it a night," Prudence said. "All this excitement caught up with my nervous system." She offered Matshediso and Tara a somber smile.

"Pru, I'll give the waitress the valet ticket," Davis said. "At least finish your appetizer."

She wanted to remind Davis that the valet had parked the car just outside the restaurant door, that they could be gone in less than three minutes, but Matshediso was now pushing his phone back into Davis's hand.

South Africa, indeed, looked lovely in his photos. Table Mountain, the Cape winelands, Mandela's houses, safari pictures of zebras and giraffes and too many wildebeest to count. Most of her memories of South Africa were wonderful, and leaning over Davis's arm, looking at those photos, reminded her of all the good moments.

"Man, I just realized you're not in any of these photos."

"I was traveling alone." Matshediso laughed. "Keep swiping. I think I took one selfie." He chuckled, and Davis swiped until he came to a photo that made him cock his head. He pushed the phone back toward Prudence as if to ask her what she made of it.

"Is that a gas station?" Davis smiled a confused smile.

"Ai, it's a stupid picture," Matshediso said. "An old friend and I used to hang out there. I wanted to send the photo to remind her of the crazy times we had in Yeoville."

Prudence looked closer. In it, Matshediso stood on a crumbly blacktop, glancing up into the camera. In the background were two outdated gas pumps and a run-down filling station convenience store, where a plump, dark-skinned woman with a face partially blurred by the dusk light stared at him from a distance. The woman's mouth hung slightly open, and inside it, if Prudence were to guess, sat a lump of gum. Purple gum.

Something hard rushed into Prudence's throat. She reached for her glass, taking a gulp of water as she stole one last glance of the petrol station that she and Matshediso drove away from twenty-two years earlier. She pushed the phone back toward Matshediso.

What the fuck was he doing?

14

They need you to rediscover their humanity.
                                    —Desmond Tutu

Johannesburg, 1996

Prudence hurried into the apartment bathroom, kicking off the
dress and pulling off her father's sweater before sitting down in a
half-filled tub. Surprisingly, she found herself comforted by the
water, the stillness of it, like a bed of chilled grass on a sweltering
day. After her mother lost the house, they often slept in her Chev-
rolet Impala, and in the mornings, their old neighbors, pitying
them, would allow them to bathe in their basement bathrooms so
long as they "didn't use too much hot water." She could forget they
were homeless for those few minutes a day, but this . . . would she
ever be able to forget this? She felt different. In her bones. In her
skin. She felt stained.

   After the bath, she tried to sleep. But thoughts of the officer kept returning. His big hands, the bloodcurdling smirk, his
clipped Afrikaner accent, his pubic hair. *Oh God.* Each moment
slowed without warning, her mind freezing on every scene, as
though someone had pressed pause on a VCR. The picture always
sharpened on his face. That ugly pocked skin, those blue eyes
widening like a river with no visible shoreline. He'd touched her.
Touched her! Why didn't she fight harder? Why did she let it
get that far? Why didn't she run or scream? Why did she need
to be rescued? Rescued? What kind of Black woman was she?

Weak. A weak Black woman? It felt so shameful. Oh, and that sinking feeling in her stomach when she recollected the sound of his zipper. It was like the drop of a roller coaster; her heart raced, the horrible fright followed by an incessant head shaking, as if a fucking head shake could make those sounds, those images, disappear from her memory. They never disappeared. They remained, occasionally interrupted by visions of the cashier girl. Her wide mouth. The purple gum. Her long, filed fingernails. Prudence wanted to smash her fucking face, wanted to crack her fucking teeth. What had the girl thought when she saw the officer removing his revolver and walking Prudence to the back of the building? Had she hoped for the worst? Was she punishing Prudence for seeming to have more than her?

Prudence would not cry again. She would not. She massaged her eyes and watched the light display behind her lids. "I want to go home," she whispered. But "going home" meant time travel, didn't it? Because Prudence had no home to return to. A dead father. A dead brother. A sporadically unhoused and mentally deteriorating mother. Maybe this was why this had all happened to her. Maybe the cop could smell the instability on her skin, could see she was already a victim many times over. She tried to conjure a good memory now. Just one. She remembered the last trip her family took to Trinidad. Swerving along curvy roads atop steep green hills. Waves tossing her to the ocean floor. Green-sauce cucumbers eaten on gritty sand. Her father laughing, proud at how long she could hold her breath in the sea. Her mother's long legs crossed, toes painted red. Her brother's hair glistening with water. Yes, yes, those thoughts were better than remembering that petrol station, weren't they? Except, Prudence realized that even her best memories featured the dead.

After her bath, she took a drive, and when she returned to the flat, she rang Matshediso. She didn't know where he'd been staying and with whom, didn't know what time he was leaving the country. He didn't answer her calls. When he'd taken her back to the petrol station to retrieve her car, he told her to forget it all, told her that it was the only way forward. Perhaps they had also agreed to forget each other? Prudence left him a message but she knew somewhere inside he would never call her back.

It was almost noon when she arrived at the internship office. The Joburg summer was making itself known in the scorching concrete of downtown. She was covered lightly in sweat as she passed the receptionist's desk. She could hear Sheryl chatting, casually, loudly, to someone, her cigarette perfuming the air. Prudence picked up the files they would take for that afternoon's visit to the prison and fanned herself with them before walking into Sheryl's office. Sheryl took a puff of her cigarette and her icy smile suggested that she would have a word with Prudence later about her tardiness. Bandile was seated near Cheryl's office window. His security guard uniform looked freshly laundered, the lapels crisp beneath his stubby neck. Often, around lunch, he gossiped with Sheryl, seated at her cluttered conference table, shrunken by the enormity of her chair. He nodded disapprovingly at Prudence as well, as if he too would have a word with her about her late arrival. Weeks earlier, Bandile had confessed to Prudence that he didn't understand the need for her since law students in South Africa would have paid Sheryl and Barbara for the opportunity to work for them. Since then, he had watched her closely, as if to determine why she had been the chosen one, as if to determine what difference a place like Harvard could make in a human being.

"SAP. Murdered about four this morning," Bandile said, holding up the newspaper. He peered up at Prudence as though expecting a smart response, a Harvard-generated one. "They printed a second batch of dailies for this." He rolled the paper while Sheryl flicked cigarette ash into a glass tray. A car horn blew with a steady cadence and Prudence shuddered at the sound of it, her stomach suddenly twisty and rubbery like layers of wires.

Bandile set the paper on his lap and shook his head. He was saying, without saying in front of Sheryl, that the murder of the police officer would make it harder for the new Black-run government to proclaim its successes.

"Shame. Eish." Sheryl looked over at Prudence. "Seems the officer came out of the house and found his tires ripped up. His wife says she was still in bed—the children had been up late. Poor thing. He was all cut up when she found him outside."

The car horn blew again, this time in a bass staccato.

"The paper wrote that a neighbor heard more than one set of footsteps." Sheryl put out her cigarette, lifting her bobbed curls off her neck, gazing out of the window.

Below, there were cars aplenty, bumper-to-bumper, office workers in hard-sole shoes clomping their way into buildings and others rushing toward the middling Small Street Mall that was likely already filled with early-lunch shoppers.

But Prudence heard only her heart beating between her ears.

"Jissis, the media will never let this one go," Sheryl added.

Prudence leaned into the wooden doorframe, trying to steady herself. "What was his name?"

Bandile looked over at her oddly before reading the officer's name out loud. She hadn't known the name of the officer from the night before. Why didn't she know his name?

Sheryl's office phone rang and Bandile stood up to leave. Sheryl had been courting a younger woman, a married advocate whose husband was a budding politician. Sheryl turned away from them so they couldn't hear her greeting.

"Is there a picture—a picture of him—in the paper?" Prudence asked Bandile.

He unfolded the paper, the fresh ink smudging his fingertips. He handed it to her but Prudence didn't dare to look at it then. No matter the photo, her expression must remain the same. Bandile, visibly uncomfortable listening to his boss giggle with her married lover, headed out of the door. He told her she could return the paper to him later, and he walked to the receptionist's desk where he was to guard them against all the criminals they supposed were outside the office.

Now, Prudence rubbed the edge of the newspaper, the chalkiness of it soothing, as her palms were sticky with sweat. The flushing sound between her ears gave way to a more insistent echoing as if it had grown legs and feet and had begun to stomp. She turned from Sheryl and placed the paper and the files against her chest. Sheryl laughed into the phone while Prudence listened to the receptionist and Bandile comparing details of what they had heard about the murder. It was reported that the officer's wife, expecting their fifth child, had gone into premature labor.

Prudence had counted the heads of those children. She'd seen only three through the window, and, of course, the woman's belly, hulking, when she'd leaned over to touch her husband's knee.

She pulled the stack of files and the paper away from her body, gathering the courage to look down at the picture. The car horn outside sounded louder, angrier. Her hands trembled and she accidentally dropped the files. Sheryl spun around in her chair to face her, and Prudence knelt to pick up the papers, trying to slow her thoughts, as she began to gradually reveal the photo beneath the fold. Sheryl looked at her over the edge of the desk, as if to tell her she needed to make haste, but Prudence didn't dare rush lest she lose her legs from under her. She glanced down at the daily and there before her was a full-body photo of the man wearing the same bulky black boots he'd used to push down her panties, the same man whose dick had smeared her face, the man who had put a gun to her head and forced her to disrobe. It was the same set of blue eyes and the same flat, frightening face, but here, in this photo, the man smiled, a slightly overbitten smile that made the man in the photo appear pitiful and even a bit tender.

Prudence placed the newspaper and the files on the receptionist's desk and rushed to the restroom. She lost her breath before bending over to vomit in a sink speckled with cocoa-colored foundation powder.

Matshediso had promised her that she would forget, but she knew then that forgetting was too big a task.

15

We pledge ourselves to strive together.
—The Freedom Charter

Washington, D.C., 2018

The engine purred and Prudence felt the slight unevenness of the car's carriage as they turned onto Wisconsin Avenue.

"What a shit show that was," Davis said.

The rain had stopped, but the air still felt dense and wet, and the windshield whitened with fog as they crossed into Maryland. Davis had canceled their entrées and tipped the valet, and all those things that were required to happen at the end of a night—"goodbye," "nice to meet you," "let's do this again"—had occurred in one blurry motion. Now, he wanted to perform their usual postmortem, except Prudence didn't want to talk about any of it.

"And those fucking people and their little boy, and that 'Africa' comment."

She nodded.

"Imagine how bad that could've gotten? Those cops and those parents. For a second, I was really worried they wouldn't find that kid. Or maybe they'd find him dead somewhere like in the bathroom. And then what would've happened?" He turned to her now, but she was still only nodding.

"Mat's a real trooper," Davis went on. "My ass might've gotten arrested if they'd been in my face like that."

"And what's with Mat not telling me his girlfriend was work-ing at the firm? I mean what the hell . . ."

"I know . . ." Prudence whispered.

"And what was going on with you?" He didn't want a truthful answer; this she knew. "You weren't very nice to ole girl."

He grew quiet, taking the swerves in the road gently as if expecting the car to lose its frame. She was happy for this new silence, happy that he didn't say the thing he wanted to say, and though she wasn't sure exactly what that thing was, she liked that he knew there were things that shouldn't be said to her.

And yet the one truth she understood about relationships is that the people closest to you were like the most lethal land mines, dormant, and just waiting for you to trigger them with your presumptions and your hubris. The fact that she had actu-ally imagined that she could escape Davis's full emotional fallout from the night seemed laughable in hindsight.

"And after everything that happened on the way there," he began. "And then everything that happened at the restaurant, you're actually sitting here quiet? I mean, look at the fucking car." He pointed at the hood. "There's no way anyone has the parts to fix it for less than ten grand. It's *your* dream car and you're not even upset? You always do this, Pru. I'm trying to talk things through and I'm getting nothing from you."

Intellectually, she understood that his frustration was less about her and more about how violated he felt by the whole night, but still . . . what did he want her to say? Did he want her to cry over a car? Cry over what *could have* happened at the restaurant? Shit happens. And *real* shit happens to only a special few. He'd said it himself at dinner—*brutal childhood* and *really fucked Pru's head up.*

"You don't want me to talk things through," she said. "Believe me, you don't."

He looked over at her, seeming to understand this as a warning, seeming to remember that before all the nonsense with
Charlie's parents, he had shamed her, trotted out her past for
some purpose she still didn't quite understand.

"I do," he said. "And I said I was sorry. You don't always know
why you treat me the way you do either."

He wouldn't say more, and he turned on the radio, as if to
self-soothe.

She had married Davis and had remained married to Davis
because the version of her when she was with him was the
closest she'd ever come to feeling healed. In their twenty years
together, she had, on occasion, convinced herself that she could
permanently change, that she could learn to process without
emotional suppression, but all she could muster in response
to his present entreaties was a warning and a shrug. The truth
was that she often felt burdened by Davis's most basic emotional needs, as if the labor of it tipped the scale of what she
already carried, and the one persistent thought she had as she
sat next to her husband that night was simply that she might
not deserve him.

Davis turned down the music. "You wanna go to Mickey
D's for some fries? You gotta be hungry because I'm starving."
He looked over at her and seemed to nod on her behalf. He
turned up the music again, as if to punctuate their silent agree-
ment, their pact, to always keep it going. As they pulled out of
the McDonald's drive-thru line, the opening bars of Ashford
& Simpson's "Solid" played. They had their fresh French fries
propped in the middle console and were stuffing them into their
mouths, three and four at a time, when they saw the man again.

The man who had climbed the hood of their now-dented car.

He was parking his shopping cart outside the side entrance of
the McDonald's. She wondered whether he had taken the bus

or walked in that terrible weather all the way from 16th Street, Northwest to River Road. His long coat hung like a matted mop, the pockets bulging, and as he lifted his hand to open the restaurant door, Prudence spied a rope, a leash, which he wore like a long, dangly bracelet. Davis tapped her hand, as if to ask if she saw it, but how could she not? The man turned toward their car. He seemed to be pointing at her now. Wasn't he? His mouth moved reluctantly, as if the thing he needed to say couldn't be said.

In the following days, Prudence tried not to think about that dinner and Matshediso, tried not to think of South Africa, or about that man and his dog. But how could she not wonder, worry, question? Memories were dangerous things, grenades with shaky pins, much like how motherhood felt. She chuckled aloud at the comparison, as she got Roland ready for bed at the end of that next week.

"Roland, why do I have to fight you to bathe every night?"

They were in his bedroom doing the usual bedtime routine, an exercise that felt like maternal torture. She had to work to get him undressed, work to get him in the tub, work to get him in pajamas, work to get his teeth brushed. They'd given him the next biggest bedroom in the house, with a triple bay window and a large walk-in closet. He had a queen-size bed and his room resembled a Montessori classroom with blocks and colorful beads and magnet tiles and live plants each with their own water pitchers, and still nothing about those evenings was easy. The most recent squabbles were because Roland didn't want her help bathing anymore. He was tall, big for only seven years old, and his privates were his privates. But when he closed the door to his bathroom, she was sure that all he did was fiddle with his penis for an hour.

"Okay, if you're not going to bathe, then come on out and let's play a game."

He snatched open the door, as if beginning a negotiation. He didn't like board games, but she had begun teaching him card games and thought she could get in one round of gin rummy before bedtime. Roland shook his head at the deck of cards she set on the floor.

"Let's toss the ball?"

He pointed at her phone and clapped his hands.

"Oh!" She laughed. "But the only way you're getting that is if you go into that bathroom and wash your little butt."

Five minutes later, her son, half washed, pointed at the phone again. She cued up the song while she lotioned his damp skin and helped him into his softest pajamas.

"Okay, stinky boy, I hope you remember the steps."

Roland kicked aside his stuffed animals and his mini basketball to make room for their dance. Prudence pressed the play button on her phone.

His shoulders shimmied at the sound of the man's voice. The drumbeat barked like a Go-Go tune and the horns blared. The Wobble song. There was no song that made Roland as happy as this one. She and Davis had learned the dance at a wedding a year earlier and had come home to share it with Roland. Now, she didn't have to teach him how to shake his hips or move to the right, then to the left, then one-two-three-four. He was better at it than her, and smooth with it too, all his coordination issues vanishing as the music rang out.

They played that song over and over again, adding their own moves when the song asked them to wait a minute, throwing up their hands like crossing guards at a traffic light, and giggling as they watched their reflections in the long mirror affixed to

Roland's wall. After the fiftieth time or so, they both fell down onto the carpet, exhausted, laughing, thrilled with themselves.

"Guinness Book of World Records, baby! I know we killed the Wobble record tonight!"

She smothered him with kisses and Roland crawled onto his bed. She thought she might wait until he fell asleep before leaving the room, but when she woke to the sound of her cellphone ringing, she realized it was almost midnight. She'd fallen asleep on his beanbag.

Quietly she closed Roland's door and tiptoed down the hall to her bedroom. It wasn't Davis calling from his conference in Texas, so Prudence rejected the UNKNOWN caller and climbed between her sheets, smiling at the thought of her wobbling boy. The phone rang again and again. Finally, she answered.

"Lunch?"

"Who is this?" She knew almost as soon as she said it that it was Matshediso. She didn't wait for him to respond. "You're not serious?"

"I need to talk to you."

"You told me to forget everything. Back in Joburg, that's what you said. And now you show up in my city, at dinner with my husband, and you want to have lunch? We have nothing to talk about."

"We do."

"No, no, we don't."

She hung up, turned off her phone, and somehow managed to get to sleep but was awakened by the buzzing of her iPad. She placed a pillow over her head, certain it was another email from Land's End, an ad for some furry winter boots and earmuffs no one in the house needed. But when the device buzzed again and again, she picked it up to switch it off only to find there were words on the screen.

It looked as if the windows were bleeding into one another, like a virus. The screen went dark and individual letters began appearing. They converged and grew taller and larger.

MEET ME SATURDAY MORNING @ 8
BEACH AND CEDAR

The curdling sourness that had been buried in the pit of her stomach for days rose swiftly into her gullet, burning hot.

16

You show me a Black man who isn't an extremist . . .
                                        —Malcolm X

Prudence parked in a gravelly space a half mile from where they were to meet. Beach Drive was a long stretch of tree-lined pavement where cyclists, runners, and walkers packed themselves into narrow, marked lanes, particularly on weekend mornings. But it was still early, the sun just bronzing the backs of leaves, the dew still burdening blades of grass, and only a few walkers were strolling. She'd told Alice she was going for an early run and was now dressed in running gear, her mid-calf pants in a tight-weave synthetic, her water bottle hooked on a clip at her waist near a fanny pack stuffed with her phone, her earbuds, and her pistol.

Davis never wanted a gun in the house but she had taken lessons, completed the registration, and purchased one anyway. He didn't understand the comfort it offered her. She had never taken it from the top of her closet before, but today felt different.

What did Matshediso want? Was he a danger to her? If he could break into her iPad, what else could he do?

As she approached the intersection where they were to meet, she noticed, across the road, a man with a child. The man pushed the girl on a swing while reading his phone and Prudence thought of Roland, thought about some of the ways she could parent him better. Parenting was always about reinvention, but had she reinvented herself enough for her particular child? Of course, there was no end to self-condemnation when you became a mother. Every imperfect parenting moment was etched into one's memory and lay ready for deep analysis. And somehow this destructive level of scrutiny managed to bleed into every other aspect of Prudence's life. As if both she and the greater world had to be suddenly righted, perfected, because Prudence Wright had decided to raise a child. It was foolish, and yet those were the thoughts that had kept Prudence up at night before Matshediso came along. And as she moved toward the curb to wait for the light, she thought about how she wanted the simplicity of those musings again. This is when she felt the hand in the dip of her back.

"Thanks for coming," Matshediso said.

He'd frightened her and she wriggled to shake off his hand, prompting him to tuck his fists into his vest, a vest that seemed too thick for the warmth of that late summer morning. In fact, she could smell his perspiration, the faded scent of an expensive musk, and as he breathed out through his mouth, she caught the odor of his minty breath.

They crossed the street beside one another and walked alongside trenches of thick mud until they found themselves near the father-daughter duo on the playground. The little girl, in faded pink shorts and a yellow tee, had moved to the sandbox, so Prudence and Matshediso circled the swings. She waited for him to begin explaining himself, but instead, he sat down, the black plastic seat sinking beneath him, and he watched the child. His expression softened, and she wondered if he had children of his own.

"So?" she said.

He let himself fly forward a bit. Despite the perspiration on his brow, he seemed so easy in his body, such a contrast to the tension she felt in hers.

"What is all this creepy shit you're doing?" She looked down at him as he gripped the metal rope chain, his shoulders rising to meet his long neck.

"I thought lunch would have been easier," he said. "But you turned me down."

"I barely know you."

"You *know* me."

"You haven't seen me in over twenty years, so what do you want?"

The man with the little girl looked over at them. She wasn't sure if he could hear them.

"I need a favor." Matshediso nudged himself back, his left foot dragging on the synthetic blacktop.

"What kind of favor?"

"In South Africa," he began. "What we did—"

This felt like entrapment. "No, no, no. What *we* did? Slashing tires is a kiddy prank. But that cop ended up dead. Did you do that? I had nothing to do with that."

He grinned an uneasy grin. "The knife tells a different story."

"What? What knife?"

"The knife that has his blood on it is the same knife you used to slash his back tires. One and the same," he explained.

"You kept the fucking knife? The one you handed to me?"

She walked to the front of the swing where he sat; her breaths were sharp and a thin layer of phlegm crackled in her chest as she clenched her back teeth. She felt wild, harried, felt the way she had when a knock at the door in the middle of an afternoon reported the discovery of a father in a Hefty bag.

"You can't—you can't put that shit on me."

But she knew he could. He had returned to take that photo at the petrol station so that she might one day see it, so she might know it was all within his power to tie her to that murder.

"You, with your credit card, arguing with a township teen about petrol station policy . . ." Matshediso sucked his teeth, as if the thought of her, cashless in 1996, had disgusted him. "You think the cashier wouldn't remember you? Wouldn't remember how you cursed at the officer, telling him you were an American who could take his job, forcing him to pull out his gun to get you under control?"

Had she said those things? Had she done those things?

The little girl dashed past them, moving swiftly toward the slide with her father stumbling behind, plucking at his phone. The man looked over at them as if to assess the situation. Black man. Black woman. Unfriendly expressions. His eyes lingered over Prudence's ten-year anniversary ring—a three-carat solitaire in a matte platinum setting. The ring seemed to have the effect Davis intended—to render her more respectable, because the man soon apologized for the interruption, which meant little to Prudence, because by then she had decided to leave the park, refusing to entertain Matshediso any further. She began walking away, just as the little girl, running back toward the sandbox, tripped and smashed her pretty little face on raised wooden planks. Her groans made Prudence ache and she thought of Roland, home with Alice. She'd promised to return with a hot chocolate for him, a cranberry scone for Alice. "It'll be an hour, maybe," she'd told them. She needed to get back to her boy now.

As Prudence moved toward the intersection she'd crossed earlier, Matshediso marched behind her. The street had filled with walkers and joggers, cars, and a line of Harleys rumbling beneath the bridge where Beltway travelers zoomed overhead. Indignation and fear fueled her pace, and soon, she broke into a jog, her keys clanking against the pistol. She was almost to the corner when Matshediso snatched her by the waist.

"Remove your hands." She pinched her lips and felt him back away, but she was still nervous. He had the potential to be unpredictable, and there on that corner, in her little suburban pocket, Prudence didn't want unpredictable.

"Look at me. Look at me," Matshediso whispered, angrily.

Slyly, he removed a clear plastic bag from his vest pocket and pushed it into her hip. She didn't want to look but she couldn't miss the red-handled knife. Had the buck knife she'd used to slash those tires been red? It had been dark, so dark in his rental car, and everything had happened so fast, the hissing sound of the leaking tires, her kicking the rubber, the two of them running back across the road, her shoving the two knives deep into his glove compartment. He had refused to take her home when she first asked, said that he wanted to see the man's reaction. Then, she'd fallen asleep in the backseat only to wake at the petrol station where her Rent-A-Wreck was still parked.

"I took the knives with me to Sweden. To protect us."

"And now you're here, threatening me with them. I guess that's by accident, huh?"

"At dinner you said you have photos. Did you take them the day of Colonel Volter's hearing?"

Prudence paused, considering for a moment that all of this might harken back to the hearings. She didn't know if she even remembered which man Volter was.

"A picture? You want a picture?" She wanted to be in her minivan, to breathe normally again, but she knew he could easily follow her home. She turned back toward the playground where there was less chance he would hurt her, less chance that a friend or a neighbor could pass them at the intersection. Two Black people on the same street in this neighborhood made it a presumptive coupling.

"Everything was filmed during the hearings. Everything was on the fucking news." She stepped back from him, and an Asian woman pushing a stroller eyed her hard as if to question if she was okay. Was she okay?

"Not everything filmed was made public," he said.

She began to walk again and he matched his steps with hers. They passed the father and daughter once more. The father's Mystics jersey, covered in blood, was now untucked as the little girl lay in his arms. Looking at them, Prudence felt herself faint and warm, too warm.

"Volter must be there. Every night on the news, they showed the hearings that were held that same day. I saw video clips of all of them testifying," she said.

She tried to remember the details. The boys in the kombi, the Black agent whose name she couldn't remember, how he had plied them with alcohol, then the torture and the explosion. All of that testimony had been recorded. From way up in the balcony, she had seen the stenographer typing, seen the journalists filming.

"I don't mean Volter," Matshediso sneered. He was getting loud, and the lump in her throat swelled, hardened. The Asian woman pushing the stroller had turned around and was now passing by again, her eyes widening, her baby's chubby little hand reaching out as if to tell Prudence that there was more than one way for a man to harm.

"It's Zwane. I need to see a photo of Zwane," he added. "Do you remember him? The askari? You went back to the hall early. They said he was there after lunch. Did you see him? Did you take a photo of him?"

Zwane. Zwane had been the Black traitor's name. Prudence recalled that they had delayed the hearings. She'd run back to City Hall after leaving Matshediso at the restaurant. She had slipped past the ropes and found the balcony empty. Looking down, she saw white lawyers and a Black man seated across from the Committee members. The man was speaking quietly into the microphone, and she remembered watching his round face and she couldn't stop thinking of him for weeks afterward, because what he confessed to had terrified her. She remembered that she *had* taken a photo of him.

For the record, we would like to request again that this testimony remain sealed until such time as a determination on the amnesty application is made.

Zwane was average in every way, with a stocky build and an outdated fade that made his face look younger. She saw how he might have fooled people into trusting him. He wore a wrinkled shirt beneath a slightly tattered, shiny black suit.

You testified earlier that you were an askari. How did you come to be an askari?

She'd looked up this word after the first day of testimony by Van der Mool. It was Persian for "soldier" and used colloquially to describe a Black African who fought on behalf of colonial powers. The Germans had used it, and so too had the Belgians, the Italians, the British, all of them who needed local Black forces to dominate the masses.

After I was released from prison, I was called into the local police station. They asked if I believed in the duty of the state to protect its citizens from dangerous activities incited by terrorists. I told them I did.

There wasn't much time left in the lunch break. She realized that she had missed some of the man's earlier testimony.

Can you please tell us what you know of the incident known as "the Mozambique Eight"?

It was 1986. My job was to identify persons involved in terroristic activities. After investigating Paul Mahlangu, I learned that his sons were involved in school boycotts.

And what did you do then?

I informed Colonel Volter of the information and he told me we were to neutralize Mahlangu.

And did you neutralize Paul Mahlangu?

Zwane raised his left hand. *Yes, of course.*

We heard from Colonel Volter that you were given orders to find out more about Mahlangu's sons, yes?

Zwane nodded. *I was told to see if they had interest in MK training.*

So, you enticed them?

Zwane sat back as if to consider the question. *I told them they would be heroes, that their schoolmates would be proud. I'm not sure that is enticement.*

One of the Committee members glowered.

If you enticed them, how could you be sure the boys were an actual threat?

Zwane leaned forward. Though he spoke in English, he spoke slowly, every word considered. *I did not entice them, but after meeting, I provided their names and their ages to Volter and they were looked into. I was told that it had been independently confirmed that they were a threat.*

Volter had lied about not knowing the boys were children. He had told the Committee that he'd relied on Zwane and that he never independently verified anything. Now, Zwane was saying he had relied on Volter.

So, you and Volter knew the youngest boy to be only twelve years old and you considered a twelve-year-old boy who had never left KwaNdebele a threat?

Zwane rubbed his face and his voice grew louder, as if he were more confident of this answer than all the rest. *If he believed in the violent activities of the ANC, he was a threat.*

A threat to whom?

Zwane stared at the counselor as if he had been part of the problem in the country. *Those kinds of Blacks were a threat to the nation.*

The counselor jotted down something, then turned back toward Zwane. *So, you asked the eight boys if they would like to go to training in Mozambique and you arranged to pick them up early the morning of their deaths?*

Zwane held up both his hands and one finger dropped from sight. *Nine.*

The counselor quickly looked down at his notes again. He flipped through pages at the same time as the Committee members. He looked over again at Zwane. *Nine what?*

Zwane's hands were still in the air. *Nine boys. The last one became frightened. I told his comrades to lift him into the kombi but he fought them. I told them to let him go. You see, I did not take anyone who was not willing.*

But the other boys went willingly?

Zwane nodded. *Yes, they were very excited. Laughing, as boys do. Singing on the bus.*

The counselor asked more questions about that morning, and Prudence remembered wishing there were others in the balcony with her, wishing that Matshediso had walked back with her from the restaurant. She needed someone else to bear witness with her.

Colonel Volter testified that on the bus you offered the boys drinks.

Yes, to make it easier, I offered them drinks.

The counselor winced. *To make what easier?*

Zwane's mouth touched the microphone. *The dying.* He cleared his throat again and Prudence snapped another photograph. *It would've been harder to keep all eight on the kombi once they real-ized they were not going for training.*

So, you arrived at the safe house and convinced the oldest boy, Thomas Mahlangu, that he was there to receive instructions from the comrades in his training cell?

Yes. I told the other boys to wait in the kombi. Zwane paused, as if to decide if he should add anything more. *I could tell the boy, Thomas, wasn't sure this was true.*

You could tell? The counselor looked down at his watch.

Yes. He kissed his brothers. He kissed his three younger brothers on the lips. I'd never seen this.

Prudence gasped. She wished she hadn't snuck in there.

But Thomas went inside, anyway?

The waiting crowd pushed against the closed doors. People were returning from lunch and wanted to get into their seats.

Yes, Zwane answered. *By then it was too late.*

One of the Committee members signaled for a security guard to control the crowd.

The counselor continued. *Did you participate in his electrocution?*

No, Zwane said. *I returned to the kombi but I could hear the boy screaming.*

Prudence wiped tears from her eyes and took one last photo-graph of the man. If hell were real, she was certain all those men involved in this case would end up there.

Did the other boys hear Thomas screaming?

Yes. I told them he was being tested. To make sure he was strong enough for the training. That they all needed to be strong.

So, the boys waited on the bus while you installed the device underneath the kombi?

Zwane did something with his hands, as if trying to show how skilled he was with the bomb, and yet, Prudence couldn't be certain it was that. *Yes, by then, the drinks were making them sleepy.*

Did it seem they were used to drinking?

Zwane seemed undeterred by all the commotion outside the doors. *It seemed they'd never been given a drink. They quite enjoyed it and became drunk fast.*

Colonel Volter testified that the boys were poisoned and that Thomas was then placed under the kombi before detonation. Why did you put his body under the kombi with the bomb?

Zwane reached for a glass of water. *To make certain he would die.* He held the glass up to the light before drinking from it. *I believed I heard him breathing.* He smacked his lips into the microphone.

You believed he may have been alive?

Zwane set the glass back down. *Yes. And putting him there would make others think he had been trying to work on the device when it detonated. SAP internal reports were that the boy turned on his brothers.*

So, the public would be told that some unnamed men affiliated with the ANC were harmed in a detonation of their own doing? And they would also be told that the missing boys, going to training, were somehow mishandled by the ANC?

Zwane looked as though he couldn't believe the banality of the questions, as though he couldn't believe all of this hadn't been already known. *Yes. The people in the Bantustans and the townships would not believe this. But what the Blacks believed didn't matter.*

He went on. *I was told that if the general public believed that it was Black-to-Black violence, it encouraged fear in whites since they would believe it was coming to their homes. This disinformation system was very effective.*

The security guard nodded at the Committee members, as if to tell them their time would be up soon.

Thank you for your testimony. Oh, one last thing, Mr. Zwane, we understand from Colonel Volter that you kept trophies of your eliminations. Is this true?

Zwane sat back in the chair. *Trophies?* He looked toward the double doors of the hall as if suddenly realizing that people were outside, as if to remind the counselor that he could be in danger if they were allowed in.

Something of your victims, to remember them, the counselor said. *Is this true?*

No, I don't have any such things.

The counselor stood and moved toward him, blocking some of Prudence's view. *We would like to remind you that as part of your application it is expected that if you have anything to identify the victims, that you would submit it to the Committee. Is that understood?*

Zwane leaned toward the microphone. *I said I have no such things.*

Now, as the little girl with the bloodied face continued to wail, Prudence looked at Matshediso, his mouth parted with this strange expression, as though he could see 1996 Johannesburg in her mind's eye.

"What do you need the photo for? What does this all have to do with you?"

Matshediso didn't answer, but Prudence didn't much care about his reasoning. Somewhere in her basement, she had what he wanted. She'd worked herself into a full frenzy and it seemed now to be a straightforward transaction.

"And if I can find the photo of Zwane, we're done with all this," she said. "We'll be good, right?"

Matshediso closed his eyes and suddenly the air between them felt charged, impenetrable, as if the two of them were fused and trapped within it. When he opened his eyes, he bent forward, and the tension narrowed into a pocket of heat.

"No, no," he whispered. "You are going to help me kill him."

17

It is through weakness and vulnerability that
most of us . . . discover our soul.

—Desmond Tutu

Alice and Roland were digging for earthworms in the backyard
when Prudence rushed into the home office. First, she conducted a search on Lexbase, Sweden's web service for criminal
records. Nothing. Then, she turned to the South African Police
Service's criminal web page. Again, nothing. She scoured social
media sites using Matshediso's firm photo and a new facial rec-
ognition application that was all the rage, only to yield more
of nothing.

She realized she'd lost forty minutes on the internet when she
heard Alice and Roland in the basement returning from outside.

"Are you guys okay?" she shouted down to them.

Roland would be surprised that she was already in the house.
She had failed to greet them when she came in, and she could
hear him now stomping on the mudroom floor, his rubber boots
thwacking the tiles, the plastic bucket rattling against the back
wall of his cubby.

Alice shouted out to Prudence that she would leave soon
and would place the receipt on the kitchen desk for the kiddie
shovel they'd bought at the hardware store. "You can pay me
next time!" she said. Prudence replied to Alice with a request
to reheat Roland's hot chocolate before she left.

As Alice and Roland tooled around in the kitchen, Prudence performed another search, this time on the US Federal criminal database. Again, finding nothing, she moved to research the terms of the 2000 Extradition Treaty between the United States and the Republic of South Africa: Article 8 provided that "extradition shall not be granted when the prosecution has become barred by lapse of time according to the laws in the Requesting State."

Perhaps South Africa had a statute of limitations for murder? She thought it unlikely.

Alice left through the garage, and moments later Roland kicked open the office door. The doorstop reverberated as he held forth his cup of hot chocolate.

"Everything okay?"

His mouth was downturned, so Prudence reached out for his cup, a silent request that they share the drink, as they often did. He'd been on her mind the entire drive from the park. She had been worried, debating with herself about what Matshediso would or would not do to her or to her child, but now as Roland stood before her with that soured expression upon his face and the hem of his pants crusted with dirt, she no longer felt that urgent rush of protective love, but rather, she was filled with a regrettable surge of disappointment. She tried to hide this feeling with a tepid smile.

"Did they put too much whipped cream in your hot chocolate?"

Roland barely took a breath before he threw the cup at her. Hot chocolate splattered her face, soaked her shirt, the office chair, the computer keyboard. It burned her eyes.

"Fuck, Roland?!"

She had never cursed at him but did not regret it. She wiped her face with her sleeve, and the burn in the corners of her eyes eased, but as soon as she began to see clearly again, she saw him positioning himself to kick the empty cup at her as though it were a soccer ball. She blocked the kick but he started toward her. When he was angry like this, he often tried to bump her chest; he didn't understand his strength. She wasn't afraid of him—not yet—but the office was small, the L-shaped desk swallowing two walls and the bookcase another. There was no way for Prudence to put distance between them, even if she felt the need to.

"Step back, Ro. Now!" Her voice was firm, and though Roland flinched, he did not retreat.

"That was entirely inappropriate!" She sounded very much like the mothers in her support group, women whom she both despised and admired. She thought of what they might advise her to do now. Reflect. Exercise caution. Lead with love. But even with their voices in her head, she kept thinking about how disrespected she felt. The gall of this little boy.

Roland stopped moving toward her, but now he stood with his chest puffed and his legs spread apart, blocking the doorway.

"Go to your room. We will talk about what you did later."

She moved toward the door, hoping to procure a kitchen towel, but Roland wouldn't step aside. He was tall, stocky, and could almost look her directly in the eyes, and sometimes his size—the way he used his size—created more friction than Prudence dared to admit to anyone, even to those in her parent support group—most especially to those in her parent support group. One woman in the group had told her that most autistic children were not like her little boy. The woman had suggested that Roland "probably also had ADHD," and that he was an outlier because he was angry and impulsive and hard to control, but Prudence knew her child and if the words hadn't been so lost in her humiliations, she would have told that busybody woman that she didn't want to "control" her son. Rather, she wanted to model for him how to emotionally regulate, and if he could, help him to directly contend with how the world made him feel.

But Prudence was not modeling emotional regulation very well in that moment. She needed to leave that office and find someplace to calm herself. She asked Roland again, nicely, politely, to please move out of her way, but he offered no space for her retreat. So, Prudence set her hand on his chest and nudged him, gently.

Gently?

And because he was often unsteady on his legs and lacked core strength, and because he hadn't been expecting the nudge, he fell back into the door's casing with a thud.

By the time Davis arrived home, Roland had wrapped and rewrapped his chest and neck in ACE bandages. He did this whenever he wanted to indicate that he'd been emotionally or physically hurt. And despite Prudence's assurances to Davis that Roland had suffered no real physical injury, Davis enjoyed playing the hero.

"Mommy is a mean mommy, isn't she?" Davis winked at Prudence and turned again to Roland as if to commiserate. "What did she do to you? Did she scream at you? She screams at me sometimes too."

Roland pointed to his neck, his waist, his back, and Davis made a sad face, then put him to bed. After Roland fell asleep, Prudence told Davis what happened.

"He came on kind of strong, huh?" Davis said.

"His anger came out of nowhere," she repeated.

Davis hardly seemed interested. His face seemed to suggest that he'd heard all her complaints before, but she wanted to tell him not only about Roland but about everything that led to her impatience with him. She wanted to ask him if she should give Matshediso the photograph, but she knew that telling him about her past interactions with Matshediso would only bloom into a bigger issue between them.

"You know he can get like that," Davis muttered.

"When I came back home, they were in the yard. As soon as Alice left, he lost it."

"Where'd you go?" he asked.

"For a run."

"You don't look like you went for a run. You didn't wash your hair? You always wash your hair after a long run."

There was nothing in his tone or his expression to indicate anything more than rudimentary curiosity. He wasn't even looking at her. He removed his wallet from his pocket and set it atop the dresser.

"More like a light jog," she said.

Davis turned into his closet and began whistling. He'd ended their conversation rather unceremoniously, so taking the cue, she lay back onto the sofa, tightening the blanket around her body, tucking the edges of it beneath her legs, as if to lock herself in. When she woke, it was close to two in the morning. Davis was in the bed and the lights were all off but now old worries and fresh worries converged like a new dawn and a waxing moon in her mind.

In the dark, Prudence found her way downstairs to the storage room. On the wire shelving unit, buried inside a Lenox picture frame box, she uncovered her most treasured documents from South Africa. She'd placed them there many years earlier, and now sitting on the cold travertine floor, she spread out all the items she'd found. In the pile were several drafts of her law review paper, a pocket copy of the South African Constitution, a typed list of the Truth and Reconciliation Commission members, and four fully used legal pads with sheets fragile and oily. She gently turned the leaves of the pads, searching for the notes from the day of Zwane's testimony.

Yes, they were very excited. Laughing, as boys do. Singing on the bus.

* * *

As she read Zwane's words twenty-two years later, they felt more devastating than before, landing in her gut like heavy metal. Was it because she was a mother now? Those boys had been so excited, so unaware of the terror that lay ahead.

One of the boys, the smallest, did not drink so much. He cried for his mother.

Pressed into one of the pages of the third legal pad were the photos she had developed at a Rite Aid after her return. During his testimony, Zwane had taken care to hold himself upright like an aged ballet dancer. She remembered that his tone had not been as sharp as Volter's, but there had been something frightening in his manner, something in the timbre of his voice that conveyed an unyielding belief that one day he would be on the right side of history.

She sighed, breathing in the numbing air of the storage room, listening to the mechanical buzz and hum of their extra freezer, as she read on. Soon, a cone of white light slashed the spiderwebbed ceiling, and when Prudence looked up, Roland was in the doorway, his legs spread apart, his arms crossed, his eyes barely open.

"Sor-ry, ma-ma," he said. "Sor-ry, ma-ma."

She felt both surprised and proud that he'd managed to put together those four syllables for her. She crawled toward him and pulled him down, into her chest. He was stiff, but as she held him tighter and for longer, he loosened.

"Mama is sorry, Mama is sorry too."

18

"They won't even admit the knife is there."
—Malcolm X

The morning after their meeting in the park, thinking again about what Matshediso wanted her to do, Prudence woke all the more enraged. Had he been serious?

Prudence had built her entire life around trying not to be the person who could do what Matshediso wanted her to do. Did he know how many of her classmates in college and in graduate school thought a Baltimore girl like her should be accustomed to crime? One sleight of the hand by some vile god and Prudence had become a statistic: a Black girl affected by gun violence, raised by a single mother with no permanent home. If her classmates had known what her teenage years had been like—if she had ever cared to tell any of them—none of them would have asked how that had happened. None would have bothered to imagine her life before her father's murder, none would have believed that her father had been kind and warm and lovely, a beloved math teacher.

Matshediso was the only person with whom she'd ever shared all the details of her father's murder. Did he think taking a life meant nothing to her because of it?

A few years before she went to South Africa, Prudence went looking for the man who had killed her father. She confirmed the man's identity with Miss Jen, who told her that he had, indeed, been the one bragging about ordering his two associates to snatch her father from his car after a Friday night lime at a steelpan yard. Miss Jen told her that the man had long since been estranged from his son and that the boy her father had tried to protect was now a graduate of Morehouse College, soon to be a Professor of Mathematics.

"But don't go and do nothin' stupid," Miss Jen had warned her.

She told Miss Jen that she had long ago accepted her father's death.

"Acceptance is not just saying 'it is what it is,'" Miss Jen had said. "Acceptance is a deeper commitment to making the terrible thing that happened to you, serve you in some way. It's got to make your understanding about life deeper and better, or that ain't acceptance, baby."

She nodded, pretending to heed Miss Jen's advice, but over a three-night period at the end of that August, Prudence and a friend waited in the dark parking lot of a condo complex for the man to show. It was a humid Tuesday night when they finally spotted him parking what looked to be a new Jaguar. He stepped out of the vehicle with not a bit of swagger, straightening his O's cap like any regular suburban dad. He was more svelte than Prudence imagined, his features angular, his clothing preppy and fresh. He could have been walking alongside her on Harvard Square any day, heading to teach Economics or Philosophy. As she watched him, Prudence didn't have to wonder what separated the two of them, for the list was lengthy, and yet at the top of it was luck, opportunity, and perhaps also a loving father. The man who had ordered her father to be cut into pieces, the man who had left him in a bag to be found by a woman who killed herself in a psychiatric facility three days later, was walking right in front of her, and Prudence believed he deserved to die. And she could have had him killed that night too. Under the cover of a sweltering Baltimore evening, that man's life could have been snuffed out with one word from her because the friend in the car was the sort who would have willingly done the deed on her behalf. And Prudence was damn certain she would not have mourned that man. Not for a second. But as she sat smoldering in the weighty air of vengeance, feeling her body tense as the man climbed the steps to his unit, she knew suddenly that she had already begun to transform into the woman she would become, the woman her father would have been proud to call daughter, and the only thing that would have changed her mind that night was if she'd had nothing to lose.

19

"Only a fool would let his enemy teach his children.
— Malcolm X

It was nearing five o'clock on Friday afternoon when Davis surprised Prudence with a call from Dulles Airport. He'd left town a day earlier for a two-day business trip but had taken an early flight home.

"I'm in the mood to cook," he said. "Can you take out a pack of chicken thighs from the basement freezer and defrost it?"

Prudence had already ordered pizza but called quickly to cancel. She told Roland that dinner was going to be much better than pizza. "Maybe Daddy will make his famous chicken parm for dinner!" Roland murmured with pleasure, and as she ran downstairs into the basement, she heard him raise the volume on the television.

"Roland! Turn it down!"

Of course, he couldn't hear her over the noise, which made her think fondly of her brother, who also used to love listening to the television at top volume. Even during his frequent overnights in the emergency rooms, her brother would hold on to the TV remote as if it were sustenance. Without the healthcare policy from her father's city job, her mother had had to use emergency rooms to address her brother's strange ailments. It would take two years to accurately diagnose his leukemia and by then it was too late—both her mother's mental decline and her brother's physical decline were precipitous. "God rest your soul, little brother."

Prudence picked up some Legos and one of Roland's Velcro shoes and set them back into his cubby. The cubby walls were splattered with mud and there still sat a bucket of dead worms on the bench. She sighed, promising to deal with the mess later, and opened the door to the storage area. She expected to feel a rush of cool air and to see the normal, neatly stacked boxes, the cans of beer she stored in open coolers, the front door wreath she rarely bothered to hang anymore, but, instead, everything was in disarray. More than disarray. It was a disaster. The garbage bags with Roland's baby clothes had all been emptied, Christmas tree ornaments were broken, old books were splayed on their spines, bags of wrapping tissue and holiday foil were emptied, Davis's Bowers & Wilkins speakers had been tipped on their sides, and all the papers from every box—and there were scores of boxes— were strewn about, as if tossed by a tornado.

It took her a moment to realize that someone had been in there. Or perhaps someone was still there?

Prudence bolted up the steps. She grabbed Roland by the hand, pulled him out of the front door and onto the front walk until the police arrived, followed soon by Davis. After an hour of fingerprinting and photo-taking, the police concluded that whoever it was must have gotten scared off before they were able to make their way upstairs. "You should get yourself a better security system," one of the cops said.

They had the best system, didn't they?

After the officers left, she reviewed the security footage again, but there were still no signs of anything or anyone unusual.

That night they moved Roland into their bedroom, unsure how long it'd be before they felt comfortable leaving him alone again. Davis asked her about the gun. She told him she had checked and that it was in the same place it had always been. He didn't sleep that night, promising in a whisper at two in the morning to make the security system impervious. For several nights afterward, he woke multiple times to play the recordings from the cameras, and though there were no signs of anything untoward, what neither could determine was what the person who had broken into their home had wanted.

"Of all places, why the basement storage room?" Davis said.

Then, Prudence remembered the conversation they'd had at dinner with Matshediso. Davis had told Tara and Matshediso where Prudence kept her notes and her photos from South Africa, and she hadn't gotten back to Matshediso after their meeting.

Suddenly, it wasn't Davis awake at night anymore, but Prudence. The tossing and turning and the nagging thoughts wouldn't stop. And with their very regulated and organized life in utter shambles, she had forgotten that Roland would be starting at his new school in a few short days.

In a place as competitive as Washington, D.C., it had been a trying private school admissions process. Roland had shown significant word acquisition in the previous year and had had some success with the Rapid Prompting Method, but his learning profile still proved a challenge for the school's admissions committee. They asked for three parent interviews and two assessments for Roland, in addition to the requisite reference letters. Before the official decisions were even released, Prudence and Davis had had to promise that in those areas where the school couldn't accommodate Roland's "needs," they would pay for independent support beyond the already $58,000 annual tuition. Of course, Prudence would have agreed to nearly anything for admission to that school, with its lush campus greens and its teachers with a collective four hundred years of training in special education. She had heard that many of the children who'd attended for only two years had been able to transition to more traditional schools, something Prudence desperately wanted for Roland, though she was loath to admit this to anyone.

The first week of school went surprisingly well, and Prudence relaxed more each morning at drop-off. Roland seemed to be adjusting and the staff seemed to understand him, delighted, they said, with his exuberance. But by the beginning of the second week, Roland seemed moodier and had lost much of his appetite, his lunches returning untouched. Was the break-in still affecting him or was it something else?

Prudence decided to arrive early for pickup to see what she could glean. It was an overcast but muggy day, and she watched the children on the playground from the farthest parking lot, immediately spotting Roland, who sat alone on a picnic bench. Self-isolation wasn't unusual for Roland and not for many of the other kids at that school, but Prudence always ached to see him this way. Standing outside the car to get a better look at things, the heat felt like a warm canvas pillowcase overhead, so she reached inside the van for a hair tie and when she turned back, she saw a smaller boy approaching Roland. She felt thrilled to see the boy trying to befriend her son—until the boy picked up the stick.

Lodging the long branch under his armpit, the other boy began to wriggle his body, as if to imitate a machine gun. A teacher approached. She said something to the boy, took the stick, threw it onto the school lawn, and nudged the child away from Roland, who again sat by himself. It was then that Prudence climbed into the minivan, planning to drive into the carpool lane, but with the teacher's back turned, the little boy picked up the same stick and stalked again toward Roland.

Prudence sprinted across the parking lot and as she ran, she saw another parent, a white man in a well-tailored suit, perhaps in his late fifties, moving swiftly toward the boys too. She was glad she wouldn't be alone in trying to separate them, as the other teachers and aides were at the bottom of a hill, chatting and supervising other children.

Now, the small boy pushed the stick into Roland's belly. He did it once, then twice, but before he could do it again, Roland rose from the bench and turned his back to the boy, crossing his arms high on his chest. But when the boy stabbed Roland between his shoulder blades, it looked as if Roland had had enough. He yanked the stick from the boy's hand and pushed him to the ground. The teacher arrived at the same time as the boy's father. As Prudence drew closer, breathless and sweating, she heard the man asking his son if he was all right. The man turned to the teacher, incredulously. "Who is this fucking ape?! Look at him! What the hell?!" He seemed to be reaching for Roland's shirt with pinched fingers, but by then Prudence was pushing his hand away.

"What the hell are you doing?" she shouted.

Roland, wide-eyed, rubbed his belly. Prudence lifted his shirt to find large red welts oozing small pindots of blood onto his stomach.

She turned to the man. "And what did you call my child? I saw your son stabbing my child with that stick and you're calling my kid an ape? That fucking little runt . . ."

The man squared his shoulders but she gripped Roland's hand and led him away. When they reached the minivan, she could see, in the distance, the teacher chatting with the man, nodding, grinning. She buckled Roland in and dialed Davis, insisting that he meet her there immediately.

Both Davis and Alice arrived within the hour. Alice took Roland to his therapy appointment while Prudence and Davis waited until the Head of School, Mr. Columb, conferred with the teacher about what took place.

Prudence hadn't been in a principal's office since the day she and her mother met with Sister Elizabeth to beg her to allow Prudence to continue the rest of the school year. It was her final year in middle school, eighth grade, and after her father's burial, her mother didn't have enough money for the rest of the year's tuition. Sister Elizabeth had asked Prudence's mother to bring proof of her financial hardship—checking and savings account statements, and insurance policies—but after the review, realizing that her mother wouldn't be able to contribute anything, Sister Elizabeth said, "I'm sorry again for your loss, but we don't have any free spaces at this school."

Now, Prudence looked around the Head of School's office. His degree certificates dotted the walls above the upholstered couch: an undergraduate diploma from Boston University and a doctoral certificate from the University of Connecticut. She and Davis waited on the other side of a polished oak desk where Mr. Columb would take his seat across from them. The office was the size of a large classroom, glass windows extending the entire length of it, statuesque trees and hills as its sole view, so why did it feel so uninviting? The walls were a strange dark brown, hickory perhaps, intended to lend the office and Mr. Columb some gravitas, but instead it felt heavy and cold.

"A New England boy," Davis had called Mr. Columb when they first met him at the open house. They both knew what that meant, yet Prudence and Mr. Columb had hit it off. They shared their common dislike for the Patriots, which she thought odd for a suburban Boston boy, and an interest in poetry. Columb was a fan of Walt Whitman and Prudence said nothing about Whitman's comparison of Black people to baboons. Oh, the irony, she thought, sitting there now.

When Mr. Columb arrived he closed the office door quietly behind him. He offered them generic bottles of spring water and began the usual pleasantries before finally getting to what they came to discuss.

"Roland's teacher, Mrs. Stims, believes that she didn't clearly hear the other parent call Roland that word." Mr. Columb adjusted his cotton tie, while Prudence felt herself stunned by the teacher's betrayal. "She says she was distracted by the boys."

The teacher had been there. She'd even gasped. Prudence shifted in her seat and Davis tapped her leg as if he could feel the change in her, as if to remind her of *the dance*. "The dance is a beautiful plié," Davis had once told her. "A show of strength and grace. It's what Black parents at private schools have to do to get their kids through." Davis had spent his life in those environments. He wanted her to let him handle it.

"I see . . ." Davis said. "That's most unfortunate because I can assure you that my wife was not distracted, and that she heard the words clearly and saw the man reaching for Roland's collar."

"The other parent admits he may have overreacted when he saw Roland push his son," Mr. Columb said.

Davis removed his phone from the inside pocket of his jacket. He scrolled to the photo Prudence had sent him and held up the phone so Mr. Columb could see. "This is Roland's stomach. As you can see, there's blood on his belly. The boy stabbed our son with the stick so hard that he broke skin, and when Roland turned away from him, he poked him in the back." Davis swiped again. "This is Roland's back. Can you see? I'd be happy to send you photos of his torn shirt this evening. Do you know how hard it would be for a seven-year-old boy to withstand this kind of torment?" Davis returned his phone to the inside of his suit, his pocket square slipping out of place. He readjusted it so that it sat perfectly again.

"But they're children . . ." Davis continued. "And we're reasonable people. We don't want to start the school year leveling accusations against a school or a teacher who should have been monitoring the kids, particularly after pulling them apart, and particularly after seeing that a child had been imitating the use of an automatic weapon." Davis rubbed his hands together as if warming them. "That said, let's just say that the boy's father wasn't actually going to lay his hands on our child; we still cannot accept a grown man calling our child a 'fucking ape,' Mr. Columb. We can't do that."

"My child is not an animal," Prudence whispered.

Tears welled up in the corners of Prudence's eyes, as if all the emotions of the last few weeks had culminated there. But she would not weep, not in that man's office. So, she sat quietly, watching those dark hickory walls. Anything to prevent that one tear from plunging.

"I'm not really sure you understand how offensive it is for Black people to be compared to monkeys," Davis said.

Mr. Columb's face reddened and he turned toward Prudence. Her nose leaked and she wanted to reach for a tissue or perhaps even to sniffle but she feared that Mr. Columb might soften his eyes and see her as wounded, feared that Davis might try to comfort her, and she didn't want any of that pity. Instead, she made her face stony, convincing herself that she was more angry than hurt, and she could see the immediate change in Mr. Columb's expression as he regarded her.

"I can imagine," Mr. Columb said. "But the other parent said you called his son a runt." Mr. Columb leaned over the desktop and there was something about the slithering way he moved himself forward, something about the gleam in his eye . . . it felt like a "gotcha."

"You aren't suggesting that 'runt' is comparable to 'fucking ape,' are you?" she countered.

"The boy *is* small," Mr. Columb said.

Prudence pushed her locs away from her face, tucking them behind her ear. In her mind's eye she saw Roland, saw his vulnerability, the confusion when anyone raised their voice at him. *Ma-ma. Ma-ma.* This is what he said to her as she walked him across the parking lot and fastened his seatbelt.

"Last I checked, runts weren't a protected class in this country. Dwarfs maybe but not runts." Prudence then turned to Davis. "Do you remember runts being mentioned on the New York bar exam, honey?"

"Mr. and Mrs. Gooden . . ." Mr. Columb began.

She wanted to correct him, she wanted to make him refer to her by *her* name—Wright—her father's name, a name she'd chosen to keep, but Prudence again felt Davis's hand on her leg.

"Roland is a lovely child," Mr. Columb went on. "The teachers already adore him. We know he will do well here, and we will make sure that his experience going forward is better than today. This is a misunderstanding. Both sides committed wrongdoings and it's such a stressful time, introducing your children to a new school, being the parents of children who need—"

"We can't have him here with parents like that man," Prudence said.

Davis's body stiffened.

Roland didn't have the words to ask her why the man had said what he said or why he couldn't stay on the playground longer or why Prudence was so angry or why the teacher hadn't stopped the boy from coming back to hurt him or why why why. So many whys from Black children that were rarely satisfactorily answered. But all her son could say in that moment was *Ma-ma. Ma-ma.*

She needed to know that her boy could learn there, needed to know he would feel safe there. What were they paying for if not for that? Her child needed to be protected.

Prudence reached into her purse for her wallet. Inside were credit cards, insurance cards, her driver's license, big-box store cards, and their joint checkbook. Prudence tore a check from the book and glanced over at Davis, who to great effect looked out past Mr. Columb, through the window, at the rolling fields and at the cloudy sky, trying to maintain the illusion of a united front.

"What do you need to ensure that that man and his child are gone from this school by tomorrow?" Prudence moved her chair closer to the lip of Mr. Columb's desktop, the check perched at the edge of it.

"That's not how we do things, Mr. and Mrs. Gooden."

"Oh no? You've just launched your capital fund, yes?"

Prudence and Davis had already received the glossy brochure in the mail, the architectural renderings of the proposed gymnasium with an Olympic-sized pool.

Davis crossed his legs and reached out his hand for hers, clasping her fingers. "Also." Davis let the word linger for a bit. "My mother is the retired CFO of a Fortune 200 company and my father is the pastor of what they call 'a Black megachurch' in Ohio. Lots of money in my church. I'm pretty certain a few calls to support their grandson's school would go a long way to kicking off your campaign."

"So how much to make sure that man and his son never see our beautiful child's blessed face again, Mr. Columb?" Prudence reached for a pen from the leather pencil holder on Mr. Columb's desk. It was a Super Bowl XLIX fountain pen.

20

The mother is the first teacher of the child.
                                        —Malcolm X

Prudence and Davis held hands as they walked across the school parking lot. Secretly, she worried that the parents, the teachers, even the other students, might find a way to make Roland pay for the position they'd put Mr. Columb in when he accepted their very generous donation. She'd have to make nice with everyone there. She'd have to join the parent board, volunteer in the classroom, ensure no one found fault with her child. They would all have to be more acceptable, more respectable. She would need to play the game to protect her boy. It was an exhausting, reckless dance with power, yet she understood there was a consequence to every affirmative and demanding Black act.

"See you at home?" Davis said. "Roland's probably about to wrap himself like a mummy." He kissed her on the cheek, and they climbed into their separate vehicles, but Prudence didn't turn over her engine until Davis was long gone. She was thinking about how easy it had been to make that man and his son disappear from the school with a pen and a healthy checkbook, as if that could wipe away the memory of the words and the physical fear they evoked in her child. When she and Matshediso slashed that officer's tires all those years earlier, she'd felt that immediate relief only to understand later that it did nothing to dull the terror she would feel for the rest of her life. She was tired just thinking about how much there was to fight. Between Matshediso, the break-in, and this school issue with Roland, something had to give.

She called Matshediso and left him a voicemail. She would give him the photo, so long as he never contacted her again. "I'll meet you on Monday and I don't owe you anything after this."

On Sunday morning Prudence packed Roland into the car and they headed to the Bethesda Farmer's Market. The little market, with its snaking rows of white vendor tents in the parking lot of a local elementary school, was nothing like the blocks-long summer markets in Manhattan, but still, there was plenty to excite them: hot chocolate and cheddar cheese biscuits for Roland, and for Prudence, fresh kale, dill pickles, and crêpes.

It was a brilliant, sunny morning, the light taking on a shimmery sort of haze that Roland found particularly remarkable when it struck the feathers of two parakeets, one a neon green and the other a powder blue with a headdress of yellow. Mesmerized, he stood with his mouth agape, admiring the birds as Prudence walked to the crêpe tent across from him. As she debated whether to order one, she could hear the parakeet vendor telling Roland that the green parakeet's name was Kiwi. She reflected on whether she'd ever given Roland a slice of kiwi to eat, wondered what happened in his mind when presented with unfamiliar words for which he couldn't associate a tangible thing. She watched him, so relaxed and unbothered, and it was then that a clear-faced teenager with a nose ring, working for the crêpe vendor, circled the tent and handed her a perfectly golden crêpe, filled with banana slices and swirls of Nutella, wrapped in fresh parchment paper.

"Pour vous," the teenager said, smiling.

How could they have known her favorite crêpe order? Prudence wasn't exactly a regular but perhaps she was more memorable than she knew.

"Is this really for me? Merci!" she said.

She took the first bite, feeling glorious, and the parakeet vendor put up his hand as if to let her know that Roland was okay, as if to say that she should enjoy herself too, and she smiled at the kind man, then searched for a napkin and held out cash for the teenager to take. There was a snaking line of customers at the crêpe tent now, and the girl waved her away.

"Please, it was so delicious. I have to pay for it."

As Prudence continued to wave the money at the girl, the parakeets began to squawk. She turned and saw Kiwi marching about, his movements sharp and ireful. Roland stepped back and Prudence, feeling worried, called out to the girl again to collect the money.

"No worries!" the girl shouted. "Your husband paid for it. He asked me to deliver it to you!"

Kiwi screeched, and Prudence, shocked by what the teenager said, began to feel strange. She gripped the side of the crêpe vendor's table while the parakeet man spoke calmly to the bird. Roland was staring over at her as her sight blinked in and out. Her eyeballs felt slick, out of control, moving like marbles. She would have laughed at the cartoon-like absurdity of it if it weren't so frightening. Had the girl said "husband"? Davis was at the office picking up files, wasn't he? And if he was at the market, why hadn't he joined her and Roland?

As the other bird began screeching too, Prudence's tongue turned leaden. She felt the need to sit and searched for a chair, a bench, a barrel, but there was nothing. Just tents and wobbly folding tables. Her heart raced. Thumped. Pounded. Her head spun and the sunlight bore down as she lost her balance.

"Roland," she heard herself saying.

Prudence fell onto the asphalt, as the parakeets squalled and shrieked. She could only manage to lift one arm before it plopped back down onto the pavement. Pain shot through all her fingers and her senses seemed to be misfiring. She heard the sound of shoes on pavement and soon the teenager from the crêpe tent was standing over her. The girl raised Prudence's arm, trying to help her up, but Prudence could not be lifted.

"Roland!"

"Get her some water!"

"Roland!"

"Is she high?"

Prudence wanted to tell the people standing above her that she'd never taken any drugs. "Just say no!" Nancy Reagan had told them. But even there, in that loopy, wiry world she had entered, Prudence knew that the idea of a Black woman from Baltimore having never done an illicit drug wouldn't be believed. She knew, lying there, that the story people would tell later that day would be of a Black woman behaving peculiarly at the farmer's market, interrupting the morning's calm for the fine and good people of Bethesda.

A water bottle touched her hand. The plastic felt damp, cold, and the crowd buzzed around her.

"Roland!" She was shouting louder now. It was the kind of shout that only children seemed permitted to do—unbound, unrestrained. Prudence had screamed this way only once before in her life, when her mother took her brother with her to make the funeral arrangements for her father. Prudence had been left alone in the house for the first time since the policemen came.

"Roland! Roland!"

Half an hour later, as she sat on the inner edge of a parked ambulance with an ice packet, a policeman agreed to release Prudence. The lead EMT, a Black woman, told the officer that

Prudence was suffering from dehydration. The policeman, skeptical, asked Prudence for identification, and as he consulted with his partner at their patrol car, the EMT whispered to Prudence that she'd likely "been on a trip."

"A what? No, I don't think so."

"It could have been an anxiety attack too," the EMT said. "You ever have one of those?"

"Yes, once when I was fourteen, but nothing like this."

"They come in all shapes and sizes, at all times of your life, but especially when women get to our age. And Black people have them too. You been stressed lately?" The EMT examined her pupils once more. "Either way, if I take you to the hospital, it could get complicated for you and your little boy." The EMT glanced over at Roland, who was standing next to a woman Prudence didn't know. "You look like you work out and take good care of yourself, so go to your doctor if you don't feel better by tomorrow."

She hadn't consumed anything that morning except the Nutella and banana crêpe. As the EMT finished the paperwork, the woman who had collected Prudence's groceries and phone from the pavement, who'd also been standing with Roland, approached her.

"He seems fine," the woman said, gently. "I kept him with me the whole time."

"Thank you," Prudence said, trying, unsuccessfully, to grip Roland's clammy fingers.

"Do you want me to call someone for you?"

She thought of Davis, but she was also thinking about what the EMT and the teenager had said. *A trip? A husband?* She wouldn't know how to explain it. The crêpe tent was already packed, all the employees gone, so she wouldn't be able to ask the teenager what the man had looked like. Did someone slip her something or was it really only a panic attack?

She told the woman, who was now handing her the container of pickles, that she would be fine and thanked her again. She inspected Roland, and thankfully, he seemed unaffected. No shaking legs, no tense shoulders. But she also knew there were no more certainties in her world.

At home, Davis was prepping meat for his Sunday grilling. A muted tennis match played on the family room television. The kitchen recess light, closest to the fridge, flickered.

"You guys were gone for a while." He was taking out an onion, gawking at the match.

"Were you at the market?" she asked.

"Whole Foods? Yeah, I stopped—"

"No. Were you at the Bethesda Farmer's Market?"

"Me? You know I hate that place."

It was true. Before Roland was born, she had tried to make farmers' markets their Sunday morning routine, a stroll to take in the tastes and scents of their local grocers, but Davis always rushed her past the stalls.

"You okay?" He peeled back the onion atop their wooden cutting board.

"Had a little fall at the market, but I'm fine."

"You sure?"

She looked up at the recess light, the fluttering worsening her headache. "I'll be fine if you change that bulb, please?"

Davis nodded and unmuted the television. The announcer shouted as she started toward the upstairs staircase. As she neared it, she saw that the front door, which they rarely used, was unlocked. She thought to ask Davis about it, but instead, she moved to secure it. When she reached for the lock, she spotted a man through the transom window.

She froze.

"Davis . . ."

She heard the clang of the grill lid in the distance, the tennis ball echoing from the television. The man outside began turning the door handle.

"Davis!" She couldn't move. Why couldn't she move?

"Davis!" she shouted louder.

Finally, she could hear Davis's footfalls. "Whoa, whoa! What's wrong?"

Her eyes filled with water, blood rushed between her ears, and her swollen finger pulsed. The crack in the door widened and in strode Matshediso.

"You remember Mat, right?"

Her heart thudded like a bird tossing itself into a glass window. Matshediso closed the door behind him and cocked his head, innocently, as he reached out to pump her hand. He squeezed it firmly but the pain from her fall made the shake feel agonizing.

"Mat came to take a look at the exterior cameras for us." As Davis spoke, he stared at her, as if trying to understand what had come over her. "He's staying for dinner. I have enough meat to last us all week."

Upstairs, Prudence felt closer to vomiting than she had in the ambulance. Sitting next to the toilet, the banana and Nutella wended their way up into her mouth. She tried to slow her breath and calm herself before brushing her teeth. After, she looked out of the bedroom window and spotted Davis down below, on the deck, at the grill, laughing. Beside him stood Matshediso and Roland. They all seemed so normal, but how could she forget her suspicions about the break-in? How could she not wonder if Matshediso had had something to do with what happened to her at the market?

Prudence made her way downstairs and found Matshediso at the fridge, filling a cup of water. She furtively handed him the envelope with the photo she had planned to give him the next day.

"This is him," he whispered, looking down at the picture.

"Please leave now. I gave you what you wanted."

Outside, Roland, at the deck table beside Davis, was lining the grill grate with foil. Matshediso stared at him through the glass doors.

"He's a nice boy. You two are lucky."

She didn't want his compliments, and she especially didn't want his attention on her child.

"Did you drug me at the market this morning?"

"What?"

With her husband and child just on the other side of the deck doors, she realized it wasn't the right place for that conversation. "Forget it. I wouldn't expect you to admit it if you did."

"Market? What drug?"

He seemed surprised. Was it possible that she'd really just had a panic attack, one so severe that she had fainted? She needed her mind to stop racing.

"I'm trying to figure out what you're doing in my house."

"Helping your husband," he answered.

He pointed then, at the photo of Zwane. "I couldn't remember his face."

"I thought you didn't know what he looked like. I thought you said you weren't at the hearings."

Outside, Roland dropped the grill grate. It thundered as it hit the deck floor. He looked as though he might cry, but Davis, not shaken at all, lifted it and returned it to him.

When Prudence turned back to Matshediso, she noticed he was still staring at the photo.

"They were my brothers." He looked up at her now, staring directly into her eyes. "Thomas Mahlangu, Steven Mahlangu, Mark Mahlangu, Elijah Mahlangu. Four of the Mozambique Eight were my older brothers. The others were my brothers' friends."

She covered her mouth. She could still taste the sourness of the vomit, as she digested his words. She was unsure what to say. She was angry, yes, but mostly she felt hurt. Why hadn't he told her? She had shared her father's story with him, and he had said nothing about knowing those boys, nothing about being the brother and son of those people who had been murdered.

She opened the deck door. Davis and Roland looked over at her as if startled.

"I'm gonna take Mat into the basement and show him our security issues down there."

"I already took him downstairs," Davis said.

"He says he needs to see one last thing." She held up her finger. "Right back." She pointed at the grill. "I hope you have corn."

Prudence blew a kiss at Roland, but Davis held her gaze as if to ask if she was all right. She closed the deck door without acknowledging the glance and led Matshediso down the steps into the storage room.

"I don't know why I didn't tell you. I was planning on telling you at the park, but this has never been easy to talk about." He began his story before she even asked. "KwaNdebele is a beautiful place. A truly lovely part of South Africa. We lived in a sort of paradise of orchids and lilies and proteas and wildflowers I never knew the names of. We had little pockets of houses built along tracks of dirt roads and we walked everywhere, me and my brothers, sometimes sharing only two or three pairs of shoes.

Everyone knew us, the Mahlangu brothers. Our little plot of land was slightly bigger than the rest of the houses on our road so my father enjoyed hosting neighbors on Sunday afternoons. He would cook like your husband cooks, for anybody who needed to eat. One Sunday, Andrew Zwane came to our home." Matshediso paused, and she remembered that every time Andrew Zwane's name was mentioned during the hearings, the room grew quiet. "Zwane walked there with one of our neighbors and he ate my father's food. He and my father and the other men talked all night about the revolution, about what needed to happen next in the country, about the regime change that was necessary. They spoke of the things that all thinking Black men in South Africa spoke of back then. My father was no different than any other man. He wanted to live free, wanted his five boys to live free."

Matshediso couldn't have been too much older than Roland when Zwane first came to his house.

"The next day Zwane came again. This time he was alone. I thought he was looking for my father. I told him my father was not at home, but Zwane said he wanted to speak to my eldest brother. I called for Thomas, and because he'd been at our house for hours the previous night, Thomas trusted him. Zwane asked Thomas if he wanted to go for MK training. He told Thomas that he was a big man now and needed to do more for his country. I would follow my big brother wherever he went so I was there that day, listening to Zwane convince Thomas. It was windy and I remember seeing the dust falling onto his sandals as he spoke. The man's feet were good feet. The kind of feet a man would have if he worked in an office. I pointed at them and told Thomas to look. Thomas touched me on the head to quiet me. Later that night Thomas told my other brothers that he planned to go for training, that the man would take him to Mozambique. My other brothers told Thomas he would not go alone. They said they would all go, though they knew our father would disapprove."

Matshediso fell quiet. They could hear footsteps overhead. It sounded as if Roland and Davis had come in from outside and were throwing soiled items into the kitchen sink.

"After Zwane murdered my brothers, he returned to our house and bombed it. My mother and I were out asking neighbors if they had seen my brothers. My father said he would wait at home for them to return. We heard the explosion and when we ran back, I was without my home, without my brothers, without my father."

Matshediso dug the tip of his shoe into the corner of a basement tile. The fidgeting felt like a way to contain himself, a way not to remember the contours of his home's walls, not to remember where he once slept with his brothers, where they once ate, a way not to remember the dark passageway that led to his mother and father's nighttime embraces.

"Pru!" Davis called out from upstairs. "Can you bring up the grill tongs?"

There were grill tongs in the bottom drawer next to the refrigerator. Davis knew this. She nodded at Matshediso. It was time to return to the kitchen.

Upstairs, Matshediso opened the deck door, handed Roland the metal tongs, and offered Davis the bowl of sauce that Davis had prepped and left sitting on the counter. Davis, organizing meat on the grate, told him that he called his special sauce SASHA, "So-Awesome-So-Hoppin'-Amazin'."

Matshediso laughed and said something about being excited to taste it as he watched Roland sticking his fingers into the SASHA sauce bowl and licking them.

"A ringing endorsement!" Davis laughed at Roland. "I know my SASHA is good!" Davis turned to thank Matshediso for helping out. "You wanna come back out on the deck? You can pull up a chair."

"Coming now now," Matshediso said. "Let me just finish chatting with your lovely wife about your security system. Plus, we like watching you two work."

Davis chuckled and shot a glance through the gap in the door at Prudence. Matshediso returned and took the seat beside her at the counter. She hadn't said a word to him since he began his story, though he seemed not to have noticed.

"I am not over it," he said. "You hear people say you need to forget, to forgive, but how do I forget and forgive Andrew Zwane? When a white journalist from Sweden came to report on the story, which the South African news barely covered, my mother begged him to take me with him. She needed to do that not to just give me a better chance at life, but to keep me alive."

Matshediso pursed his lips and sighed, as though he wished he could take back his mother's words. "My whole life as I knew it was gone. Like yours, when your father was killed, and when your brother died, and when your mother stopped mothering you. Everything happened in what felt like an instant."

"If you knew him, why did you ask for this photo?"

"I wanted to be sure of his face. I was a child."

"But I still don't understand why you didn't tell me any of this before?"

"I never told anyone until I met my ex-wife. And you know what she said? She told me I was irrevocably ruined. That I was too invested in my own argument. That I had let that man eat my humanity. She told me I suffered from *child shock* and that that was the reason our babies miscarried. Something in me killed them, she said." He sucked his teeth but Prudence had heard this term "child shock" before. It was coined for the children of

Apartheid, and it meant they had suffered the trauma of growing up in a society with political unrest, a society in the midst of
major social change. The suggestion was that they were at risk of
being dehumanized by their environment.

"I don't think you're telling me everything," she said.

"You're the one person I trust. I wouldn't lie to you."

She moved away from him, pretending to need to wash her
hands. "Trust doesn't feel like this," she said. "You pulled out
that knife at the park to threaten me. You asked me to help you
kill a stranger. I am pretty sure you broke into this house. And
I don't know what you did or didn't do to me at the market this
morning. But what I do know is that you're here now pretending to be my husband's friend, and nothing about any of that
feels right."

He looked through the deck doors, then turned back to her.
"I'm here because you, of all people, know how it feels to be
cheated out of a justice that could have easily been yours."

"Don't bring my father into this. Please."

She wiped her hands moments before Roland burst through
the door. He stopped and stared at Matshediso as if to study
him, then he washed his face in the kitchen sink, splashing water
onto the floor. Prudence handed him a paper towel before he
ran upstairs.

"You can trust me. You can," Matshediso whispered. "But let's
really talk. All right? Some other time?"

Davis came in from outside. He held the tongs upright, like
a torch, before dropping it into the sink. He stood next to her,
his hip pressed into hers. "Y'all all right?" He was focused on
Matshediso. "Did you figure out how to keep my wife from having to shoot the next person who tries to break into our house?"

Prudence laughed a strained laugh.

"We'll be eating in thirty minutes," Davis added. "I can't believe you two are gonna eat my good food and not lift a finger to help!"

"Put me to work. I'm ready, ja." Matshediso clapped his hands but Davis waved him off.

"Naw, it's good. I only get to cook on the grill like once a month or so. Prudence loves my grilling, so I do it for her." He quickly glanced over at her. "And lucky you, Mat, you showed up on the right day, huh?"

He motioned for Matshediso to sit back down and the two men chatted, but Prudence hardly heard the rest of the exchange. She was thinking of how Matshediso's presence had forced a sort of mining of memory that she hadn't wanted. There was a reason she had never looked for Matshediso, a reason that after learning of the officer's death, she never even went to Yeoville again. There were people from one's past who were present at the worst time in one's life, people whose very name evoked a time and a place one didn't want to revisit. Those were people you never wanted to see or hear from again. They were casualties of memory, casualties of too-hard truths.

The four of them were seated around the deck table an hour later. Davis's barbecued lamb chops and chicken quarters were a hit, delectable, as always. The late September sunrays fell like long stilts over the back of the house, but still the afternoon air felt crisp enough to signal fall. It had been an unusually warm summer, but the buds on the Sweetbay magnolia had already given up, fallen down; and the Japanese maple in its dramatic burgundy color might have felt discordant anywhere else so early in the autumn season, but in their backyard, with its purpleheart wood deck and its family of singing cardinals, the burgeoning color of that maple made complete sense.

As the men continued to talk, Prudence smiled when there was occasion to do so and leaned in when she needed to fake interest, but no part of her wanted this man in or near her home. She felt powerless against him, however, for his charms and his worldliness seemed wholly magnetic to Davis and Roland. There he was coloring pages with Roland and making Davis laugh in a way he hadn't laughed in weeks. She hadn't spent much time with Matshediso back in South Africa, but she, too, had fallen for that same enigmatic quality when they met for lunch in Orange Grove. And now, here he was, decades later, long after she had managed to forget about him, drudging up old shit.

Why was he trying to drag her into this long-awaited murderous transaction? Matshediso was a master manipulator, she was thinking, when suddenly, Roland set down his crayon and rose from the table. She expected he would return with a juice box, but he came back with colored pencils and a pad of construction paper. Matshediso laughed. He was a good artist and Roland was now pointing out things for him to draw on demand. As Matshediso began to sketch the hostas, big and green like banana leaves, Roland ripped out a picture from his drawing pad.

"What's that?" Davis reached for the thick cream-colored sheet. "That's a real good drawing." He pushed the picture toward Prudence, who looked down at it. Roland had some real talent. The way he shaped the bodies in the drawing was impressive. He had sketched a woman wearing a fanny pack and a muscled man in a vest standing near a swing set. There were no children in the drawing, only the man and the woman.

Prudence looked at the drawing more closely and her heart felt as if it were stomping across her chest.

She flipped the paper over, but Davis reached for it, examining it longer this time.

"Is that Mommy and Daddy at the park?" he said.

Davis was eating another slice of sweet potato, while Matshediso had his head down, concentrating on getting the shape of the hosta leaf exactly right.

Roland answered Davis with a shake of his head and pointed at Matshediso.

Davis chewed slowly, seemingly confused by Roland's response. Finally, Matshediso glanced up and Prudence could see him trying to understand what he had missed. It was clear to Prudence that Roland had seen them together. Her thoughts returned to the Saturday she left him with Alice, the day she met Matshediso at the park. She'd gone to Starbucks afterward, returned home with Roland's hot chocolate and Alice's scone. They had been in the backyard when she raced into the office, and later, when Alice and Roland came inside, Alice mentioned a receipt. She'd left the receipt for the kiddie shovel they bought. They would have passed the park on their way to the more kid-friendly hardware store in Kensington. Roland had definitely seen them together.

"Did you draw that today?" Davis asked Roland.

Matshediso looked down at the drawing now, moving it closer to his face before clenching his jaw ever so slightly.

Roland shook his head and pointed to Matshediso again.

"Do you see dead people too?" Matshediso quipped.

Davis snickered loudly at the joke Roland would have no way of understanding. Then, as Prudence watched, Matshediso pushed his own drawing forward, covering Roland's sketch.

"Look at you!" Prudence pointed at the Roland in Matshediso's artwork. Matshediso had drawn him standing between hostas, his foot dipping into a pool, his life vest zipped to his chin.

Davis nodded with approval at the drawing, then offered everyone another barbecued lamb chop. Matshediso accepted the offer and asked him about his secret SASHA ingredients.

"Oh no no no, brother, I can't give that up," Davis said. "You must have some secrets you can't share, right?"

Matshediso blanched, wondering perhaps like Prudence why Davis, grinning, would bring up *secrets*? Was Davis trying to sniff something out? She needed to make sure he didn't find a trail that led to her.

21

There is nothing more difficult than waking someone who is only pretending to be asleep.

—Desmond Tutu

Matshediso called and she didn't answer. That day she erased the security footage from his visit to the house. He then sent flowers to thank her and Davis for having him over for dinner. She tossed the bouquet into the garage bin before Davis ever saw them.

But now, he wouldn't stop calling.

"You're fucking with my family," she hissed over the phone.

"I wouldn't do anything to hurt your son. He's a special boy. I mean that."

She'd seen the way Roland took to him. At the door, when Matshediso was leaving, Roland held his hand. Both Davis and Prudence had complicated feelings about what they witnessed. Roland was never like that with strangers. They talked about it after he left.

"That's a strange man," Davis had said.

"Very. I felt that the night we were in D.C. at dinner."

"Did you tell me that? I don't remember you telling me you thought that."

"I don't know, maybe because I felt sorry for him after those white people accused him of stealing their child . . ."

"Oh yeah." Davis shook his head, as if he didn't want to revisit that night. "So, what were you two talking about?"

"South Africa and his bad ideas about the security system. That dude is a total weirdo. I was hoping you'd save me from having to talk to him."

She rose from the bedroom couch to turn on the shower, but Davis followed her into the bathroom. He propped himself against his sink and watched her undress.

"You seemed angry when he was here."

"Well . . . I fell down at the market this morning, come home in pain to find him creeping outside the door, then you invite him for dinner without discussing it with me." She shrugged and examined her still-throbbing hand. "I was trying to be nice but I really didn't want him here."

She thought that would be the end of it, but now, on the phone with Matshediso, he was asking her to meet him for lunch.

"It's only lunch," he insisted.

"I gave you the photo. Leave me alone. I would never do what you want me to do. Never. It doesn't even make sense that you would think I'd do this. We have enough Black people dying in this world. You want me to add to that? What's wrong with you?"

"I'm asking you to meet for lunch. I can't talk to anyone else about this. Just one hour."

She imagined all the things he could do to upset her life and the list was endless.

She chose an Italian restaurant in Van Ness, the sort of place frequented by Botoxed women who liked to drink midday prosecco and old men with newspapers and NRA cards. When she arrived there, her plan was to convince Matshediso either not to involve her or not to do anything at all.

She chose a table at the far end of the restaurant and waited for his arrival. She was ravenous and already knew what she would order—the artichoke and arugula salad with brined lemon zest and Sorrento citronette dressing. She would take the salad home so she could enjoy it. She planned for the meeting to be short.

"Howzit?" Matshediso rushed toward her and sat down in a flurry of motion.

"How is it?" she repeated. "Not good. I'm at lunch with a man who's trying to get me sent to jail."

He smirked and turned to peek at the crowd around them. The restaurant was only a quarter full but still he leaned forward, speaking softly. "I have a lot to tell you."

"I already know that Zwane is awful," she said. "He killed your brothers and their friends. He killed your father. He killed countless others. I was reading through my notes again. The list of victims is so long. I know, I really know all this."

She hadn't remembered writing some of the stories that were in her notes. They were terrifying. In one notebook, she wrote about Zwane and other askaris being asked to help the Port Elizabeth Security Branch suppress unrest there. The SAP had gotten wind of the arrival of three men, ANC activists, who they were convinced were involved in terrorist activity.

We wanted to neutralize their involvement. The man testifying was named Fritz, formerly Colonel Harold Fritz. Prudence hardly remembered what he looked like, except she'd written in her notes that he was missing a thumb.

I didn't know at that time that they were to be killed, though I did know that many activists were routinely eliminated. Zwane picked them up and took them to the meeting place in Cradock. By the time I arrived, the men had hoods on their heads. Zwane would do the interrogation. Fritz seemed nervous; his injured hand twitched as he spoke.

What were the victims' names?

Fritz said he didn't remember the names. He seemed to want to talk about generalities, not specifics. He began his recitation on the need to suppress the liberation movement, then he added, *The methods of interrogation were well-known.*

The Committee's counsel jumped at this opportunity. *What were they?*

Fritz refused to answer.

You said the methods of interrogation were well-known, so what were they?

Fritz shrugged. *I don't know because I wasn't present.*

Counsel looked up at the Committee as if to insist that they note Fritz's lack of cooperation. Fritz noticed the glances between them.

I can sketch the normal means of interrogation. The normal way was to use violence, humiliate people, assault people, and intimidate people to get information.

Counsel for the Committee introduced another lawyer, a man in an eggplant-colored suit who said he was a representative of the families. Prudence didn't know until then that the victims' families could question amnesty applicants. She sat forward on the bench.

Why were those three men arrested at the airport?

Fritz shook his head. *I was only told to have the askaris take them away so they could be handled by the Security Branch.*

The family's lawyer seemed displeased. He dropped his shoulders. *So, you were called all the way from Vlakplass to go to this small airport in Port Elizabeth only so you could watch a few men get taken away?*

Fritz nodded, looked over at the other applicants. *I waited in my vehicle. Zwane approached the bakkie. He and the other askaris grabbed the men.*

There was a tsk-tsk sound down below; someone in the gallery hoped to shame him.

Zwane was one of your charges and yet you say that you weren't involved in the interrogation.

Fritz shrugged, then added, *Zwane was very capable.*

It says in your written statement that while the men remained hooded for three days, many of the officers and askaris were having a braai and drinks in the same place the men were being held. Is that right?

Fritz's hand trembled more. *Yes, we ate,* he said.

Did you hear gunshots?

No.

So, you don't know what happened to the men? If you were in command, you didn't feel like you had a duty to ask?

Fritz shrugged again. *I asked Zwane and the other askaris whether the job was done.*

The family counsel stretched out his neck. *What job? What job were you expecting them to do?*

Fritz firmed himself. *I didn't ask Zwane what the job was because I didn't believe he was involved in the elimination.*

You asked if "the job was done" but you want us to believe that you only meant the interrogation? What if I told you that two of the men died the night they were picked up? At the same place as the braai? You were at the braai and you didn't know this?

Fritz put his impaired hand through his hair and kept it there, as if to hide it away. *Zwane may know more,* he said.

Now, Prudence needed to convince Matshediso that all of that was in the past. That despite everything she knew about Zwane and those other horrible men, despite what she may personally believe, what Matshediso wanted to do wasn't resistance, it was vengeance. There was no imminent threat, no imminent danger. And yes, perhaps brutality was an inevitable and understandable response to brutality, but it was in no way justified, no matter the historical context, right? The hearings showed how many of the men from the Apartheid era were under the orders of the government. They had been doing their jobs. That had been the whole

point of Apartheid, hadn't it? To make people puppets. Zwane
was just a puppet. She would have to convince Matshediso that all
those men were puppets. That had been the argument, the basis
for amnesty. They were following orders. And so, the Amnesty
Committee held everything that happened up to the light so that
the whole country—the whole world—could examine it. Trading
amnesty for truth was the best they could do to ensure no one
would forget. But a democratic South Africa couldn't exist unless
the country forged forward, focused on the future.

"I'm so sorry about what happened to your family. I really am."

Had she said this before? Had she stopped even for a moment
to put Matshediso's pain under the light, to examine it? She would
now. He deserved this, at the very least. But Matshediso winced
while she spoke the names of each of his brothers and the other
four boys. He didn't want what she offered.

"I hope you know that if I could help you, I would—but I
can't," she said. "You have to move on."

His jaw tightened and he bit his lip but said nothing. The
repression was finely tuned, well polished, terribly familiar. He
was in full control of his eyes, so he knew that she could read the
searing expression he was offering her now. He had taken offense
to something or perhaps everything she said. He had been searching for Zwane for who knows how long, and finally he had found
a way—and she was refusing to help him.

"You think your regret is enough?" he said.

He looked as if he wanted to say more, but then a woman
approached their table. Prudence thought she may have been
the server, since no one had taken their order yet, but the woman
touched Matshediso's shoulder. He turned around, rose to his
feet, fell into her embrace.

"It is so very good to see you again." The woman spoke with an
accent. It wasn't South African but Prudence was certain it was

from somewhere in southern Africa, and it was also clear from it that she had not been educated abroad.

The woman sat down next to Matshediso and across from Prudence. She was older than both of them, her face with fine etches, her shoulders hunched, her fingers arthritically curled. She set her bag, a black nylon bookbag, atop the table.

"Prudence, I want you to meet Aneni. She is a friend."

The woman, Aneni, had a warm smile. Prudence reached for her hand and Aneni held on to Prudence longer than expected, as if to signify her desire to be friends.

"Aneni is from Zimbabwe."

Prudence had taken a few days off from her internship back in 1996 to venture to Victoria Falls. Whitewater rafting was still the most amazing outdoor adventure of her life. She had been certain she would die on the raft and remembered peering up into the wide mouth of the canyon and thinking that if she did, in fact, die, she would have no regrets, for it was enough to have seen such beauty. It was exactly what a twentysomething-year-old would think.

"Aneni flew in two days ago. She's going to New York tomorrow to meet with people at the UN. I asked her to stop here to see us on her way."

Prudence was confused. Matshediso had said nothing about meeting anyone, nothing about a woman flying in from Zimbabwe.

"Matshediso is humble. He made all this possible—my first time in America." The woman looked around the restaurant. The seats were filling, and the smell of fresh bread scented the air. "He has been a very good friend to us, a very good friend to my village."

"Aneni has always been willing to speak out," Matshediso said. "When you have someone willing to fight, it makes it easier to help."

The waitress came with bread. The straw basket nearly tipped over, pregnant with fresh ciabatta, focaccia, pane toscano, and pano pugliese. Prudence thanked the server and asked her to return quickly for their lunch orders. Aneni reached for a roll and Prudence poured a bit of olive oil onto a saucer and sprinkled a pinch of salt in it for her. Aneni dipped the bread, took a bite, and smiled at Prudence, her mouth gloriously full.

"I need you to start from the beginning," Prudence said to Matshediso. "I don't know what's going on here."

Aneni, still chewing, looked confused, and Prudence wondered what Aneni had been told about this meeting and about her.

"Aneni used to live near the Marange mine in Zimbabwe. It is the richest deposit of diamonds in the world. De Beers once owned it, and after independence, the Zim government took it over. Diamond mines are always rife with criminal activity, but the Marange mine has been one of the worst."

Prudence knew about Zimbabwe diamonds, knew about the Mugabe government, knew that American and UK sanctions had helped to destroy Zimbabwe's economy, making it ripe for even more corruption, but these facts didn't seem much different from the corruption in most other countries in the world.

"Since the mine's opening, villagers were hired to help dig. It was once a decent living, though none of them were made rich by it. But soon, an underworld of digging started, run by police officers and military officials. A few miles away from the main camp," Matshediso said.

"This is where many women worked. My big daughters. My sisters. All my friends." Aneni put down her cut of bread and took a sip of water. She looked to Matshediso as if to ask if she should continue. "At first, it was not so bad. They give us a bit extra if we find something important. I send my sons to school on this money, feed my mother. I never complain about work.

"But they stopped giving us the bit more," she went on. "And when we asked after it, they beat us. On the bottoms of our feet and on our ankles. Then, they begin to beat us for no reason. But we need to eat, so every day we take the beatings. Forty lashes. The beatings were not pleasant, but we knew what to expect.

"Men from South Africa came in the early 2000s. White men and Black men. They made us work hard but stopped the beatings. They told us there would be more money if we sped up our pace. Rhodesia, as my country was once known, was a white nationalist state. We fought ninety years to get our country back, and then were betrayed by Mugabe, so when the South Africans came we believed they would help restore order," she said. "But they wouldn't let us go home. We stay for months in the camp working into the nights. And when we go to our tents, we women are not always alone."

Aneni tore at her bread as Prudence's breath caught on the words "not always alone." Aneni ripped a small piece of the focaccia and set it into her mouth.

"What do you mean?"

Aneni wiped her fingers on the tablecloth and reached for Matshediso's hand. He seemed already to know what she would say. He rubbed his thumb over the back of her fingers.

"They rape us." Aneni swallowed hard, looking at Prudence from across the table, as if trying to determine if Prudence really understood. "My daughters suffer. I beg the men to choose me over my daughters. I try to help them run, but my big daughter ask me where they would go. If they return to our village, they will be found and killed. Those men don't want anyone to know what is happening. The mines were shut down before. They can't risk that again."

Matshediso's eyes were watery, almost spilling over.

"Then Matshediso came with his father, the hairy photojournalist." Aneni elbowed Matshediso, as if to tease him. He wiped his eyes and smiled weakly, though affectionately. "His father took pictures. I don't know how he found us, but he began asking questions. After his father had the pictures put in newspapers around the world, the EU came, the UN came. It got quieter but this thing never stops. It will never stop. I am here and will tell everything that has happened to us, but I know it will not stop."

Prudence didn't have to ask. She knew that none of the Zimbabwean officials were punished.

"Tell her about the man," Matshediso said to Aneni.

Aneni set a portion of her bread back into the basket, pushing it with such force that it smushed the ciabatta, but she didn't seem to notice. Her lip was quivering. Prudence remembered her mother's bottom lip trembling like this. An indication, perhaps, that all the emotion remained but that the eyes had simply tapped out of tears.

"I—I know you asked me to come here for this, and the whole way on the plane, I told myself I can speak of it, but I—I do not think I can," she said to Matshediso.

Prudence could see that Aneni felt like she would be a disappointment to Matshediso. What did she think she owed him? Why did she feel so indebted to him? And why would he ask her to come to America and relive this most horrifying story?

But Matshediso seemed unwilling to contend with her disquiet. Prudence knew he could be like this, tender and also brutal. He opened his jacket and removed an envelope. From it, he pulled out the photograph Prudence had given him, the one of Zwane.

"Is this him, Aneni? Is this the man who was in charge of the camp?"

Aneni peered down at the photo. "He is very young in this picture but that is him. The South African."

"We call him Nayarai," Aneni whispered. "In Shona. We call him Nayarai."

"Shame," Matshediso explained to Prudence. "They call him 'shame.'"

"You call him 'shame' because he is a Black man who betrays his own people?" Prudence asked.

A deep line appeared in Aneni's brow. "Black?" she said. "What use is Black to us if he does not see us as he sees himself? Black? You mean his skin? Black isn't skin." She leaned over the table as if to ensure Prudence was listening. "Black, as you call it, is a word they make for us. But we decide for ourselves who is for us. Not because of skin."

Prudence remembered that for her parents who'd also lived in a majority-Black country, "Blackness" was a complex notion.

"So, now he is here in Washington?" Aneni looked over at Matshediso.

"Here in D.C.?" Prudence was taken aback and she, too, turned to Matshediso. "You knew he was here? Is that why you're here?"

"He moves around the world," Aneni interjected. "He leaves Zimbabwe, he comes back, he leaves again, but his men are in all things. I don't live near that village anymore but my family is still there." She perused the restaurant, as if taking in the fact that she'd traveled eight thousand miles, away from her family, to sit there with them. Her eyes landed upon Prudence's ten-year anniversary ring. It was only a second long, this glance, but they all noticed it.

"With luck," Aneni went on, "he and his friends will rot in jail. He will still be a very rich man there." Aneni clasped prayer hands to her chest. "I am a woman who believes in Jesus, our Lord and Savior, but he is not a man that should be redeemed, not even by the blood of Christ."

Zwane was no longer just an SAP puppet. He had taken his skills elsewhere and again used them to hurt others. But Prudence knew that there would always be men like him, reinventing their violence. What surprised her most, however, was that he might have been here in Washington and Matshediso hadn't told her.

Now, Prudence glared at Matshediso. "Did you tell Aneni what you want to do to him?" Prudence said.

Oh, how his eyes widened. She loved that he was visibly worried. He hadn't told Aneni his plans. Aneni believed Matshediso was going to help her get Zwane prosecuted.

Aneni turned to him. "Do what?"

"You know I want him in prison, but no one knows what he looks like. Even most South Africans don't know his face. He was never seen on television. And we never got photos of him in Zimbabwe."

Matshediso was a good liar, but still, Aneni shook her head, profusely, fearfully. "No, please don't show his photograph to the public. If he is not jailed, he will not tolerate it. He will find us and kill us. Please do not do this. I am only now getting my daughters better. Even being here is a risk. You promised me we would be okay." Aneni's lip trembled again and Prudence ached for her, and Aneni, perhaps sensing it, reached for Prudence's hand. A woman with Prudence's life, with her privileges, should not need comfort from a woman who had suffered as Aneni had. And yet Aneni didn't seem to see her this way.

The three of them ate lunch in relative quiet that afternoon. Aneni ate mostly bread, and when the basket was emptied, Prudence realized she hadn't eaten much at all. She had arrived at the restaurant thinking she could convince Matshediso to let this all go, but she knew now that would be impossible. And this freed her to think of her father. He had crept into her thoughts as Aneni held her hand. She thought about how he'd feel sitting across from a woman like her, hearing her story. He hadn't wanted the father of his prize student to steer the child away from her studies. He'd confronted the man, a dangerous man, risked angering him, all because he wanted better for a boy he hardly knew. She wondered if her father would have put Zwane's humanity on par with the humanity of the people Zwane had degraded and debased and terrorized. She wondered if her father would have wanted Zwane dead. She wasn't sure.

22

Where there is injustice, invariably peace becomes a casualty.
—Desmond Tutu

The lawyer for the families called the wife of one of the men who'd been picked up at the Port Elizabeth airport to testify. Mrs. Khumalo was short and stocky, with a full face and big, sad, expressive eyes.

Mrs. Khumalo, did you know your husband was politically active, a member of the ANC?

She nodded, then shook her head, as if the answer could be either yes or no. *He drove a red Gallant,* she said. *I last saw that car when I saw him for the last time. He left with that car. He used to visit his brother in Botswana.* It didn't seem as if she had heard the question. She appeared shocked, her chin down, her mouth tight, as the cameras flashed and rolled, as the mic amplified her small voice. It was as if she hadn't expected to find herself a widow and a witness called to speak in front of the world.

Mrs. Khumalo, what are your feelings about the amnesty applications of Colonel Fritz and Andrew Zwane, as well as the other men you've heard who have testified to being involved in the death of your husband?

She touched the microphone, as if trying to control it better. *I am here because I suffered. So much. My husband left me with children. If it wasn't for these men, he would be alive. What should I do with his children?*

She stopped and the lawyer waited. She wiped her eyes.

I have four children. The first is eighteen; the second is eleven, in standard four; the third and fourth are ten years in June. I don't accept amnesty well. They could have asked forgiveness long before. They could have come to me before. I don't accept it because it is painful to us how they killed him.

One of the Committee members nodded, as if he had forgotten his commitment to impartiality.

Where did you hear about the amnesty application?

Mrs. Khumalo frowned. *On the television.*

When did you hear for the first time that your husband was killed?

She frowned again, her whole mouth downturning this time. *January 28, 1996.*

This year?

Mrs. Khumalo didn't answer. Everyone in the hall seemed to be doing the calculations. Ten years. Over three thousand, six hundred, and fifty days.

After lunch and a warm goodbye with Aneni, Prudence picked up Roland from school. She brought him home and put him in front of the television while she tapped away at the computer. Afterward, she lay on the floor behind the sofa, where it was dark and cave-like. She didn't know that she'd fallen asleep until Davis touched her back.

"You feeling sick?" he said. "You haven't seemed like yourself lately."

She nodded and he helped her off the floor. "I'm gonna sleep in the guest room tonight. We can't both be sick."

That night she dreamed she was back in Cambridge. She arrived at her dorm and found four girls assigned to her one small room. She would have to share a bed with another girl, a full-sized bed with flowered sheets. Her father had dropped her off there and she ran after him in a parking lot to tell him she wasn't sure she wanted to stay. He opened the front passenger door of his car, as if to invite her in. "You don't have to be anywhere you don't want to be." The dream ended and Prudence woke, thinking of her last visit to Trinidad. They had traveled to a little seacoast village to see a piece of land that had been willed to her mother by her grandmother. Back then, the land had seemed only a cut of bush in a dead village but Prudence remembered her mother telling her to close her eyes, to listen for the ocean, and it felt to Prudence that all the world had decided to whisper "shhh" in that little place. This would be her land, her mother had said.

"I wanta stay," her mother told her father. "Let's not go back to America."

Her father had simpered, told her mother that nobody scraped like they did to make it in America just to turn back. "And our children are Americans." Her mother told her father that she had no one in the States who loved her, who loved her children. "What if somet'ing happens to you, Calvin. Me, there, all alone, raising dem chil'ren?"

It was then that Prudence's father pushed back the three of them so hard they'd almost tumbled to the ground. He reached for a branch, ripping it from some tree and began ramming it into the earth. Prudence had never seen her father like that. Her mother held her and her brother tight until her father, sweating, raised the dead snake, its colors a bright red and deep black. Her mother gasped then laughed, but Prudence couldn't stop crying. Her father tossed the dead snake into the bush and reached for Prudence, pulling her plaits, as if to tease her.

"Pru, it's good to cry but only after the t'ing comin' for yuh is killed," he said. "Cryin' before the t'ing does bite yuh does do yuh no good."

Turning atop the guest room mattress now, Prudence realized that Roland had come in to lie beside her. He had brought his special blanket for them to share. She scooted closer to him and the heat from his body warmed her. She didn't always know how to be tender with her child, but as he slept, she touched his face, and his lips turned up for a smile; it was as if he had taken her out of her dreams and into his.

That night the moon was full and the guest room awash in a creamy light. There was a strange charge in the air. Since leaving the restaurant, she had been thinking about Matshediso's request, thinking about Aneni and the kind of man Zwane had to be to do what he had done in so many places, to so many people. Zwane seemed unstoppable. When she had arrived home from picking up Roland, she read everything she could find about the mines and the corruption and the village terror and pillage. She had hoped that with President Mugabe gone, things would be different, but there was no indication that much had changed in Zimbabwe. Neither the EU nor any government in Africa nor the UN nor the United States seemed able to keep the situation controlled. And perhaps they didn't want to stop it. Zwane and the men who set up that camp were relatively anonymous prospectors, finding opportunities where they could. There was no doubt that many people reaped the rewards of his quiet terror. Could she abide by that? What difference did it make if she could not? What Matshediso wanted to do was not reasonable, and yet, she knew how he felt. She had wanted to avenge her own father's death, but what were the moral costs, the spiritual costs, to her, to her family, in that sort of vengeance? She didn't think she could be involved in anything like this and yet, as she lay under the moonlight next to her child, something so certain began to rise in her belly, something that felt like heat. She turned away from Roland.

When the sun broke through, Prudence's body felt sore from the internal resistance it had endured for hours. She had tried to render her mind still, tried to sleep, but now she could hear Davis readying for work, flushing the toilet in their bedroom down the hall, turning on the shower water that ran through pipes that cut beneath the guest room. Davis was passing a normal morning.

She sat up slowly, watching Roland, and dialed Matshediso. "I want to hear your plan," she whispered.

23

I live like a man who is dead already.
—Malcolm X

Matshediso had found Zwane's house. He lived in a gated mansion in Potomac. In America, his name was Roberto Pina, and Roberto Pina was not married and did not have children. Security guards were present whenever he was in residence. He was the owner of two bars in the District, one a very popular nightspot that Matshediso believed he used to launder cash. Zwane didn't operate the places himself, but frequented one of the bars every Thursday and Friday night. He loved parties and live music, adored beautiful women.

Matshediso told her all of this as they sat in a parking lot of a local high school. The two of them were alone in his car like they had been all those years earlier. It was a dreary day and they sat unnoticed by the few passing high schoolers who were late for class.

"Your job will be to attract him and distract him," Matshediso said. "I am not asking for much. I'll do the rest."

He couldn't promise they wouldn't be caught. "This isn't an American movie. Things can go sideways."

He said he didn't know if his plan was foolproof.

"But what exactly *is* the plan? I need you to tell me what you're going to do," Prudence said.

"I prefer if you don't know everything. It will protect you later . . . if anything should happen."

"That won't work for me." She threw up her hands. "I need to know that you thought everything through the way that I would."

He reared back as if surprised that she'd question him in this way.

"He will be at his nightclub with his main bodyguard, a big white fella. Beefy Afrikaner type. You'll know him as soon as you see him." He showed her a photo of the man. "Zwane will notice you. You resemble the kind of women he likes. You will need to make sure he asks you to drink with him. He has a VIP table. You will sit with him there. He won't talk much."

"And I guess you want me to slip something into his glass?"

Matshediso's brow furrowed. "This is Zwane. He is not an amateur. You understand that, don't you?" Matshediso unbuttoned the top of his dress shirt, but he wouldn't meet her eye. It occurred to her that he might be nervous, unsure of his plans.

"I booked a room in a hotel that's near his club. Go up to the room, and at eleven o'clock, leave the hotel and walk to his bar. At two o'clock, the club will be preparing to close and he'll want to count the cash at the back. He'll leave you there, at the VIP table. But before this happens, you must tell him where you're parked and he will tell you that he's parked there too."

"So, my car will be in the same garage as his car, and you want me to drive away with him?"

"No, you will tell him that you will follow him in your car wherever he wants to go next. He will be eager. When he is with a woman is the only time I have seen him let his guard down."

"Does that mean the Afrikaner muscleman will disappear?"

"No, probably not. Zwane will only dismiss him when he is sure he will be alone with you."

Listening to Matshediso, it felt to Prudence that she was more than bait. She would have to interact with Zwane, converse with him, intrigue him, throw him off. She hadn't been prepared for all of this and wasn't sure if she was ready for it.

"When he leaves the VIP table, you will have to make your way out of the club quickly."

She imagined that he wanted her to do this because he was afraid of her being caught with Zwane on the city's closed-captioned cameras, but she didn't ask. In truth she was having a tough time focusing. She had asked for all the details but now felt dazed, almost punchy.

"When you get to the car, you will wait for Zwane to get into his, then you'll pull your car in front of his vehicle, making sure to block him in."

"Wait. But there are cameras in the garage, I'm sure."

"I will take care of the recordings from the garage cameras," he said.

"The bodyguard will be driving another car," he went on. "And he will drive around your car to get to the exit. He'll want to be ahead of Zwane so he doesn't lose him when they go through the garage gate. When you see the bodyguard turn the bend to the next level up, you will tap your horn to let me know."

"That will make Zwane suspicious. I can't do that," she said.

"I'll roll down my window and turn up the music really loud."

"Sure. That's good. I will already be there. As soon as you turn up the music, you wait ten seconds, then you leave. Calmly. You mustn't look back. Drive to our meeting place."

"And what about the bodyguard? Won't he be waiting outside the garage for Zwane to exit?"

"Yes. We have to hope he waits for Zwane long enough for you to get away."

"Fuck, this feels more like blind hope than a plan."

"I need for you to trust me."

She thought the plan would be more intricate, more complex. Could she trust Matshediso? Could she go through with this if she didn't?

"I need more time to think about this," she said.

He paused and gnashed his teeth. Everything in the car felt instantly still.

"Prudence, I saw you that morning," he said. "At the police officer's house."

Still, he wouldn't look at her.

"What? Which police officer?"

"I parked a few streets away and I walked back to his house. His wife had just found him on the carport when you drove by."

Fat drops of rain began to fall from the sky. It had been expected, but still she was surprised by it. She focused on counting the droplets of water on the windshield.

"You must've gone to your flat in Sandton, then you drove back to his house because you knew what I would do. You knew I would take care of it for you. When you passed in your car that morning, the woman—his missus—tried flagging you down for help. You drove past her. With that strange look on your face. The way you are looking now."

Prudence's chest constricted. These had been her most private truths. She turned away from Matshediso.

Yes, after he dropped her off at the filling station, she had driven to Sandton, bathed, but unable to sleep, she went back out for a drive. She found herself traveling along the same road Matshediso had taken to the officer's house. Because the sun had not yet risen, she hoped that under the cover of darkness, she could watch the officer leave his home, watch his expression when he discovered his slashed tires. Like Matshediso, she too had wanted to see what defeat looked like on his big, flat face. She planned to circle the block a few times hoping to see him exit the home, but as Prudence drove by the house, the scene was not at all as she expected. He was lying there, in his uniform, his head barely under the cover of the carport, his wife in furry pink slippers and a robe—a lovely white robe—kneeling beside him.

"I didn't know he was dead," she said. "I thought maybe he had collapsed. I didn't see the blood, so I didn't know about the murder until I got to the office hours later. I read about it in the paper. You did it. Not me. And no one can hold it against me that I didn't stop the car." Prudence felt panicked. She didn't know that she'd ever have to explain that she'd passed that woman, his wife, screaming out for help.

"I'm not judging you." His words were plain, as though he didn't suffer from the guilt of what he had done. He turned on the car, switched on the windshield wipers. The swish-swish sound was comforting.

"He is the only man I have killed. I know you won't believe that," he added. "But I do not regret it. I am not a murderer of innocents. That piece of shit was no different than Zwane. No different than the men who killed your father or those men who testified at the hearings. They were made under different circumstances, but they are the same."

"And what about us? Aren't we the same as them?"

She could sense that he felt her words as an indictment, an accusation, a judgment. She didn't mean for them to land that way. She needed him to help her answer those questions about herself.

"Who knows how many would have come after you? He would have thrown your body into a bin if he'd had a chance. He might even have killed that cashier girl to cover it up."

For years, she had mulled over the events of that night. All the ways she could have died if Matshediso had not shown. She

remembered thinking through each of the steps that Matshediso
took to be there. Listening to her message. Hearing in her words
what she didn't even know yet to be true. Entering his car. Driving
to Yeoville. Stepping out onto the asphalt. Making the decision
to intervene. Implicitly, he understood all the ways things could
have gone wrong between a Black body and a police body, and
he acted, all on behalf of a girl he didn't really know.

As they watched the rain, Prudence didn't ask Matshediso how
exactly he planned to kill Zwane. She was remembering another
story from the testimony given by Colonel Fritz, the nine-fingered
former SAP officer. On the first day of November 1996, Fritz told
the Committee about the use of the generator.

*The interrogation was done in the bush. I grew up in this area. An
open piece of property where cattle grazed. The generator was used to
pump water for the cattle.* Fritz closed his eyes as if remembering
the smell and the feel of the thick scrub. *Zwane and the others put
the man in the kombi and took him into the bush. He stayed there
overnight. We left water and food for him, then the next morning
we went back to the property and shocked him with the generator maybe three or four times. It took roughly an hour. He quickly
made all the facts available. He said he had received instructions
from Henry Sibisi. He was in an ANC cell with Sibisi. That day, I
went to the Security Branch head office to find Sibisi's file. He was
an ANC supporter. Involved in limpet mine explosions, and he had
given instructions to others in his cell to kill Black SAP officers. That
night, Zwane, Volter, and I returned to the property. We had found
Sibisi at his sister's home. We shocked him between five and ten times.
He admitted to being an ANC organizer, admitted to limpet mine
explosions, admitted to being a trained terrorist.*

The Chief asked Fritz if Sibisi had mentioned where he'd been
trained.

I can't remember but I will say for him that Sibisi was a strong person. He believed deeply in what he was involved in. Zwane forced a knife in Sibisi's nose and it was the only time he begged for his life. He asked if he could sing. He sang "Nkosi Sikelel' iAfrika." In between his singing, he said the ANC would rule, that Apartheid would be over, that democracy would be the end of the Boers. I never believed that. Zwane threw the ANC flag over him, and as Sibisi sang, we shocked him to death with the generator.

24

Life's most persistent and urgent question is,
"What are you doing for others?"
—Dr. Martin Luther King, Jr.

Prudence told Davis she would be gone for two nights for a new consulting project. Before leaving, she drafted a schedule for Davis and Alice, which included things as important as the soap Roland was to use, how much toothpaste should go on his brush, the washcloths he preferred, and after checking the weather forecast, she set aside Roland's clothes for each day, including his underwear, socks, and the light jacket she insisted he carry. On the fourth and final page of her typed instructions, Prudence wrote advice for meltdowns, agitations, outbursts, and in the case of full-blown violence, she made it clear that no one was ever to call the police on Roland.

"And where are you going again?" Davis asked.

"New York. To give a presentation," she answered, impatiently. "I'll pick Roland up from school, but then I've got to catch the train so I can make it into the city in time for a late dinner."

"So, why not come home right after the presentation?"

"C'mon, Davis, I never ask you why you're not rushing back when you have meetings."

It was the usual double standard bullshit and yet she wondered if maybe he felt something. He trusted her implicitly and yet he was also a smart man, an intuitive man, so she hoped that her

anger would obscure any suspicions he might have, deflect any
further questions he might think to ask, because she really wasn't
sure how much more she could lie to him.

He fell quiet for a moment. Then, seemed to think better of it.
"You still don't seem to recognize all the ways someone can show
love. I just want you to be okay. You don't seem okay."

She nodded and felt tears burning the corners of her eyes. She
wouldn't be able to leave if she thought too long about how much
she loved what they had created together. The truth was that some
part of her feared that Matshediso would never allow her to go
back to her life until he got what he wanted. She needed to get
the deed done, get back home, and tuck this memory away like
she'd done with many others. She turned away from her husband.

After dropping off Roland at the house after school, Prudence
waved goodbye to Roland and Alice then made her way to Union
Station. Matshediso had instructed her to drive her minivan there,
then to get on a northbound train. She needed to make sure her
ticket to New York was scanned by a conductor before exiting
the train at Baltimore/Washington International Airport Rail
Station. There, she would look for the car Matshediso had rented
under a fake international license. In the car, she would change
into the disguise he left for her, and before driving back into the
District, she would have to retrieve the burner phone that she
should use only in an emergency and the two D.C. hotel room
keys from the glove compartment.

"One key is for before you go to the club. And one key is for
after, where we'll meet."

Prudence climbed into the spacious second row of the Toy-
ota Highlander Matshediso had left for her, pulling her hair
under a stocking before setting the wig on top. She squeezed
into control-top undergarments that she wore beneath the slacks

that were a bit too tight in the butt and a bit too loose in the waist. Thankfully, Matshediso had included a leather belt. Gucci. It was soft and not too thick but also solid enough to neatly cinch the extra fabric in the waist. She slipped into pumps, inserted gel pads into her bra, then clipped on expensive teeth veneers. She felt absolutely ridiculous. The getup reminded her of Halloween when she was a child. Her Baltimore neighborhood had buzzed on that last day of October, trick-or-treaters sloshing across chilled grass, her father in his Count Dracula costume with a slick, straight-haired wig, the white powder on his face greying his lovely brown coloring, and ohhh . . . the sound of her mother's laughter each time he opened the door for a new batch of children. "I am Count Dracula! Hahahahaha!" Prudence had loved those nights. She and her friends would travel from house to house, running back home with their bags bursting with candy, only to retrieve another brown paper bag so they could make their way to another street to meet up with more friends. It seemed endless, that joy. A joy she imagined she'd pass on to her own son, until realizing how Halloween night and the increasing decibels and Prudence's elaborate costumes frightened Roland into semiparalysis. She insisted he would get used to it and for years she'd pull out her Elvira costume, until finally, Davis, losing his patience, told her that Roland was never going to enjoy that day. "He's not you!"

Now, as she drove back toward D.C., she hoped more than ever that her child would be nothing like her. But she also imagined that what she felt—the jitteriness, the uncontrolled worry—was much like what Roland experienced every day. She hadn't always been compassionate, hadn't always been accepting, hadn't always understood his many layered anxieties, and she pondered, not for the first time, if she was the right mother for him. She loved him, dearly, but maybe Davis had been right about her childhood being fucked. Would she ruin her child because of it? Had she *already* ruined her child because of it?

She couldn't think of all of this now. She needed to focus on the plan, execute the plan, so she could get back to her boy.

Forward.

25

Let us all be brave enough to die the death of a martyr.
                                                    —Mahatma Gandhi

In the high school parking lot, Matshediso had shown her more recent photos of Zwane. One was of him in a local park and another was of him grabbing takeout from a roti shop on Georgia Avenue. Matshediso had told her to memorize his face and the features of the big fella who was always with him.

After Matshediso had put away his phone, he seemed to be reaching for the right words to say next.

"He was never granted amnesty," he said. "He was given immunity because they wanted him to testify against the others, but he was found to be lying to the Amnesty Committee. There was talk of him being prosecuted after the hearings, but he quickly left the country."

Matshediso would go on to tell Prudence that once she crossed into D.C., she should turn off the burner phone, park at the garage he mapped out for her, then walk to the hotel and wait in the room.

"At precisely eleven o'clock," he reminded her. "Make your way to Zwane's club."

When she arrived at the hotel, the lobby was jammed with tourists who seemed to be part of some large conference. They were a rowdy bunch, replete with Brooks Brothers suits and red ties. The hotel décor, however, was far more restrained than the guests, and quite beautiful too: teardrop chandeliers in platinum settings, silk Turkish rugs, velvet banquette chairs, fresh lily bouquets. She wasn't sure how she'd never been there before.

Matshediso told her the elevators would be off to the left of the check-in desk. She couldn't yet see them from the front entrance, but she slid between the crowd of people, wearing her sunglasses, clutching her tote, and strode confidently around the front desk. It had been almost three hours since she left home and everything seemed to be going as planned. Until she saw him.

Zwane.

The lump in her throat hardened and her breath quickened. He was taller than she remembered. He had wide hips and his sagging cheeks had the appearance of suction cups. He also looked like a man who needed to get somewhere quickly. He was waiting at the elevator bank, fidgeting with his shirt collar. She thought to snap a photo of him to let Matshediso know he was there but the burner phone didn't have a camera and she was not to use her personal mobile. Zwane looked over at her as she stood beside him. His gaze lingered, as Matshediso predicted it would. She didn't know what to do. This was not the plan and yet she also knew she couldn't double back and leave now that he'd seen her. So, she remained beside him, waiting for the elevator, while his bodyguard, whose face she had studied from the photo, but who seemed much brawnier than in those pictures, stood a few feet behind her.

Trembling, Prudence pressed the elevator button twice. Zwane nodded as if appreciative of her efforts. He gave off an air of raw masculinity. Sturdy and powerful. She decided to assess him, as he had done her. She lifted her glasses and scanned his frame so that he would notice, then she pressed the elevator button once more.

"Don't be fooled." She shrugged, demonstratively. "I don't think I can make this elevator get here before all those other tourists crush us."

Zwane grinned and Prudence felt the removable veneers challenging the natural contours of her mouth. Zwane didn't seem to notice the awkwardness of it. Rather, he was mining every detail of her figure, her clothes, her shoes, his training with Vlakplaas never too far off. Prudence inched even closer to him.

"You look like you know your way around," she said. His eyebrows went up. "I'm meeting some girlfriends later. Do you know anything about the bars around here?"

Zwane looked down again at her Gucci bag and the belt Matshediso had given her. He seemed to be making some sort of assessment about the kind of woman she was, about the kind of place he should recommend. "Absolutely. Inanda is a lovely place. I'm going there myself in an hour or two. Would you like to join me?"

She wondered how long he'd had to work to flatten his South African accent.

"Oh, that's so nice. I'd love to."

What had she agreed to do? The reality of this moment panicked her. She wasn't sure she could get her heart to stop beating with such intensity. She was afraid she would faint.

"And your name?" Her voice quaked and he looked at her oddly as if to wonder why she asked that question or perhaps why she seemed so nervous.

"Roberto." The name slipped from his tongue as if it'd been with him his whole life.

He inched toward her, his shoulder almost touching hers. He smelled spicy and she couldn't believe how easy it was not to perceive him as a monster. She placed both hands to her heart to thank him for his kindness, then reached into her purse for her hand cream, the one she had tried to use to get Roland to say "Wonka." The scent of it calmed her, and she rubbed it on her hands and her wrists, then placed it back into the bag, just as a white couple arrived at the elevators. Prudence smiled at them, which prompted the woman to speak.

"We just flew in." The woman wore a mullet and her husband a bright-blond toupee. The man looked especially weary, as if he'd flown his wife in on his back from whatever small town in Idaho they were from.

"I heard they've had a rash of break-ins in this hotel," the woman added. "They think it's a pretty sophisticated ring. We would've changed our reservation but the whole city is booked." The woman stared at Prudence, as though trying to understand why she wasn't reacting to the news of the burglaries.

Prudence couldn't tell the woman that she was, in fact, part of a plot to murder the man standing beside her.

The husband grinned at Prudence now. "You should use the safe in your room," he suggested.

Prudence nodded and Zwane, who'd taken a step toward the elevators, putting some space between them, let out a small chuckle, as if he felt sorry for her, as if he were thankful it had been her and not him wrestled down by the two Midwesterners.

"It's our first time bringing the kids to Washington." The woman pointed at two children standing behind them. They looked to be about nine and eleven years old. Both strawberry blond, both slumped over typing on phones as if their sugar high had plummeted them into the next phase of jittery exhaustion. "We're from Montana. Where you from?"

Montana, not Idaho.

"L.A.," Prudence said.

The husband elbowed the wife as if to tell her he'd been right. Zwane jammed his fingers into the elevator button again.

"Los Angeles! That's so exciting," the woman said. "What do you do—" She turned to her husband. "Oh, darn it." She placed her hand on her husband's arm. "I left my medicine in the luggage, dear. You know how long it's gonna take them to bring it up. I have to get my bag."

The family of four turned to leave and Prudence felt both disappointed and relieved. Looking at the children dragging behind them made her think of Roland.

Zwane stepped back to stand beside her again. "Would you like to come up to my room for a cocktail before your friends arrive?"

She stroked her wig, pushing back some other woman's hair behind her ear. Would she have to fuck this man so Matshediso could kill him?

"I hear an accent. Where are you from?" she said.

"London."

"Oh, I should have known." She smiled, held up her finger to ask him to wait a minute, then removed her phone from her bag, pretending to type a message to the phantom friends she was going to meet. Zwane glanced back at his bodyguard and lifted his chin. The muscleman backed away and immediately left through the throng of tourists. It seemed Zwane expected she would soon be in his bedroom.

Shit. She needed to stick with the plan.

"How about later tonight?" she said. "After my friends go back to their hotel? I need a little time to freshen up and they'll be here any minute."

Zwane's nose flared, and she saw the man she'd seen twenty-two years earlier in Johannesburg. The raised eyebrows, the shrug, the gritted teeth. It was all there. He thought she was blowing him off, and he wasn't a man to be blown off.

"This fucking lift," he mumbled.

He walked away from her without another word, heading for the front desk. She could hear him asking loudly if there was something the matter with the elevators.

"We've been having problems, sir," the desk attendant answered. "There's only one working. And even that one stays stuck on the top floor. You're welcome to take the stairs if you want, sir."

"I'm on the top floor!"

"The penthouse suite?" the woman said, surprised. "I'm sorry. Let me see if I can call maintenance again. They should be getting one down soon."

Zwane left the woman in a huff and moved toward the stairwell. Was he going to climb all those stairs simply to avoid standing next to Prudence after she rejected him? She called out to him.

"Meet me in the lobby at eleven?"

He looked back at her, surprised. "Yes," he said. "Enjoy your room."

He didn't mean it. He meant to tell her that she was a dick tease, but she pretended she couldn't see that in his expression.

He opened the stairwell door and disappeared. Prudence had never been so relieved in all her life, but she was also worried she wouldn't be able to fix things between them soon enough not to ruin Matshediso's plan. Seconds later, a Black man in a Washington Wizards cap and sunglasses strode past her, heading toward the stairwell too. She looked at the back of him, at the eagerness of his stride, and knew in that moment that it was Matshediso. What was he doing there? She could hear him running up the stairs before the heavy steel door closed behind him.

Nothing about his plan was working. She was getting the hell out of there. Her life could be destroyed by going any further with this. Her child needed her. Her husband needed her. This was a mistake.

She turned toward the hotel exit, then heard someone shout, "Slow down, fella! Slow down!" Matshediso bolted past her, then someone gripped her arm, spun her around.

"Do you know that man?!" Zwane's face was flushed, his bald head glistened. He was clutching a black nylon backpack she didn't remember him holding at the elevator.

"What?" She held on to him tightly, hoping to give Matshediso a few seconds of a head start. There was blood at her feet, on the white marble floor. Was Zwane bleeding? Or was it Matshediso?

Zwane was glaring at her now, his breaths heavy, his nose widening, and Prudence knew that if they had not been there in the lobby of that fancy hotel, he would have hurt her. She had seen that expression before. It was unmistakable. Unforgettable.

"Release my arm." He said this quietly. No one was looking at them yet, but he seemed to want to ensure that no one would.

"I thought we were meeting later." She plastered on a demure expression of confusion.

"Lady . . ." He pulled away from her, muttering something in a language she didn't know.

She waited a moment before following him through the revolving doors. He was already a half-block away, walking rapidly, his arms pumping. On the sidewalk she saw far more blood than on the hotel floor and knew then that she and Matshediso had taken too big of a risk. He could be dying. And now she had to worry about what he might leave behind that could connect her to him.

Distracted, she walked into traffic as she began tracking Zwane.

"Fucking stupid bitch!" the driver of a car shouted from his window. He offered her a long middle-finger salute but Prudence hardly registered it. She thought if she walked faster, she could maybe spot Matshediso somewhere in the distance, lumbering but alive. But she could only see Zwane. He reached the street corner and removed a flip phone from his pocket. He was speaking to someone with great animation as he seemed to be examining the trail of blood at his feet.

The light turned red and Zwane, moving between cars, was still speaking into the phone when he looked up and spotted her. His brow collapsed and his eyes narrowed, but then he continued following the blood like a hound. He would never give up. This was what Volter had suggested about Zwane—his training under the Apartheid regime on how to hunt "the Blacks" would not fail him.

She wouldn't follow him any further. She had trusted Matshediso and of course she wanted to know if he had left her exposed, compromised, but following Zwane wouldn't give her these answers. She turned back toward the garage. She would drive the rental car to Union Station, she would retrieve her minivan, and she would get home as quickly as possible.

26

Freedom is something you have to do for yourself.
—Malcolm X

Prudence marched into the bowels of the parking garage, snaking herself under the dim lights, deeper underground. She hadn't wanted to wait for the garage elevator, but walking down the ramps now, she felt disoriented, panicked, unsure of where she'd parked the car. Despite Matshediso's warnings, she turned on her phone. She hoped he might have left a message saying he managed to shake off Zwane, hoped he might offer her a plan to end the nightmare she had allowed herself to be dragged into, but there was no signal in the garage, nothing but the loudest silence.

She thought about the last time she had found herself with no cell phone signal. She had been alone in another garage, that time in the basement of an office building in Chevy Chase just after a meeting with a child therapist. She and Davis had met with the therapist together, then separately. Davis had his appointment a week before Prudence's.

"Davis asked me to speak to you." Prudence hadn't been in the office for ten minutes before the therapist moved the conversation to fit her agenda. "He mentioned that sometimes . . ." The woman looked down at her notes, moving her finger across her notebook as if to keep her place. "He said that sometimes you 'buck,' and I take that to mean that you seem to be on the verge of initiating violent contact."

Prudence sat back in the uncomfortable leather lounger. *Buck*. Why would Davis tell this woman that?

The therapist went on. "He told me you keep a weapon in your closet. A gun you hid from him at first. Is that true?

"He said you have security cameras everywhere in the house and that you're obsessed with checking the footage. That you watch recordings of your son and the babysitter? Is that true?

"He said that sometimes he sees you making an incredible effort to restrain yourself, says he feels as if any moment you might explode.

"He loves you, wants what's best for you and your family, but he fears you might be capable of being violent with your son," she went on. "Are you, Prudence? Have you ever thought about hurting your son or anyone else?"

Prudence could hear the woman's voice echoing in her head now. The condescension. The misogynoir. Davis had undoubtedly told the therapist about Prudence's father's violent death, her anger about that loss, her childhood in and out of shelters in one of the country's toughest cities. She told the therapist that she didn't think she was any more violent than anyone else around her. All those people living in Bethesda and Potomac and Chevy Chase were violent too. She'd seen her own neighbors on recordings from the camera at the front porch, pounding the doors of friends who'd slept with their spouses, pimping out their teenage girls to boys from wealthier families. She'd seen them at dusk with their kills on the backs of their usually hidden-away pickup trucks. She'd seen them bare their teeth and throw each other down concrete steps at football games, hockey games, the way they lost control at bars on Sunday nights, pissing in public trash cans, and returning to the Capitol or to their law firms or their lobbying firms or their accounting firms on Monday morning, barely speaking to their secretaries.

"Violence? What is violence?" she'd asked the therapist.

Prudence had never thought of herself as violent. And she especially didn't now. She'd found the rental car on the third level below ground and wanted nothing more than to go home. As she sat down inside the vehicle, the garage floor tremored beneath her and even that small quake frightened her. She breathed deeply, turned off the interior light, pulled off the wig and sunglasses, removed the fake teeth, then climbed into the second row for the bag she had packed for her alleged trip to New York. Inside was Davis's grey hoodie with the pull strings and the letters SORBONNE written across the front. It smelled like him, smelled like home. She slipped it over her blouse, and threw the wig and the heels into the other bag, the one Matshediso had left for her. She quickly slipped on the flats she'd been wearing when she left Roland with Alice. There was no time to change pants, so she tightened the Gucci belt around her waist and wiped away as much of the red lipstick as she could. Rubbing her hand across her mouth again, she saw that the red dye had stained her fingers. She reached for the pack of wipes she always kept in her bag for Roland and decided to clean everything she'd touched. This very act made her feel more in control. She pulled on her leather driving gloves, and finally felt herself calming. She would be home soon and would figure the rest out there. She would have to tell Davis that the meetings in New York were canceled. He would question why she didn't just stay overnight and she would say that she wanted to be with her child, wanted to be with him, wanted to sleep in her own bed. She found the car key at the bottom of the purse, and as she began pushing herself forward to climb back into the front seat, she saw, through the passenger-side back window, someone moving between cars.

Shit.

She threw herself against the backseat, her body clenched as she tried to focus on the person's movement. She needed to concentrate on breathing, in and out, without a sound. Fixed in position, she squinted harder, pushing only her neck forward to see better. It was him. It was Zwane.

A small yelp escaped from her throat. He was using his phone light to search inside the vehicles parked on her level. Within minutes his face would be pressed against the glass of her driver's side door. He must have stopped searching for Matshediso to follow her there.

There was no time to think. She flung open the rear door and stepped out of the car, crouching down as a car passed, then another, tires whining, engines gurgling, her legs in a squat, moving almost without her thinking. The sound of the scuff of her shoes was drowned beneath the hum of the passing vehicles, which meant that Zwane's footsteps couldn't be heard either. Her thighs vibrated, the muscles straining as she waddled her way behind parked cars. Zwane was somewhere behind her. Had he seen her? She would have to find a stairwell to go up to the street level. Going down to the next level was not an option.

Another car rounded the ramp but then began to slow. She hadn't seen any empty spaces on this level. She pushed herself back into the tiled wall and listened as the car's brakes screeched, the sound heightening until the vehicle came to a full stop. The sound of its idling felt too close. She inched past two more cars, then knelt behind a silver Lexus, her knees throbbing. She covered her mouth. She could taste bile on her tongue.

"I don't know!" a man shouted. "Keep looking!"

Zwane must have called his bodyguard to meet him there. There were two voices in quick succession. Prudence swallowed the bile, too scared to spit, but feared it would soon make its way back up into her throat.

The car moved on. Did Zwane get inside it? Had she heard a car door open, a door close? She couldn't be sure. The vehicle turned down onto the next level and she waited, the tips of her gloves flat against the garage surface as she balanced herself on her toes like a sprinter. A car alarm blared. Maybe it was the right moment for a quick dash to the stairwell, but she decided to move slowly, crouching behind one car and then the next, deliberately, carefully. Yet, with no clear plan, she could feel herself panicking even more. She would soon be at the end of the row and would have to come out from behind that last car. She wasn't ready to show herself. She lay flat on the surface, her chest pumping against the concrete, the smell of oil and gas overwhelming her as she waited, listened. The alarm stopped. She heard, clearly, the sound of a door closing. Was that Zwane or someone else? Maybe she could flag down a stranger? Could she do this without putting someone else at risk? She was thinking too fast to be any good to herself, so she searched for something with which she could use to fight. Perhaps a scrap of metal or a pipe someone had abandoned. But she saw nothing. A car horn tapped and the same vehicle as before began lurching up the rampway. It was definitely Zwane's man's car again. The brakes screeched and the engine raced as the car climbed, slowed, then halted in front of a space only three cars from her. It chugged, like a rabid dog, and the sweat from her face dripped to the garage surface. Could they hear her heart pumping, hear the blood crashing into her skull?

A car door opened. Music and light from it spilled out. It seemed that Zwane had been inside his car and was now walking toward his bodyguard's vehicle. The two men began talking again.

"She absolutely came to the car. I have her things. I know where she lives now."

It was Zwane speaking. The "she" he was referring to was her. She'd left the back door of the Highlander wide open. The wig, the pumps, the overnight bags, the purses with her identification had all been resting on the backseat. Fuck. And she'd left the gun too. She had stuffed it into her purse before leaving home, then changed her mind about carrying it into the hotel. It was in the Highlander's glove compartment. Fuck. Fuck.

The other man, Zwane's bodyguard, began to speak. Prudence couldn't make out his words. Her stomach lurched and she pulled the strings of the hoodie, tightening its fit around her face, as if to hug it. She could see the interior light of Zwane's SUV brightening the row where she now crouched. He'd left his door ajar and his music played as he continued giving directions to his man. She started toward it, a black, heavily tinted Chevy Tahoe. He had backed into the space, so when she crouched down behind it, her face met its enormous rear bumper. Zwane was only a few feet in front of his truck, only a few feet from her.

"You go and see if she made it outside on foot. I'll—"

Prudence didn't hear the end of his sentence. A song she loved was now playing through his speakers. "Grazing in the Grass," by Hugh Masekela. Masekela had been forced to leave South Africa when the Apartheid government forbade more than ten Black people from gathering after the 1960 Sharpeville Massacre. She had always liked the iconic 1970s sound of that song, but now, as she climbed into Zwane's truck, the blare of Masekela's horn didn't bring her any joy.

The SUV felt stuffy. Next to her were wads of tissues, an old jacket, a peppermint container rusted at its edges. If she moved just one inch to the right, that tin would surely rattle. Prudence made herself small, folding her body behind the driver's seat. It would do her no good to question why she was there, to question all the things that had brought her to this terrible moment. Everything in her mind began to slow and expand but the pace of her breaths doubled. She could hear, only faintly, as Zwane finished up with his body man. Her adrenaline pumped and her hands shook as she slowly pulled off the Gucci belt. He meant to hunt her, meant to kill her. He had her license, her address, maybe even her gun. He would make it to her house before she could. Her child was at home, sleeping in his bed.

Zwane's man drove off and Zwane began walking back to his car. He opened the door and sat down. She held her breath, remembering that her father had timed her underwater at Maracas Bay. She'd made it to three minutes and twenty seconds and he'd clapped, bringing onlookers to see his little girl perform the feat again. She thought now she'd need every one of those two hundred seconds of withheld breath.

Prudence tightened the belt between her hands.

Zwane shut the door. Masekela's horn overfilled the car. A bitterness rushed to the roof of her mouth as her heart wouldn't stop racing. Then, Zwane turned off the ignition.

Masekela's horn ceased, mid-note.

Zwane sniffed the air.

Prudence suddenly remembered that she had nervously creamed her hands while she stood beside him at the elevator. *Willy Wonka.* She could feel the precise moment when he realized she was there. She threw the leather belt over his head, around his neck, pinning him to the headrest and bracing the bottoms of her feet against the back of his seat, as she pulled with all the strength in her thighs, her arms, her back, her core. Zwane wedged the fingers of his left hand between his throat and the belt, trying to thrust the belt forward, trying to capture air. Outstretching his right arm, his fingers clawed for the glove compartment. His gun was there, she was sure, maybe even her gun. She pulled harder. The muscles in her arms shook, pulsed, burned. Other than childbirth, she had never felt this kind of physical strain. She had never thought about how much a human might fight to live, how very violent a person might become to maintain their hold on life. Desperate, he began to slap at the headrest, blindly attempting to locate some part of her. They were both fighting with everything that had made them. All that he felt for his life was imbedded in every second of his resistance. But still, Prudence gripped tighter, pulled harder, dug her feet deeper into the back of his seat, as he punched up and around his head, pumping the brake pedal, stomping the accelerator, his knees knocking the underside of the wheel, the sound thunderous and fierce. As the belt strap began to cut into her leather gloves, Zwane slammed the palm of his left hand into the horn. The sound was desperate, aching, unending, and Prudence didn't know how much she had left in her. She imagined a garage security vehicle making its way around the corners, imagined them parking in front of Zwane's car, their yellow-bulbed siren light spinning as some man in an ill-fitting uniform approached. What if they saw her? How would she explain this? She felt herself tiring. Her body seemed unwilling to hold on much longer. The horn rattled in her mind. Someone would come soon. She would go to prison, or worse, she would lose her life right here in this car. She tried to control her breath until a rush of something overwhelmed her. She screamed. She didn't know if the sound made any sense, for it felt primal, necessary. And as saliva dripped to her chin, the blare of the horn faded. Zwane gasped louder and looked into the rearview mirror, searching for her face. The power of his confused expression nearly made Prudence lose herself. His legs spasmed and his thick hand fell away from the wheel, losing its fight, leaving Prudence to wonder if this was how it had happened to her father.

Colonel Fritz, you watched Zwane use the generator on more than one victim, is that right? What does it do to a person when they are shocked to death?

Fritz grimaced. *Their bodies convulse and their eyes close.*

27

Never wound a snake; kill it.
—Harriet Tubman

She held on to the belt for far too long afterward. And yet she still found it hard to take in enough air. When she removed a glove and touched his skin, the feel of him, clammy and soft, made her feel ill. She needed to get out of there, but she had to be methodical, careful. She pulled the belt off his neck and looped it back around her waist, trying not to think of what she had just done with it. On the passenger seat, she spotted her driver's license next to the black nylon bag he had been carrying when he ran out of the hotel. She stuffed her ID into her pocket and reached over the middle console to search for her gun. She found it, next to his, in the glove compartment. Holding it, she began to feel the throbbing in her hands and arms. Her fingers were swelling.

"My God."

She pushed his body over so it would be hidden from passersby. His head fell onto the passenger seat, the sound just a pillowy thud. Her breaths slowed a bit as she sat in the back of his Tahoe, trying to ensure she hadn't forgotten anything, while also in various stages of shock. There was a burst of tearful recall, then silence, then relief, then seconds of analysis and "what ifs?" She remembered his much younger face in City Hall, twenty-two years earlier, and remembered something else too.

Zwane had told the Committee that he didn't keep trophies, but Volter had testified to seeing it. *What kind of trophy?* the Chief had asked. *A tin,* Volter said. She was now looking down at a tin box on the floor beneath her. It was old, rusty at its edges. Could it be? She read the label. Callard & Bowser were candymakers. It was just candy. Butterscotch. But Prudence trusted nothing in the moment. She reached for it, pried open the lid, and there staring back at her were rows, columns, piles of human teeth.

"Fuck!" She dropped the tin and human teeth scattered across the back floor like squirmy larvae.

She didn't want to think about the dozens, maybe hundreds who'd died for him to have them. She wanted to know what had turned Zwane into that kind of man. But as soon as the question crossed her mind, she knew. Perhaps she'd always known that there was very little that separated a man like Zwane from anyone else, including her.

28

There is nothing like returning to a place that remains unchanged to find the ways in which you yourself have been altered.

—Nelson Mandela

She couldn't return home. Not yet. The second hotel room for which Matshediso had given her a key was across the city. When she arrived there, the room was abuzz with the kinetic sound of computer monitors, processors, drives, modems, equipment Prudence couldn't name. It was a spacious room, if a bit grimy, with a red, flowery duvet, heavy yellow curtains, matted navy-blue rugs, and a dismal view of the parking lot and New York Avenue.

Prudence stood inside the doorway with tears in her eyes. Selfishly, she was relieved to see Matshediso alive. She wanted his help to figure out how to keep Zwane's body from leading the police to them, but she also knew it was probably too late. They held each other, the solace of being together, surprising.

"Are you all right?" he asked.

"No, we have to talk."

He had bandaged himself, but the blood from the stabbing was soaking through at a worrying rate. Zwane had overpowered him, turned the knife on him. He was in pain, and she spent the next hour tending to the wounds, re-bandaging him in the bathroom where he sat atop the plastic toilet cover, wincing quietly. It felt strange, this new ease between them, and she wished to sit in the

peace of it for a moment, but she also needed to tell him everything that had happened, needed to admit to what she'd done.
Everything would not be fine, she needed to say, but how could
she tell him that she'd left a mess that neither of them could fix?
She had ruined everything.

"Look, you need to listen. We really have to talk." She helped
him onto the mattress, and as he lay back on the bed, he reached
for her hand.

"Listen to me," he said. "It's over. It's all done."

"But it's not."

"Zwane took the black bag. It was as I planned it."

"What? What bag? What part of the plan was this?"

Matshediso's phone buzzed and he reached for it, read something, then rose from the bed, limping over to one of his keyboards. Holding his waist, he began typing, his eyes scrolling
across two monitors. He searched for the television remote. His
right leg shook as he pressed the buttons.

"What bag?" Prudence said again, her back to the television
screen.

The newscaster said something about a developing story and
the discovery of a murdered man in a downtown parking garage,
but by the time Prudence turned to view the screen, the young
reporter was replaced by a laundry detergent commercial.

"Was that about Zwane?" Her heart quickened. She didn't
imagine they would discover his body so soon.

"They found the bag in his car." Matshediso held up his phone
to show her a police scanner app. "The black backpack. It was
filled with dirty diamonds. From Zimbabwe."

"What? How? Did you—"

"It's over," he said.

"Can you start from the beginning? I need to understand.
What exactly are you saying?"

"It doesn't matter. He's dead."

Did Matshediso know that Zwane was dead before the news announcement?

She walked to her handbag and pulled out the Callard & Bowser tin. She handed it to him and watched him as he held the tin, gingerly. His lips moved as if he were praying over it, but quickly he set the tin down on the hotel nightstand. The teeth rattled. He didn't flinch.

"They're going to uncover everything about him," he said. "The diamonds, Zimbabwe, the warrant for his arrest in South Africa, everything." Matshediso hobbled back to the bed. "They will have so many other suspects. They will have no reason to believe a soccer mom would have killed him. No reason to believe some IT guy from Sweden would either."

"You're avoiding my questions."

He snorted, and it landed in her gut as dismissive and arrogant; then she remembered something from Zwane's testimony. Recently, she'd gone back to her notes, gone back to the legal pad pages hoping to understand something Zwane had said when he was trying to prove that he was not a monster.

Nine what?

Nine boys. The last one became frightened. I told his comrades to lift him into the kombi but he fought them. I told them to let him go. You see, I did not take anyone who was not willing.

Prudence stilled. Something stunned and fleshy and dark moved through her as she remembered that later, the counselor came back around to the day Zwane picked up the boys, the Mozambique Eight.

You mentioned there was a ninth boy. You said you left him on the road. Didn't you think he would report what he'd seen to his family who would, in turn, report you to the leaders of the ANC?

Didn't you see that as a potential risk to the story you wanted people to believe about the boys having done this to themselves?

Zwane smirked. *No,* he said.

No?

He said it again. *No.*

Why not?

The child was scared. And he'd taken a gift from me. The morning I returned to talk to his eldest brother, I offered him a pair of Nikes. They were used takkies, but it didn't matter. His eyes grew big when he saw them. He hid them away, then told me his father had gone to see his uncle in Soweto and wouldn't return for two days. He told me that Thomas would absolutely want to go away to be trained. He gave me the information I needed.

Zwane had been talking about Matshediso.

Matshediso had been the youngest brother who Zwane had tricked into entrapping his elder brothers. He didn't tell his mother where his brothers had gone. He left the house with his mother the day after the boys disappeared, pretending to search for them, shamefully knowing that they had boarded that kombi with Zwane.

She stifled a gasp.

She wouldn't mention knowing this to him because then she would have to make room to pity him, she would have to acknowledge what a terrible burden he carried, when what she mostly felt was rage. He hadn't told her his real plans for getting to Zwane, he hadn't told her about his past, and yet he had asked her to put her life on the line for a shitload of half-truths.

"You didn't open the box." She pointed to the tin that he had set down on the hotel nightstand. "You know what's in it, don't you? You know that I got it from him, don't you? When you came to the restaurant with Tara, did you already know you would find me there? Did you know Davis was my husband?"

Matshediso pressed his back against the headboard, his shoulders slumping. "I knew," he said. "But you already knew that I knew."

"Seriously, fuck you. I knew *what* exactly? How long have you been tracking me? How many years?"

"On occasion. I wanted to see what you made of yourself. But I didn't come to Washington for you."

"You're a liar."

He reached for the bandage at his waist now, his fingers pulling at the edges she had smoothed. "After my wife lost the last baby, she left me. My mother died weeks later. When I returned to South Africa to bury her, I had nothing left. I wanted a fresh start."

Prudence didn't even know that his mother had died.

"You knew that Zwane was going to check into that hotel tonight, didn't you? It was never your plan to get him after the nightclub closed. And you knew that he followed me into that garage. Did you watch him hunt me down?"

She felt feverish, almost delirious, as truths flooded from her.

"Did you put some kind of surveillance device in the clothes you gave me, or in his car? Tell me."

Matshediso didn't explain anything, and he didn't deny anything either.

"You weren't going to interfere until you believed he might get away. You would've let him kill me."

Was this true? She wasn't sure. He had saved her before, hadn't he?

Matshediso got up again, but his focus did not leave her face this time, not until he handed her a paper bag.

She peeked inside and saw two knives.

"Everything I have that could tie both of us to that policeman in Yeoville is in that bag. I wiped clean the security recordings at the hotel and at the garage. Believe me. They're not going to be looking for us. It's all going to be fine. You know that, don't you?"

"No, I don't know that. How could I know that? How could *you* know that?"

"Because this was never only about him."

"Please stop. I don't want to—"

"Listen to me," he said. "There's a book called *Meditations on Hunting*. Have you heard of it?" He paused as if he needed to know that she was still listening, carefully listening, and though she was, she also didn't want to hear about some book, and yet, there he was, continuing to talk about it, continuing to move toward her, reaching for her hand, interlacing his fingers with hers. It felt unnatural, their knuckles wedged between each other's, their palms forced together, and yet she didn't remove her hand because she needed, wanted, wished for someone to offer her a resolution for this chapter in her life, a resolution that had eluded her for the last thirty-four years.

"Some people—conservationists—think the book is terrible but hunters consider it a bible. The author writes that 'one does not hunt in order to kill, but on the contrary, one kills in order to have hunted.'"

He squeezed her hand. "Are you listening to me?" She looked at him, and there was something different about his face, an expression she hadn't seen before.

"You are no longer the hunted, Prudence Wright."

Something passed through her as he said those words, something that felt palliative maybe, close to relief, and under the light of the computer monitors, which had cast Matshediso in a sad aqua blue, she saw in his face her own face and Prudence understood him to be simply human—a sad, beautiful, lonely human being—and when she closed her eyes and opened them again, she found that Matshediso had pressed himself closer to kiss her forehead. And though Prudence could appreciate the gesture, she suspected he already knew that she wasn't the sort of woman who needed to be comforted in this way. That very night, she had confirmed this about herself. The exhilaration she felt when she pulled that leather belt against Zwane's throat was the same exhilaration she experienced the day she wrote that check at Roland's school, the same exhilaration she found in allowing her father's killer to live, and the same exhilaration she reached when she slashed the SAP officer's tires and surreptitiously and silently suggested to an innocent and vulnerable young man that a policeman needed to die.

Now, tired, she lay down beside Matshediso, their cut and swollen bodies closing in on the other, her back to his back, the warmth between them like mellowing embers. He was kin to her in some way, perhaps only in that strange world the two of them shared. It seemed clear that he knew all along that if given the right opportunity, she could have done exactly what she did. And she knew this of him too. They'd proven this to each other, and lying there, she began to wonder if it was true, what he said, about her never again being the hunted. And if this were true, did this mean, she wondered, that she was now and forever the hunter?

29

True reconciliation exposes the awfulness.
—Desmond Tutu

She is back at City Hall. It is a warm Johannesburg day and the sun bursts through stained glass windows. She is wearing her blue pantsuit, her navy pumps, sitting at the conference table where the lawyers sat during the original days of testimony. A man approaches. He stands at the table before her.

Ms. Wright, are you serving as counsel today?

She shakes her head. She begins to explain that she graduated from law school but has never practiced. *No, I don't know why I'm here.*

The man, bull-faced, in a too-big grey suit, grins at her. *You don't know why you're here? Everyone knows why you're here.*

Who is everyone? she wonders. She turns and, behind her, up in the balcony where she once sat, is indeed, nearly everyone. Her mother, her father, Davis, Roland, Miss Jen, the Girls, Nadia, her little brother, and a young woman in a navy-blue pantsuit. She finds herself waving at them all. It is a small wave, but none of them wave back, none of them smile down at her.

Ms. Wright, do you believe what you did was honorable?

She feels confused. *What did I do?*

The man scoffs. *Do you believe what you did was just? What did I do?*

The man shakes his head. *Come, Ms. Wright.* The man stalks in front of her, leaning his body over the table, casting a heavy shadow.

I don't know why I'm here, she says.

He throws his head back. *Don't you know that violence begets violence?* He taps a pencil on the table, then drops it, and it rolls and lands on the carpeted floor. She looks down at the sea of red beneath her feet because she cannot look at this man again.

Yes, I do know that violence begets violence, she whispers.

Did you kill a man, Ms. Wright?

She shakes her head. *It wasn't like that.*

Is that the kind of world you believe in, Ms. Wright? Is it? She feels herself growing angry in a barely repressible rage.

You see how furious you are now, Ms. Wright?

I am not sorry.

He taps the table. *What did you say? What did you say, Ms. Wright?*

She wakes.

Davis could hardly remember what it looked like, so when she called to inquire about it, all she could provide the technician was the date and the time of the accident.

"We did our best." The woman was speaking fast, as if she needed to get to something else in a hurry. "It says here that someone donated the funds for the two surgeries required. They took it home, but after a few weeks, they returned it." She clacked on the keyboard. "It was aggressive." She clacked again. "It's scheduled to go under tomorrow evening. We don't have space for it. Are you interested in seeing it? I recommend coming before three p.m. today in case one of the techs gets eager."

Prudence and Roland arrived at the veterinary clinic soon after school let out. Dogs barked furiously and the desk attendant stapled papers and ran credit cards for an hour before she took Roland and Prudence into the back. The crated dog was sound asleep when Roland stuck his fingers between the slats. The tech urged him to step back.

"We have to muzzle this one when he comes out of the crate."

"We'll take him," Prudence said.

"Ma'am, you don't want this dog. I have never said this in my life, but this one is broken. Unless you're a dog whisperer, you can't train a dog who's been through whatever he's been through."

Later that evening, she cleaned the ashes from the outside firepit where she had burned everything from the night of Zwane's death. Now, in the backyard, she thought about jacaranda trees, thought about how her father would have loved her Japanese maple and her hostas. When she returned inside she helped Roland out of bed.

"It's time," she whispered.

They had set the dog crate in the garage and the dog hadn't once stopped barking. Roland helped her lift the crate into the back of the minivan. With Davis away for work, she gave Roland permission to sit in the front seat. It was his first ride in front and he was contemplative, searching the sky and the road that opened before them, and when it began to rain, she could see him staring at the streetlights as they made sparkles inside the falling drops. The night air felt particularly cold, so she cranked up the minivan heat, then the music, to drown out the sounds of the barking dog.

It was nearly ten o'clock when she set the crate down at the side entrance of the McDonald's and quickly returned to her car. She'd gotten Roland a milkshake and fries, and they listened to Kidz Bop until Roland fell asleep. One of the teenagers who worked in the McDonald's came out to see about the barking. The young woman reached inside the crate, and when the dog snapped, she jumped back and returned inside, perhaps hoping it would become someone else's problem by the time her shift was over.

By midnight, with the engine steadily running, Prudence's gas was running low. The mission was a bust. She would have to recover the dog from the entryway and return him to the clinic in the morning to be put down. Thankfully, the dog had stopped barking a half hour before, and she could only hope it would remain relatively quiet until she could set it back inside the garage at home.

She slipped on her coat, but decided to wait until the one car in the drive-thru—a lone woman in a Subaru—left the parking lot. But the woman checked her bag first, then took several gulps of her drink, then ate half her burger, before driving off. By then, Roland had awakened. The whole afternoon he'd been trembling with excitement, but now he wiped his eyes and looked around as if to locate himself. He yawned and seemed ready to go home when suddenly he began tapping on the window.

"Go back to sleep, Roland."

He was pointing at something.

"What is it?"

It was the man she had described to him: "The man with a grocery cart, who is sad because he lost his dog."

The man looked different than Prudence remembered, though the heavy coat was the same. His skin was paler and there was a new hat with ear flaps. He was pushing his cart, which spilled over with all manner of things.

Prudence turned off the engine. She asked Roland to quiet down as the man passed their car and approached the side entrance of the restaurant. The man moved wearily, suggesting none of the vigor of the person who had smashed the hood of their Porsche. The teenage girl who'd come outside earlier was now cleaning the glass doors with earbuds firmly perched in her ears, shimmying her shoulders. She seemed to recognize the man at once. She opened the door for him and offered him a little smile before saying something that caused the man to look down at the crate. The man kicked at it and the dog barked. He flinched before bending down to look inside. The barking was immediately replaced by soft whimpers, faint whines. Roland tapped the windshield and dragged his fingertips down the glass.

"He's taking him out now, Roland. Look."

Slowly, the dog limped out. He was thin but muscled, and his recently brushed jet-black coat caught the yellow light of the parking lot lamps, making him look flecked with gold. The man watched the dog, as if to ensure it was what he believed it to be.

"I never told you this but when Mommy was a teenager, she and your grandma and your uncle had to live in a car for a while. I think this man was probably sad like Mommy was sad, but he looks like he feels a bit better now, doesn't he?"

Roland nodded and offered her a sip of his milkshake. As she drank from the cup, she noticed that he'd wrapped himself in his special green blanket.

Now, the man knelt on the chilled ground before finally falling onto his bottom and splaying his legs so the dog could curl himself into the space between them. Roland tapped the glass again. She didn't want the man to see them, but she didn't ask Roland to stop either. She was proud that he had the capacity to be excited for another. They'd done this deed, mother and son, surrendering to the great possibilities that exist even in perceived ruin. The teenager brought the man a cup of water and the man drank from it before tilting the cup so the dog could drink from it too. The man didn't yet notice the billfolds that Roland had clipped to the dog's collar. Undoubtedly, it wouldn't be the end of all his worries, but it might feed them for weeks, maybe even a few months.

30

The order of the day is forward march.
—Nelson Mandela

It was Spring Break and they surprised Roland with his first trip to Disney World. Prudence and Davis weren't sure if he could manage the crowds, the heat, the overstimulation of an Orlando vacation, but he'd had a good few months at his new school, had acquired more words, new skills, and one new friend. And things with Davis and Prudence felt good too, or maybe better than good, as they were communicating with more ease and had each gained a little professional steam. Prudence had been hired as a consultant for the Baltimore City Public School System to bring them up to date on their advancement policies, while Davis had not only brought in one of the largest construction companies on the East Coast as a client but also helped the firm find an equally capable IT strategist to replace Matshediso, who, not long after Prudence left him at the hotel, had submitted his resignation noting that he had reconciled with his wife and would be returning to Sweden. Davis had asked Prudence what she thought of his quitting and she had only shrugged, but what she actually felt was an immediate and immense sense of relief. Of course, this relief didn't mean that the memories of that night weren't still playing in her mind. In fact, she found it hard to function for many weeks afterward and was currently on a need-to-use basis with Ativan, which made the Disney crowds far more bearable too.

But in Florida, despite the heat, the three of them happily stood in those atrociously long lines. They had a private meeting with Mickey and Minnie, they rode the Kilimanjaro Safari six times, cooled down inside the watery tunnels of "it's a small world," flew atop the pink and blue Dumbos, ate roasted turkey legs and poofy cotton candy. Their family photos were embarrassingly sweet: Roland in the middle with his big red sneakers nearly the same size as his father's; Davis smiling, showing almost all his teeth; while Prudence's grin seemed to suggest that her life was, if not on an upswing, definitely steady.

The night they returned to D.C., they didn't make it into the house until just after midnight. A lightning storm had shut down all the airports in the nation's capital. Roland was near explosive with exhaustion, threatening to ruin the lovely memories they'd brought back from their Florida adventure. It was almost two o'clock in the morning by the time Prudence got him settled enough to sleep.

The next morning, Davis woke before everyone. He was already downstairs flipping hotcakes when Prudence and Roland met him in the kitchen. Roland watched cartoons on an iPad, shoveling strips of turkey bacon into his yawning mouth, while Davis, still waiting for his eggs to boil, went to retrieve the mail. It was a big stack.

"This is for me, this is for you, this is for me, this is for you, you, you, you." He organized the mail in piles, setting down envelopes near each of their plates. Roland reached out his hand as if expecting mail too. Davis plopped the cable bill down in front of him.

"And you can pay for all that television you like to watch." He laughed, while Roland only shrugged.

Then, Davis handed Prudence a large bright-yellow envelope. "A package for you. Looks like it's from overseas but it doesn't have a return address."

Prudence poured honey over her pancakes.

"Are you gonna open it?" Davis tapped the package with his finger.

"Is it a surprise from you?" She looked up at him, honestly wondering if this was some ploy to have her open a gift from him while he stood over her.

But there was nothing in his eye to suggest he'd sent it. There was just a blazing expression of curiosity.

"Oh, you just being nosey!" She laughed and picked up her fork and cut into the golden-fried dough, the steam rising into her face. "I don't want my pancakes to get cold," she said, with her mouth full. "It's probably that special Korean face cream I like to order."

Davis stood over her a bit longer, watching her eat, as if to consider her reasoning, but soon he seemed as convinced as Prudence that the package was hardly consequential. Later that morning, while Davis and Roland were upstairs unpacking their suitcases, Prudence brought the package into her office. Looking at it more closely, it did, in fact, strike her as odd. Her name and address were handwritten and there was more postage than seemed necessary, as if the sender wanted to make sure the package didn't get returned.

She reached for her office scissors and cut open the envelope. "I know it's from you," she whispered. Inside sat a necklace box, rectangular and cardboard in a deep burgundy color. She smiled. Davis *had* bought her a gift. He would be disappointed that she didn't open it in front of him, and she started to raise herself out of her office chair to call for him when she decided to take a peek at it first. She opened it and there, sealed in bubble wrap, nestled between a pad of foam, was not a necklace but a shiny USB drive. There was no note but the fluttery feeling in her belly gave her all the warning she needed. She rose from her chair to close the

office door. She could hear Roland and Davis, upstairs, separating
their laundry in the hallway. Davis was instructing him on why
whites and red-dyed T-shirts should never meet. They would be
distracted long enough for Prudence to boot up their old desktop
computer, which neither she nor Davis had used in years.

The computer warmed, and as she waited for the screen to
indicate that she could click open the drive, her heart raced. Then,
the screen darkened and in an instant it grew bright again.

Her breaths were coming hard now. She moved her chair closer
and rotated the monitor so that the trees on the screen appeared
tilted. She soon realized they were, in fact, growing crookedly on
the side of the hill.

She could almost smell the oily blacktop at the rear of the gas
station building.

She swallowed hard as the security camera panned the area
and passed over a twenty-four-year-old Prudence and a tall police
officer. Every thirty seconds she saw Prudence again. First, there
was the gun to the back of her head. Then, her daddy's sweater
over her arm. Then, Prudence, without her dress.

She didn't remember knowing that a camera was mounted on
the back roof of the petrol station. And yet, Prudence had looked
up at it, into its eye, her face so young, so clear, so very afraid.
Had she been looking skyward when the policeman's elbow rose
then descended, as the sound of his zipper's teeth pierced that
howling air?

"Oh my God . . ."

She slapped at the monitor until her hand burned, then deleted
the file before snatching the USB drive out of the computer. Prudence jammed her fingers into the keys to make sure the file had
been permanently erased from the hard drive. She needed it gone.
And yet, even with that biting rage, even as she trembled, hoping

never to feel the terror of watching herself in that recording again, she knew nothing was ever permanently deleted.

During all those intervening years, the images she'd kept in her head had grown dull, hazy, and she had imagined herself braver, more resolved, less childlike than what appeared on that screen. With this recording, however, Matshediso had taken memories that she believed she controlled and he had transformed them into something unfettered, graphic, and even more horrifying.

Nothing ever remained the same, did it? There were terrorists now in graves with iron clenched between their fingers, there were strong fathers weeping and mothers wielding knives, and children in beds, their thoughts filled with new worries. One day you were healed, the next day you were wounded, one day you cannot remember, the next day your body marks each memory with a blistering pain. There were wondrous disappointments and also terrible surprises, but this thing, this thing that Matshediso had done, if she were being honest with herself, was not unexpected. She knew he was capable of this. Oh, yes, one could argue— and she began playing out this argument as she switched off the computer—that the content of that package might be intended to signal that he had seen her, had borne witness, that he understood that what had happened to her over two decades earlier was as horrific as she had remembered, and that he wanted her to be the keeper of this memory, to do with it what she pleased. It could have been a generous, beautiful gesture, one that might have signaled that she was never alone in the world, but that was not what she believed Matshediso meant to say. This thing, this package he had sent to her home, without a note, without a return address, was a threat. A way to let her know that he would never release her from a past he couldn't be released from, and that he would be holding a plethora of gruesome possibilities for her future. And the truth was that he had always been a threat to her future. Just as she had also been to his.

Prudence sat straight-backed in the office chair, looking at the greyed, blank screen of the desktop. She knew he might come for her with his USBs or his knives or his security footage or his photos or whatever else he had stored in some Swedish closet, but she also knew that if he did, she would be there, ten toes down, prepared.

She pocketed the drive. She would burn it later. She would put its remnants with the bones of all the rest of her dead.

Still in shock, she didn't hear Davis enter, but he was there now, rubbing her shoulders, the pressure firm, as if he knew that something inside her needed to be tamed for a spell. She looked up at him and smiled the sort of smile that she hoped hid everything that could hurt him. Then, she noticed Roland, behind him, in the doorway, his jacket buttoned, his iPad in hand. They were going to a diner for lunch. It would be their last lunch of Spring Break.

"You ready?" Davis said.

She shifted her weight to nudge the trash can with the torn yellow envelope further beneath the desk before Davis gently pulled her out of the office chair.

"Yes, yes, I'm ready," she said.

Author's Note

I lived in Johannesburg in late 1996 and bore witness to some of
the testimony given during the Truth and Reconciliation Commission's amnesty hearings. Some of the stories told of the Apartheid era inspired portions of this novel. I changed the procedural
workings of the Amnesty Committee but tried to preserve the
spirit of such on these pages. Though I was only in South Africa
for a short period, I left there altered by what I saw and heard.
Despite its growing pains, I watch this young democracy from
afar with all the hope I had for it in 1996. I believe in its future
and I hope you leave this book feeling the same.

Acknowledgments

It would be disingenuous to say that I did not have a desire to write early in my life, but certainly by my second year of law school when I found myself seated at the amnesty hearings of South Africa's Truth and Reconciliation Commission, I had long since given up the idea. So, how to explain my furious and meticulous note-taking during the hearings? And the salvaging of such notes written on flimsy legal pads for more than twenty years? Perhaps, I knew, even in my youth that I might never witness anything like that again and/or perhaps some higher power had already preordained this writerly life, this particular story. If so, thank you to that higher power without whom none of this is possible.

Few books are written and shared with the world without the help of others. I am deeply indebted to Tebogo Skwambane, my beloved friend, who shared her love of her country long before my first visit and whose willingness not only to answer all my queries over WhatsApp but also to house me while I conducted research in Johannesburg, feels invaluable. Her parents, Abner and Johanna, opened their home to me in 1996 during my first visit, and they, along with her brother, Thabang Skwambane, helped to begin my love affair with South Africa.

While on my most recent trip, I had the most tremendous luck in finding Badresh Kara, who patiently answered my questions. There were so many others whose names I don't know who gave me more than I asked and added to the possibilities of this story. Thank you also to David Goldwyn, my dear friend, who reached out to his network on my behalf and who, along with Cathy Goldwyn, a woman whose friendship has sustained me through some dark days, rarely said no when I needed help for this project or even a dog walking favor.

For me, writing has been a rather lonely endeavor, but there are a few writers who took every call over the last few years: Bernice McFadden, Elizabeth Nunez, David Haynes, Pete Turchi, Marisa Silver, as well as my ever-supportive Tennessee retreat crew, Rachel Beanland, Claire Gibson, and Blair Hurley. I would also like to thank the Freedom Writers' Retreat, established by the extraordinary Kellye Walker and Werten Bellamy, at Great Oak Manor, for the focused time and the fireside chats, as well as my Bread Loaf family, including Jennifer Grotz, Noreen Cargill, and Jason Lamb. My sincere gratitude to three others in my stable of steady friends: Tricia Bent Goodley, Raqiba Sealy Bourne, and Tanisha Lyon Brown, who all seem to hold their own special Lauren healing powers.

Thank you to my wondrous agent Victoria Sanders, as well as Bernadette Baker-Baughman, who helped me find my way to the incredibly encouraging Katie Raissian and then to the warmest and crazy-talented, Peter Blackstock, my editor, who took one look at this manuscript and knew how to make it better. Thank you also to Emily Burns for her incredible suggestions, the entire team at Grove, including Deb Seager, as well as Kimberly Burns of Broadside, who is unmatched in her enthusiasm.

Thank you to my sister, Halcyon, my father, Leonard (Terry), and my mother, Jennifer, for the laughter via text and across kitchen counters, as well as for the consistent love and support. I am nothing without you three. Thank you also to my in-laws, Khemraj and Anita Sharma, for the sustenance, the chuckles, and the consistent prayers.

To my children, Sage and Ava: my love for you two knows absolutely no bounds and the most beautiful thing about writing these words is that I suspect you both know this already. And lastly, to Anand: no one knows what transpires between two souls but what we have makes me believe that there must be some great magic at play in the world.